CHEW ON THIS

EDITED BY

ROBERT ESSIG

ISBN: 978-1-940250-46-5

Artwork by Andrej Bartulovic

Interior Layout by Lori Michelle
   www.theauthorsalley.com

Printed in the United States of America

First Edition

Visit us on the web at:
www.bloodboundbooks.net

MORE EXTREME HORROR FROM BLOOD BOUND BOOKS

TABLE OF CONTENTS

MEAT OR BE MEATEN

ROBERT BOSE & SARAH L. JOHNSON

LAZLO LURCHED INTO the front closet, tail swishing, as two police officers emerged from the master bedroom holding handkerchiefs to their faces. The younger of the two gagged and Lazlo's own malnourished gut convulsed. Rot saturated the air and stained the carpets. Even the light seeping through the windows had a yellowish murk, like eggs gone off. The house was diseased.

They'd caught him dozing. Weeks of praying to Bastet for someone to blunder through and render Plan B unnecessary, and he'd fucked it up by taking a nap. The old man's daughter must have called the cops in for a welfare check.

Cat-hating bitch, Lazlo hissed inside the musty closet. *Shame the old man blew her inheritance on his Meat of the Month club gold membership.*

Lazlo's remaining whiskers quivered. He needed to get out. Twelve years he'd been trapped in this house as the old man hoarded pound after pound of meat. Twelve years of discount beef, pork, and poultry, and then the dubiously sourced exotics. Twelve years of freezers gasping a carrion stench fit to blow a buzzard off his gut pile—or a cat off his chow. Now the old man was dead, and Lazlo was well and truly fucked, unless he could escape this abattoir. He focused on the door.

"Jesus Christ, Dave, man up. You can't puke in here, forensics'll have a cow."

"Urk." Dave took a shuddery breath, eyes watering.

"Never had a freezer die before? It's always disgusting."

"Yeah." He coughed and took another deep breath. "But normally you're talking a couple steaks. A box of meatballs. A Christmas turkey. Who the hell has an industrial freezer stuffed full of meat in their bedroom?"

"Beats me."

"It's fucked up, is what it is, Dwayne. And what's that clacking noise?"

Dwayne glanced around. "Pipes, attic vents, who knows. These old houses are talkers. No sign of Mr. Bennett. I need some air and a smoke. You can puke in the flowerbed." He pounded his partner's back and laughed.

They stopped at the door and Lazlo got ready. A few ounces of hemp milk puddled in a trash bag put enough coil in his spring for one last try. He was getting out of this charnel house.

Dave put his hand on the doorknob. "I'm betting those bloodstains are his."

"Naw, just freezer leakage. You saw it. Cracked open. Oozing."

"Yeah, but that chewed up extension cord. The old man got fried, and his cat ate him. I've heard that happens."

"Where's the bones then?"

Dave shrugged. "It's been a few weeks."

"That'd be one ravenous pussy. I don't think we're looking for a stiff. Bennett probably just took off for a few days. Let me grab a quick puff and we'll check the basement."

The door squeaked open and Lazlo leapt for the crack with everything he had. A streak. A flash. Also cross-eyed. He bounced off Dwayne's leg and dropped back, stunned.

"What the hell," said Dave.

"There's your cat," said Dwayne. "Or what's left of him. Doesn't look like the poor thing has eaten anything for a long while. Skin and bones."

"We should get him to the Humane Society or something. Tell the daughter." Dave reached down, got a hand around Lazlo's emaciated rib cage.

Oh, hell no. She'd put him down. Or worse, force-feed him Purina. Even Plan B was better than that. Lazlo slashed at Dave's hand with ragged claws. Dave howled and Lazlo skittered away, hips cracking and back legs splaying in opposite directions. The officers didn't follow, and he hid behind one of the innumerable boxes of old man junk crowding the hallway.

"Shit." Dave held up his bleeding hand.

"We'd better get that checked out ASAP. Let's call the daughter. She can have Animal Control deal with the little monster."

The door slammed shut.

Goddamnit. Lazlo crept out. *Way to go, you dumb litter tracker. Now you're trapped. Again.* Limping into the kitchen, he paused at the pantry door. Deep scratches and gnaw marks marred the once white paint. Plenty of food in the hold of this reeking plague ship. Boxes and boxes of Kitty Kale. And all of it trapped behind two inches of solid hardwood. He'd wasted days on it, and most of his remaining teeth. He'd resorted to gumming down the leaves of sun-scorched African violets lining the living room windowsill. They tasted like shit. Literal shit. Like they'd grown wrong, the soil sucking in poison and spitting up something even worse

The choice to go vegan was hard for a cat, harder still in this house, but Lazlo shuddered at the fleshy alternative. His body was a temple. Or had been.

At the top of the stairs a shadow stirred in the gloom. Clack . . . clack . . . clack . . . Lazlo's spine arched, and his tail puffed like a mangy toilet brush.

Plan B, then.

A heat vent gaped from the baseboard in the kitchen. The old man had removed the brass grille when the screws had wiggled out, and never replaced it. Lazlo stuck his head in and recoiled, overwhelmed by the stench. Did he have to do this? He knew the answer. He wiggled down the narrow tin circle. A month ago, he'd never have fit. One turn. Another. The second was tight and he lost some fur on a sharp edge before reaching a rupture in the conduit from the old man's careless handling of a garden weasel.

He hesitated, no longer having the strength to get back up. Even if he did, Animal Control was on its way. Even if they weren't, *She* wasn't about to give him another chance. He said a quick prayer to Bastet and gracefully dropped down onto a pyramid of water softener salt bags, one of the old man's many subscriptions. Two bags delivered every month. For how many years? Decades? Lazlo perched regally on the topmost bag and surveyed the dim basement.

Between two narrow windows, stood the golem. Born of meat. A menagerie of flesh, long dead and drained, packed together and resurrected. Lazlo yawned and immediately gagged. Then the precariously piled bags shifted.

Darryl observed the wretched critter tumble down the salty swale to the floor. A fine layer of saline dust covered everything in the basement, and Darryl, a practicing stoic, had long since accepted the chronic sting in his eyes and his nether region, yet he couldn't help taking a step back from the plume raised by the drop-in vegan.

Carefully, Darryl laid his book aside. A pulpy paperback, pages brittle with age, gold embossed title shining in the gloom. This one was medieval, and he preferred regency, but those swirly letters . . . Like true love, they would never tarnish.

"Hey, Laz."

The cat licked his paw and swiped the salt from his face. "Since when can you talk?"

"Since I found a pair of sheep lungs and a goodish length of tongue. How do I sound?"

"Like two fat humans fucking."

Darryl emitted a visceral huff. "Must you be so crude?"

"I don't have time for manners, meat boy. While you've been down here . . . suppurating, and reading romance novels, I've been dealing with a big problem."

"An inability to embrace your better nature and open your heart to those who would elevate you?" Darryl knew it was antagonistic, but he'd just read a thrilling passage of banter between the secretly destitute Baroness Mary and the common but wealthy merchant Charles.

Lazlo's muddy green eyes glared. "Is that a turkey wing on your head?"

"Do you like it?" Darryl raised a lumpen hand to his improvised accessory. "Something I'm trying, though I know gentlemen aren't supposed to wear hats indoors."

"Whatever, Downton Abbey, you do you, but have you noticed anything different lately?"

Darryl glanced around at stacks of dusty red vinyl kitchen chairs, three artificial Christmas trees dripping strands of tinsel, trunks overflowing with old curtains and afghans, and of course, the four deep freezers. His entire world since he emerged from the largest chest, having achieved critical meat density and thus sentience. This subterranean lair where he'd discovered books: Romance Reading Club novels, the manuals for a variety of Oldsmobile Cutlasses, and a slim volume by Seneca that taught him about stoicism.

While Darryl constructed a rich inner life in the pages of those books, his outer life was largely consumed by pilfering the freezers for an ever-rotating supply of replacement parts that formed his person. He did his best to be his best, though loneliness plagued him. Each time he opened one of those insulated lids and inhaled the gamey gust of cold air, he hoped to find another, a friend, someone to love. A better companion than that ghastly uncouth cat.

"What should I be noticing?" Darryl asked.

Lazlo extended his front paws and elongated his spine. "A putrid stink that for once isn't coming from you."

"The old man never had much in the way of olfactory off-cuts," Darryl said, ignoring the sudden dribble of ichor down the inside of one leg, ill-fashioned from Florentine T-bones and ground pork packed like mortician's wax to fill any holes. No tripe delivery in weeks, and those precious lengths of intestinal lining were literally all that held him together. He was losing structural integrity. "I did notice that the freezers aren't working."

"That's right, beef-for-brains. The old man is dead, the power is off, and I'm goddamn starving."

"Enough to eat meat?"

"Jesus Christ, no," Lazlo hissed. "I came down to get you to come up. The cops were here, and the old man's daughter'll have me euthanized. You're not gonna last like this either. We gotta get out of here."

"I can't," Darryl said. "I'd be shunned, or worse. The villagers would come with their pitchforks and torches."

"You really have no clue, do you?" Lazlo said. "Look, I don't care where you go, I just need you to open the front door."

"You'd leave me alone?" Darryl cried, tongue partially detaching in a spray of foul mucous. "No, Laz. You can't. Please don't leave me."

"A bird may love a fish, Darryl, but I ain't living in no igloo." Lazlo cocked his head and his surviving whiskers twitched. "You know the old man had a freezer in his bedroom."

A sudden chill gripped Darryl, his first reprieve in weeks from the methane heat of decay. "And?"

"And there's something living in there. Not like you. But she's definitely something."

"She?" Darryl's heart squeezed out a clot. "Are you sure?"

"Are you kidding? She's a bacon wrapped bombshell. Those Hutterite chickens have an awfully nice set on 'em. Imagine ripping the bodice off that."

"I don't know," Darryl said, glancing down at his body. "I'm awfully bloated today. I want to make a good impression."

"Trust me," Lazlo said. "She's as lonely as you are. You let me out of this house, and I'll make you an introduction to the trim of your dreams."

"Okay, I'll do it!" Darryl shouted, the force of his jubilance causing a bubble of putrefying gas to blow straight through his abdominal wall. Lazlo's eyes watered and he fell over unconscious.

Lazlo retched himself awake, devastated to find himself still in the basement.

Darryl loomed over him. "You okay, Laz?"

"Ugh, you're dripping on me," Lazlo hissed and scuttled away, reflexively licking the rancid precipitation dotting his fur. The stench. The taste. It overpowered everything, even the salty brine stinging his ulcerated mouth. "Look," he swallowed his gorge, "since you don't know shit about women, there are a few things I should mention about Savannah."

Darryl emerged from rooting in one of the smaller, auxiliary freezers, and swung around, two large salamis in hand. He held them at waist level before tossing the smaller, bent one away. "What?"

"Something wrong with your hearing?" asked Lazlo, dodging the meat tube as it squelched into a crate overflowing with older, juicier discards.

"Hmm . . . " Sticking his finger into the pig ear protruding from the right side of his blockish head, Darryl fished around before flicking away few dollops of goo. "Sorry, Laz," he said, returning his attention to the salami. "You see any string laying around? I pulled some off a roast yesterday."

"I said, there's things you should know about Savannah, and just what do you think you're going to do with that—" Lazlo pointed a broken claw at the dangling sausage. "—monstrosity?"

"Well . . . " Darryl turned a shade of darker mottled purple and showed Lazlo the cover of a dog-eared paperback. A chiseled man in a codpiece had a stunning woman in a passionate embrace. "I thought . . . "

Lazlo shivered. *Ugh. Damned meat-eaters. No vegan ever needed a backup salami.* "Stop, okay? Just stop. Stop thinking. Stop playing with your . . . whatever the hell that ends up being. We need to get upstairs now, before anything else terrible happens."

"Savannah," sighed Darryl. "What a beautiful name. Is she as beautiful as her name, Laz? Tell me."

"Sure. She's something all right. Look, you idiot, she needs you as much as you need her. Desperately. But she's not like you. Not exactly. So don't freak out if she isn't the lady you've been reading about in your trashy books."

"I love her already. She's perfect. I know it," said Darryl, eyes oozing. He slid a thick arm across them. "Perfect."

"Tik-tok. Onwards and upwards." Lazlo dragged himself up the steep basement steps, Darryl in tow.

Opening the door, Darryl stopped. "You sure she needs me? I . . . "

"Yes, yes. Come on. See those stairs there," said Lazlo, cocking his head toward the hallway. "Your princess awaits."

Darryl snagged the cat in a moist hug. "Thanks, Laz. I love you too, even if you are a foul little beast."

"Ugh. Don't mention it. Could you perhaps, open the front door?"

Darryl shuffled forward and started up the stairs.

"Darryl?" Lazlo shook off a few clinging giblets. "Well, fuck."

Darryl's feet slapped on the stairs, and he gripped the railing with greasy elk sausage fingers. His heart—once belonging to a black bear before being crated in ice and shipped to the old man in his Meat of the Month delivery—quivered in his chest. He thought of the virginal Baroness Mary and rogue merchant Charles. Their first kiss. Tentative at first, then igniting. Lips, like strips of calf liver, growing bruised and tender under the force of their passion.

"Christ, could you move any slower?" Lazlo snarled from the bottom of the stairs.

Darryl took a slow breath, inflating the fetid ovine lungs. "I'm mentally preparing."

"Animal Control is on its way. Get up there, bag that bird, and let's haul tail."

Darryl ignored the spitting feline. Lazlo was a good kitty and a bosom friend. His love language was not one of pretty words, but deeds. He'd given Darryl the gift of romance, and Darryl would not forget that.

At the top of the stairs, Darryl followed a chewed extension cord into the old man's bedroom. Savannah's boudoir. Ribbons of light fluttered through the lace curtains. For the first time Darryl felt summer sun on his dewy face.

He cleared a congealed mass from his throat and spoke. "Hello?"

Next to the befouled bed, stood an upright freezer. The door hung open, and a green sludge trickled onto the carpet. The poor creature had been without refrigeration as long as he, and in a much warmer room. Was it odd for humans to keep a freezer in their bed chamber? Wasn't for Darryl to say. The modern world was alien to him. Though he could probably operate an Oldsmobile if pressed.

Clack . . . clack . . . clack . . . squelch . . .

A mottled mass of flesh slumped out of the closet. It was all Darryl could do not to cringe. He'd thought nothing in this world could be more monstrous than himself.

Lazlo was right.

Savannah was different.

An assemblage of whole chickens and exotics, as far as he could tell. Baby seal flippers, gazelle kidneys, giant panda cheeks, and some species of tissue he didn't recognize. She undulated along the floor, making that strange clacking sound.

"Savannah?" Darryl croaked as the mosaic of meats roiled across the gore-stiffened carpet on leg-like stumps, its nubbin arms flapping at its sides. *Her*, he reminded himself. Her sides. But his spine, fashioned from a whole smoked eel, froze at the most horrifying part, or lack thereof. His lady, his love, was headless.

Darryl knew then why the old man kept a freezer in his bedroom. Unlike Darryl, Savannah was no accident of nature. The old man made her this way. Intentionally. A venal god who saw no reason to give a woman a voice or a mind of her own.

"Savannah," Darryl said. "It's an honor to meet you."

The creature spasmed at the sound of his voice and wriggled closer, as if to reciprocate the salutation. This was good. This was something. He reached out to embrace her, but she darted back with surprising agility. He tried again, and again she shrank away like an octopus folding itself into a rock crevice.

"Savannah, I won't hurt you. I promise."

Darryl found himself ashamed. He'd assumed Savannah, by virtue of being female and of like kind, would simply fall into his arms. As though she were a piece of property Lazlo was entitled to exchange, and Darryl equally entitled to take possession of. Savannah was no prize to be won, no object to be owned. While not fully formed, she nevertheless had an equal right to self-determination. Darryl felt a welcome surge of purpose.

"Well, Savannah," Darryl said. "If you'll allow me, I think I can help you."

With a wet shudder, she slid closer as he peered into the freezer to assess their options. Luckily he found several pounds of ground gorilla that hadn't yet liquified. He brought the entire burping tub of meat to the old man's desk and got to work.

After a time, Lazlo poked his face into the bedroom. "Yo, Savannah," Lazlo yowled before his mostly toothless mouth fell open. "Jesus, Darryl, you're still . . . What the hell are you doing?"

"The right thing, Laz." Darryl set the greyish green mass gingerly upon Savannah's shoulders, where it sat for a moment, before sliding off and splatting onto the floor. "Oh dear . . . "

"Holy shit, I'm gonna yak," Lazlo grunted, running back down the hall where Darryl heard the unreasonable racket of a cat disgorging its stomach contents.

"Not to worry," Darryl said to Savannah, as he slopped the meat into the tub. "Back to the butcher's block."

He sat at the desk and resumed sculpting. After a while, Savannah came up and sat behind him, sliding her flippers down his arms, their entwined fingers sinking into the hot meat. Together they molded and pinched, and pulled, and carved. Finally, they crafted a head that would stay on her shoulders, and a face fit to launch the grandest of ships.

"Look," Darryl said, turning her to the mirrored closet doors. "You're beautiful."

Savannah twisted around and gazed up at him with marbled eyes. She couldn't yet speak, but Darryl knew she could achieve anything she put her mind to. He didn't know where they'd go, or what they'd do when they got there, but if she'd have him, he'd spend the rest of his existence making her the happiest meat golem on earth.

Her cupid's bow mouth puckered, and he lowered his face to hers. The kiss was everything he'd read about. Though the sound effects were squishier. Their mouths navigated gently at first, and then with more friction. Shreds of meat detached and slid down each other's throats, which struck Darryl as embarrassing, but it seemed to arouse Savannah. The strange clacking noise emanating from her torso grew louder and more rapid. She pulled him closer and Darryl groaned as the salami he'd smuggled in his belly, despite Lazlo's admonitions, slowly emerged like a magic meat stalk.

This was happening. They would make tenderized love on the old man's bed and be washed free of the foul effluent of the past, clearing the way for a bright refrigerated future. The clacking crescendo moved lower. Darryl disconnected his mouth from Savannah's and looked down to see something hard and white punch through her lady's garden. Darryl recognized the old man's dentures as they opened, engulfed the salami, and snapped shut.

No pain as such, but Darryl knew this was not good. He tried to pull away, but her teeth had a death clench on his meathood.

"No, Savannah," he pleaded.

So she'd eaten the old man. Understandable. The villain had it coming. But how could she do this? After all they'd been through together? Darryl struggled, until his arms tore themselves off. He begged until she ate his tongue. He writhed until she slurped out his spinal column and he collapsed in a boggy heap. With his flesh between them, her teeth no longer clacked, but chewed, and chewed, and chewed.

Lazlo vomited a slurry of hemp milk, African violets, and extension cord sheathing. Then he scurried downstairs where he couldn't hear Savannah finishing her first dinner date. Besides the obvious horribleness, he couldn't stand the sound. How hard was it to fucking chew with your mouth closed? Savages.

Poor dumbass Darryl. Lazlo shrugged, and felt his shoulder bones scrape and nearly dislocate. The romantic fool didn't deserve his particular fate. But, a deal was a deal, and while Lazlo and Savannah had never spoken, they had communicated. One predator to another. The deal, however, now made what was left of his fur crawl. Lazlo knew a little about monsters. He'd lived with the old man for twelve years. All that meat. All that delicious . . . disgusting meat.

She'd eat him next. He had no doubts about that. Might as well make peace with Bastet while he had the chance.

The *woosh* of air brakes snapped him out his navel gazing. He padded slowly to the front window and crawled onto the back of the fifties-era sofa, the oldness assaulting his nose. An unmarked freezer truck idled on the curb. Lazlo felt his knees give in relief. Not Animal Control. A squat man in gray coveralls and a flat cap hopped out the passenger side. The man looked around, warily, and turned back to retrieve a clipboard. Lazlo knew the man. Horst. District manager for the Meat of the Month Club. Horst was his own kind of monster, but he loved cats. Maybe—

A flipper stroked the back of Lazlo's head. His tail shot up.

"Cat," she purred, her vocal cords, obviously liberated from the idiot, vibrating deeply.

To Lazlo, it sounded suspiciously like 'Rat'. She stroked him again and they both watched Horst open the back of the truck, drop down a battered ramp, and wheel out two coolers on a dolly.

The flipper retracted and something clacked.

Lazlo closed his eyes and braced. He'd had a terrible life really, why would the end be any different?

Nothing.

He cracked an eye and saw Horst struggling to pull the dolly up the front path. Cracked the other eye. No Savannah. He heard the pantry door creak open and scampered into the kitchen. She'd torn open a box of Kitty Kale and dumped it into his bowl, the crispy pellets overflowing onto the floor. His stomach growled and his eyes teared. He'd never been so happy to see his least favourite food of all time.

He savoured the bitter kibble as the doorbell rang.

He ate as the door opened.

He continued eating as Horst shrieked.

He only stopped when he heard the clacking. The chewing. The godawful chewing. Savages.

Whatever. Let her eat. Let her do whatever she wanted. She'd held up her end of the bargain. That was all that mattered. He gulped down another mouthful. Once he escaped this madhouse it was impossible to know where his next meal would come from. He was still inhaling when he heard the door slam shut.

Motherfucker.

He scurried back to the couch in time to see Savannah squeeze into the passenger side of the truck. The driver's door opened, and a young lady scrambled half out before being yanked back inside by her hair. After a minute the truck pulled away, back still open, and disappeared down the street.

So much for Plan B.

Lazlo stood there, nose and front paws pressed against the filthy glass, unfocused vision split between his raw-boned face and the outside world. So close, yet so far away. Time rolled on and through, extruding endlessly like sausage from a grinder. Eventually his stomach growled as the hunger returned, worse than ever.

With a heaving cough, Lazlo half hopped, half fell off the couch, and shuffled back toward the kitchen. The aftertaste of kale, once all he dreamt about, soured his thoughts. Like cinders in his mouth. Not what he remembered. Not even close. He edged around Horst's arm, fingers still clutching the handle from a shattered cooler. Fat juicy fingers. Lazlo licked his withered lips, slid his rough tongue along tepid salty skin. Remembered.

Eat or be eaten. Was that a Seneca quote? He wouldn't make the same mistake he'd made with poor dumb Darryl. Savannah had the right idea. Lazlo gnawed off a fingertip and wriggled through the pet door into the garage, where yet another freezer stood. Silent. Waiting.

CHERRY RED

CHAD LUTZKE

RAYMOND SAT IN the clearing, a line of three shiny toy cars in front of him. It was just before noon and Kevin would be there any minute. It was Kevin's turn to bring the lunch, and Raymond was starving. He was hoping for PB & J with Doritos. Kevin had taught him about the *PBJD Deluxe*. The idea of placing Doritos within the sandwich was a simple one, but genius, taking an otherwise dull sandwich to the next level, like adding bananas to unsweetened cereal, chocolate chips to pancakes, or freezing the corn syrup from a can of pears—simple, but genius.

The clearing was a large area of dirt in the middle of the woods behind Claywood Elementary. The woods were dense with a variety of trees, the forest floor covered in thick foliage, except within the clearing. That special place made for the perfect Matchbox racetrack, where countless hours had been spent carving out a city of roads within the ground. Tree bark was used to construct houses, garages, and even a gas station, while twigs made for guardrails along dangerous curves. Green army men acted as pedestrians, policemen, and gas station attendants, and matchbook lids for ramps, where the cars would launch within the boys' fingers, clearing rocky ravines and temporary streams. It was a tiny world that "even God himself would be proud of," Kevin had said.

The reason for the clearing in the middle of the woods was a mystery solved by years of hearsay. The land was owned by the Stimacs, an elderly couple with a farm who'd purchased it in the early fifties, eventually building a guesthouse for their son, complete with a fireplace. The house was far beyond throwing distance from

15

the farm and at one point had its own private drive off from River Road, a trail that had since grown over on account of the house burning down barely a year after its construction—an event that had its own urban legend, which held about as much truth as a sieve holds water. But fallacy filled with dread is far more entertaining than uneventful fact.

The story, as Raymond, Kevin, and every other pre-teen boy and girl in Lavendale recited, was the Stimacs' son—who was an obese deviant with an appetite for too much food and an obscene amount of sex— stole a pig from his parent's farm in effort to satiate one of his two vices, depending on who was telling the story. The girls tended to lean toward the son's addiction to food, as opposed to the horrific idea that someone would put their pecker where it most certainly didn't belong.

The tale goes on to speak of a struggle between pig and man that resulted in a tipped candle and eventually a fire that killed them both. The punchline was always the same: *For three whole days, the smell of bacon filled the air within a 10-mile radius.*

The truth was the son was a drunk (a skinny one) who passed out beside two lit candles and a large stack of newspapers, catching fire to the place. The man got away safely, only to die ten years later in another state from liver failure.

Decades later, the only remains were the fireplace and a cellar door in the ground that led to nothing but a three-foot hole, the cellar having been filled in a year after the fire, when the Stimacs found a young boy who'd fallen down the hole and broken both ankles. He'd been there for two days, malnourished and covered in dirt. That particular part of the clearing's history never made it to the ears of locals.

Kevin was late. Their meeting time was noon sharp. But showing up a few minutes late was nothing new for him, or for nearly any kid his age. Even an appointment as exciting as a day at the clearing wasn't enough to make sure the fun began promptly for most kids. Raymond on the other hand was always on time. He had no reason to linger at home. Every hour away from there was a welcome escape, freedom from the smell of alcohol and smoke, the sound of a too-loud TV and the insistent rubbing of his mother's corn-ridden feet.

Raymond studied his three Matchbox cars, wiped them each free of dust and placed them on display once again, perfectly symmetrical, perfectly new. They were prizes found inside Sugar Bang Cereal. He'd collected three of the four available—the fourth being an anomaly. Kevin hadn't gotten it either, and the two started to wonder if the elusive thing even existed, that perhaps its image on the back of the box was just a sly way of selling more product.

It wasn't that Raymond absolutely had to collect them all. It was the model of car itself: A cherry-red Dodge Charger. His favorite car, in his favorite color. And the fastest of them all. His dream car.

So far, he'd talked his mother into purchasing six boxes of the cereal. The first two boxes held the same navy-blue Volkswagen Bug. The next box he'd eaten awarded him the canary yellow Ford pickup—his least favorite of the four pictured on the back of the box. The final three boxes gave yet another Bug, one more pickup, and the Dodge custom van with flames on the side. He traded the duplicates at school for candy and a baseball card he was told was worth money, but being a fan of neither baseball or cards, and not trusting the offering party with its true value, he found himself regretting the trade. Nobody else he knew collected baseball cards, and the candy was gone far too fast.

After gloating over the line of cars and contemplating the effort put into their obtainment, Raymond began constructing a new road that would ultimately lead to a lakefront formed by digging a small hole and filling it with whatever beverage Kevin might bring. Or if all else failed, piss.

By using a spoon Raymond had taken from home and kept there at the clearing, he dug out a shallow path, being careful not to go too deep. There was a science to forming the perfect road, a skill he'd became quite proficient in. Once the path was formed, it would need to be firmly pressed. Loose dirt made for a slow car, and nobody liked a slow car.

Soon after the first stretch of road was complete, Raymond heard the sound of tall weeds slapping against hurrying legs. He refused to look up, hoping his agitation for Kevin's tardiness showed.

"Sorry I'm late, dude. But I've got a damn good excuse. A *damn* good one . . . you're not gonna believe it."

Raymond set the spoon down and finally looked up at Kevin, whose hand was deep in his pocket.

A grin spread across Kevin's face. "Ready?"

A nod from Raymond.

"Close your eyes."

"Just show me, already."

"Okay. You asked for it." Kevin withdraw his hand and held it out, palm side up. "Check it out."

In his hand was the ever-elusive cherry-red Dodge Charger, more glorious than Raymond had ever imagined. The picture on the box had certainly not done it justice. It was gorgeous. No. It was perfect.

"Wow!" Raymond stood and slowly plucked it from his friend's hand, carefully, as though it could be crushed between his eager fingers. "Metallic paint?" The box hadn't revealed that glorious detail.

"Spin the wheels!" Kevin said.

"Raymond pinched the small car between thumb and index finger, then spun the back wheels with two fingers. He watched with wonder as the wheels seemed to go on forever. "Dang!"

"Definitely the fastest out of 'em all."

"Definitely." Saying the word in agreement created a strange sensation in Raymond's gut—a sickly feeling, like he'd just admitted to somehow being inferior to his friend. "How many boxes?"

"Twelve."

"Twelve!" His sickened gut dropped at the thought of having to ask his mother for so much more cereal, of having to *eat* more of it. The worst cereal he'd ever had.

"Can you believe that?"

"You must be full." Raymond laughed.

"Pfft. I don't eat that shit, do you?"

Raymond *had* eaten it. Every day. One box every week. Him eating it was the only way his mother agreed to buy it. And to make matters worse, she wouldn't allow him to add any sugar, not even honey. "It's already sweetened," she'd said. "It says so right on the box. That's all we need is for you to be as hyper as that Fields boy.".

"Nah. I don't eat that shit either," Raymond lied. "I'll give you a baseball card for it . . . and Miss October." He was referring to the centerfold he'd torn from his mother's old boyfriend's Playboy magazine. Kevin had seen it and brought it up often that summer, even asking to borrow it just for the night. It was the one thing Raymond had that Kevin actually wanted, coveted even.

"No way, dude. Not worth it. Plus, what would I do with a stupid baseball card?"

"It's worth money."

"How much?"

"I don't know. I got it from Tommy Dorr."

"Tommy Dorr? Tommy don't know shit about baseball cards, and if you got that from him in a trade then you got gypped, dude. Sorry."

Raymond stared at the car in his hand. The wheels had finally stopped. There was a moment of awkward silence between the two boys and, reluctantly, Raymond offered the dream car back to Kevin.

Kevin knelt down and tested the car on a track, taking one of the dangerous curves while doing a bad imitation of squealing tires. He spotted the new road Raymond had started. "Workin' on the lakefront road?"

"Yeah." Raymond deflated, his ambition gone. He wanted to be happy for his friend, but he couldn't. He'd worked much harder on getting that car than Kevin did. Kevin didn't even have to eat the cereal. Whether his brother and sisters were eating it, or his parents had the kind of money to just dump on box after box for the sole purpose of making sure their son got what he wanted, he wasn't sure. But Kevin getting his hands on the Dodge Charger first felt . . . undeserving.

Raymond sat propped on a rickety stool at the kitchen counter, reading the back of a Sugar Bangs box for the fourth time that morning. He shoveled the bottom of his third bowl of cereal into his mouth and let out a burp that almost turned messy. He rubbed his bloated belly and felt the taut skin as it stretched against too much food.

Asking his mom for another box before this one was finished was useless. He'd tried that and it triggered a lengthy diatribe about money and kids starving and rent being due. The only thing on his side was his mother's disdain for cooking—be it a home-cooked meal or a simple TV dinner, her lazy ass just as soon let him live on cereal and chips alone. Anything to keep her from having to peel away from the TV. So, cereal twice—or sometimes even three times—a day was fine with her, encouraged even. Just so long as he ate it.

As Raymond upped his Sugar Bang intake from one box every week to nearly one a day, his mother accommodated his new diet but lessoned trips to the store by buying three boxes at a time. Raymond would tear into them immediately, being disappointed each time as the same three cars were pulled from their cardboard homes.

It became difficult to enjoy himself at the clearing, watching Kevin run his car through the tracks, boasting continuously on how no other car could ever catch up to the cherry-red Dodge Charger. "Wanna race? " he'd say with a chuckle, knowing full well that Raymond couldn't compete, not without pretending his cars were something they weren't.

For several weeks this went on—the teasing, the mocking, and the gluttony. Until one day Kevin directed attention toward something Raymond himself hadn't noticed.

The two sat shirtless under the sun, building a motel where Kevin had said prostitutes "did it" for money, or for rides in fancy cars, cars like Dodge Chargers. Kevin looked at Raymond and giggled. "Dude! What's up with your belly?"

Raymond looked down at his stomach. He noted the strange way it sat. His poor posture when sitting had always yielded little rolls— thin flaps of flesh that even the skinniest of boys sported across their midsection when hunched over. But this was different. The rolls were large mounds and dimpled like his mother's thighs when she wore those shorts that embarrassed him—the frayed denim ones she had no business wearing. He had gotten fat. And worse yet, his superior friend was pointing it out.

"Dude! Ha ha! It's the ghost of Stimac. He's got you!"

Raymond sat up straight in effort to make the folds disappear but somehow made it worse, as thin white lines highlighted each section where sweat had pooled.

"Everybody get away! It's fatty the Stimac ghost here to eat you all!" With the Dodge Charger in hand, Kevin made peeling-out noises and raced away from Raymond, adding additional screams in varying tones as though an entire village were pleading for their lives. He doubled over, grabbing his stomach in a fit of laughter. "No more PBJD's for you, boy." His eyes widened as he discovered even more to the joke. "Warning, all farmers, keep them pigs locked up. The Stimac ghost is on the loose!"

Raymond clawed at his stomach, wishing it away.

"He'll stick his pecker in your hog, eat it whole, then kill your dog."

Torn between crying or yelling his own obscenities, Raymond glared at his tormentor, the Dodge Charger in Kevin's hand like some kind of accomplice to the cruelty being dished out. Finally, Raymond's face went blank.

You could blame his next move on the relentless teasing or on extraordinary envy. But it was the cereal that really sent him over. The three meals a day of the worst shit he'd ever put in his mouth. Worse than that stale beer his uncle once offered him. Worse than the boiled cabbage his grandmother insisted on cooking every Easter Sunday. And he wasn't exactly sure what chewing tobacco tasted like, but he was pretty sure it was better than twenty-two boxes of Sugar Bangs. The sweetened, unsweetened cereal that smelled like burnt corn and tasted like cardboard.

Raymond rose from the dirty ground, his belly streaked red, and grabbed a nearby stick the size of a baseball bat.

There was no screaming, no pleading. Only one small grunt that left Kevin's mouth. The first swing split his ear against his head. His eyes rolled back, and his legs seized. The second, third, and fourth swings split his forehead, shattered his teeth and crushed his nose.

The sound of wood on flesh and bone seemed to echo through the trees, then all was silent. Except for the birds, whose song played as a disturbing soundtrack in the aftermath of the violent outburst. Blood trickled, urine flowed, then all movement stopped, while the birds continued to serenade.

Raymond stood over the scene, emotionless. He dropped the stick, pried the Dodge Charger from Kevin's hand and stuck it in his pocket, along with the other three cars he'd worked so very hard for.

The boys had only opened the cellar door a few times, including the first day they'd ventured to the clearing. They explored every inch of their new finding that day—the crumbling fireplace, a nearby hollowed log from a tree that'd fallen decades prior, and finally the cellar—a doorway that led to nowhere. No further exploration necessary. The two had once used the three-foot hole as a toilet, until they realized what a bad idea it was if they were going to be playing nearby. For the last time in his life, Raymond opened that cellar door, and filled it.

The police didn't ask Raymond as many questions as he anticipated, not as many as they should have. And as soon as school started again, rumors circulated regarding domestic violence and an evil stepdad with a criminal record. None of which pointed to Raymond. As a matter of fact, the school year was going well. Good grades, weight loss, and a new friend.

Raymond graduated from making tiny roads for tiny cars to making wide and lengthy trails for riding BMX bikes. He proudly rode his bike with its mismatched rims and silver matte primer finish—a garage sale find for a measly ten dollars.

Hours were spent in a larger expanse of trees and fields, far away from the Stimac farm and its secrets. Jumps were built with dirt and plywood by Raymond and his new friend. Hours of bonding. Hours of riding and constructing, then hours of teasing, mocking, and leaving Raymond in the dust, courtesy of his friend's new bike—a Mongoose with matching rims, Oakley grips and a light-weight frame painted a brilliant, metallic cherry red.

THE FEEDING

KRISTOPHER TRIANA

A FLYER HUNG from the front door of Walter's trailer. The other old folks in Palm Gardens liked to refer to them as *manufactured housing*, but Walter had no illusions. This wasn't some white trash trailer—it had several rooms, a full kitchen and a bathroom—but it was a trailer nonetheless, identical to all the others in the community.

One of the other things the retirement community had was a guard stationed at the front entrance who wouldn't let the bar up for just any car to drive through. Walter wondered how someone had been able to get past the guard and canvas everyone's door with restaurant coupons.

He turned the flyer over in his hand.

Dottie's Grinders!

Coupon good for one free sandwich!

Walter frowned. *Dottie's*? In his day delis had names like *Tony's* or *Frankie's* or some Italian surname like *Bianchi's*. It seemed odd for the place to have a woman's name, but then again, maybe Walter was just being old fashioned. Or sexist, as his daughter sometimes called him.

The other side of the flyer was a photo of one delicious looking foot-long.

Fresh, revitalizing sandwiches made to order!

Walter shook his head. How could *a grinder* be revitalizing?

The recycling bin was right there in the carport. Easy enough to toss it. But Walter had been a child of The Great Depression. He'd always been frugal, and ever since Agatha died he had taken over her habit of clipping coupons. He was always looking for discounts and there was no better discount than *free*.

He put the flyer in his pocket.

He placed the order the following night.

It'd been a while since he'd had a foot-long grinder—doctor's orders about his weight—but one couldn't hurt. Walter didn't have much. He was an old man who lived alone and rarely heard from his only child. Even his grandkids didn't call him. Sure, they cashed the checks he sent for Christmas and their birthdays, but he never got so much as a thank you call or cheap Hallmark. One of the few joys he had left in his life was food. Doc Flanagan would never have to know.

Walter called the security office to let them know a delivery guy would be on the way, and set out to watch John Wayne kill some Indians on AMC while he waited. He was startled when the doorbell rang. It hadn't been more than ten minutes since he'd called in the order.

Boy, he thought, *they take that twenty minutes or it's free stuff seriously.*

He got out of his recliner as fast as he could, which was still rather slow. He and his knees hadn't been friends for a long time. Bracing himself on his cane, Walter tightened his robe as he shuffled toward the door, grabbing the two-dollar tip he'd put on the table.

"Just a minute."

When he opened the door, his jaw fell agape. He had to remind myself to be polite and close his mouth.

Standing on his porch was a beautiful young woman. She was a blonde girl no older than twenty-five, with the kind of body only a young girl could have—smooth skin, lithe limbs, soft curves in just the right places. She wore tight jeans and a long-sleeve shirt with an emblem of a little sandwich just above her right breast. The dull gold of the porch light gave her an angelic glow. In her hands was a paper box. Her smile was a daydream. Walter felt like a young boy staring at clouds, making mental shapes of dinosaurs and flowers.

"Mr. Devereaux?"

Walter blinked out of his reverie, barely recognizing his own name. "Yes—I mean, hello. Sorry, I just wasn't expecting anyone so soon."

The girl smiled wider. "We don't like to keep our customers waiting when they're so hungry."

Walter instinctively returned her smile. "Well, good customer service goes a long way."

He noticed a spark behind her eyes, glimmering like Christmas. God, she was beautiful. He had to force himself not to stare.

"Here you go," she said, handing over the grinder.

Walter took it from her and she turned to go.

"Wait," he said, wanting her to never leave. "I've a tip for you."

She came back with an *aww, you didn't have to do that* look on her perfect face. Walter bypassed the two bucks on the nightstand, reached for the old cigar box where he kept his grocery money and fished out a ten-dollar bill. It was more than he'd ever tipped anyone, but he wanted her to remember him, to fight the other drivers to be the one to deliver to him in the future, just so he could look into those soft, green eyes again.

"You're sweet," she said, taking the cash. "But it's such a large tip. Are you sure?"

He nodded. "Positive."

She tucked it into a pocket so tight it was a miracle she could pass the small piece of paper through. He watched her with quiet awe, a slight tremor coursing through his arthritic fingers, making them feel more alive than they had in years.

He wasn't being a dirty old man here. He wasn't interested in her sexually. Okay, maybe he was a little bit. She was gorgeous, after all. But what really drew him to her was the aura of youth that radiated off her like the warmth of sunlight. She was bouncy and bubbly without seeming like an airhead, her smile not just a show for customers. There was genuine joy there, the kind of joy Walter wasn't used to seeing in this village for old farts. The faces he usually saw were staring down the final curtain of their lives. This place wasn't the thriving community the pamphlets made it out to be, it was simply the reaper's waiting room. Seeing youth and all the possibility that came with it, here in Palm Gardens, bordered on the surreal. The delivery girl was magic in purple sneakers.

25

"You're an angel," she said, surprising him. He'd been thinking the same thing about her. "I really appreciate this."

"Anytime," he said, and meant it.

The girl turned, walking out of the light and into the encroaching dark of the evening. As he watched her round the corner of the house, he wondered where her car was.

The grinder was okay. It wasn't Subway level terrible but wasn't special either. Too much mayo. Watery tomatoes. Not bad, but he was glad he hadn't paid for it. Still, he knew he'd order it again, as long as she was the one to deliver it.

He thought about her all night, confused by the sudden obsession. He wondered if she lived on her own or still at home, if she was working nights at the deli to pay for school. Maybe that's why she'd been so grateful for the tip. He wondered what her favorite color was, what her favorite movie was, if she loved summer or preferred fall. He wondered what she looked like under those tight jeans and felt a twinge of guilt. He didn't even know her name for goodness' sake.

He would have to ask her.

The next night, the doorbell rang mere minutes after he'd called. He muted the TV and got out of his seat with ease. He grinned, attributing the flexibility to mind over matter, the anticipation of seeing the delivery girl giving him pep. He still needed his cane, but his knees gave only a smidge of their usual resistance.

She beamed when he opened the door and Walter had to remind himself to breathe. Somehow the girl looked even more beautiful than last night. Her hair was down around her shoulders in yellow curls and there was a wet sheen to her lips. The cold air had blushed her cheeks.

"Me again," she said, handing him the paper box he didn't really want.

"I'm so glad. Say, what's your name again?"

She raised her hand to her breast and Walter's eyes went wide. For a moment he'd thought she was going to squeeze it. Instead she pointed to the little patch sewn into the shirt. There was also a white squiggle there he hadn't noticed.

Dottie.

Walter blinked. "You're Dottie?"

"Mmhmm."

"The one who owns the deli?"

She shrugged. "That's me."

"You deliver the orders yourself?"

She giggled, the sound of love songs and butterflies. "Not all the time. Only to special customers."

She gave him a sly wink and he was lost to her forever. Through that simple bat of her eyelash he felt more love than anyone had given him since his sweet wife had died. He knew he was reading far too much into this, that he was just a foolish old man and this pretty, young sweetheart was probably just being friendly for tips, but he couldn't control the way Dottie made him feel. He was blushing and hoped the busted capillaries in his face would cover that up.

"You make an old man happy."

This time he gave her a twenty.

With the fifth sandwich he ordered that week, Dottie came inside. It was bitterly cold and the wind was a vicious, biting thing. When he opened the door, she stepped right past him.

"Hope you don't mind if I come in for a minute," she said. "It's freezing out there."

Walter was more than okay with it. The girl could move in rent-free if she wanted to. Not only was he enamored with Dottie; he had also grown to really enjoy the grinders. He'd acquired a taste for both their cold and hot ones, and whenever he ate one, he felt a burst of energy and mild euphoria, like he had when he'd first started taking the painkillers his doctor had given him. He also felt oddly healthier, despite eating meatball subs and Philly cheese steak sandwiches, often with a side of fries. He'd been breathing better and hadn't used his oxygen tank in days, getting around the house without his cane. It was crazy, but true. He couldn't wait to show off to Flanagan during Monday's checkup. For all his doctor's red meat and junk food bashing, nightly doses had done wonders for Walter. Now it seemed no other food could satisfy his hunger.

"Come right in, Dottie. Can I make you some coffee or cocoa?"

He was glad he'd tidied up that morning, almost as if he'd known this would happen.

"Hot cocoa sounds wonderful."

He guided her to the sofa and went to the adjacent kitchen to boil some water. He took out the fancy coffee mugs Agatha had bought but never let them use. If this wasn't a special occasion, what was?

"Lots of orders tonight?" he asked.

"Yup. That's the weekend for you. Busy, busy."

"I imagine you'll stay that way. Dottie's has the best grinders in town. I've told all my friends that."

But Walter's true friends were all dead. It would've been more truthful for him to say he'd told his neighbor Mrs. Bloom and the man down at the post office.

"Always the big sweetheart," she said, getting up and taking off her gloves. "You always take care of me, don't you, Walter?"

He turned, somewhat surprised by her choice of words. He gave her big tips (the last one had been close to fifty bucks, making it a 500% tip) and he gave her repeat business, but that was hardly taking care of her. Still, he accepted the compliment.

"Just returning the favor," he said. "It always makes me happy when you bring my food. It's so nice for a girl like you to come to see an old guy like me."

Dottie came closer and her proximity made Walter's skin tingle. He could smell the strawberries of her shampoo and the faint hint of mint on her breath.

"Everybody needs somebody to take care of them," she said. "I worry about you being all alone in this house. Bringing you hot meals gives me a chance to check up on you, to make sure you're still smiling."

The water was boiling but Walter didn't notice. He was lost in Dottie, a released prisoner seeing the night sky for the first time in years. He wanted to tell her she would never have to worry about him not smiling. Not as long as she was in his life.

"You take great care of me, Dottie."

She reached up and ran two fingers through the hair on one side of his head. For a moment he was convinced she was going to kiss him, and a punch combo of bliss and terror stunned him. But she only patted him on the shoulder. Then she turned toward the grinder on the table. She popped open the box and the familiar aroma hit Walter's nostrils like an intoxicant. He felt suddenly lighter and freer—a dreamer, a virgin. Dottie lifted half of the hot sandwich and brought it over to him, her lips pursed as she blew on it.

"Open up."

From that point on, she always fed the grinders to him.

"I'm afraid it's gotten worse."

Doc Flanagan looked at him from over his reading glasses. Walter winced.

"Worse?" he asked, chortling sardonically. "How could it be worse? I mean, just look at me!"

Walter slid off the examination bed and made a point of making a hard landing to show how strong his knees had become. He stood up straight, his slouch gone. He flexed, showing off the biceps that were larger and leaner every day. Skin that had once hung like clothing on a line was now as tight as a fifty-year-old's.

"I'll admit, you do look great, Walter. Exercise has helped you a lot."

"Heck, I haven't so much as gone for a walk in weeks. The meds must be working."

The doctor shook his head. "The medicine wouldn't help you lose body fat or grow new muscle tissue. What it's suppose to do is make you healthier on the inside, and from the test results it hasn't been doing that."

Walter scoffed, dismissing this with a wave of his hand.

"Your blood pressure is up," Flanagan said. "Your cholesterol has spiked, your sugar is way off and your blood vessels are more damaged than last time. I'm worried about your kidneys and—"

"There has to be some kind of mix up."

The doctor ignored him. "I'm wondering if there's something you've been doing differently, something I warned you *not* to do. Have you been consuming alcohol or smoking cigars again?"

"Not at all," he answered, truthfully.

"What about eating habits? Any changes?"

Walter hesitated just long enough for the doctor to know.

"Cheating on the diet, then?" Flanagan asked. "You know how easily your blood sugar is effected, Walter, and how the wrong foods affect your weak heart. You can't indulge in ice cream anymore."

Heat rose at the back of Walter's neck. Flanagan didn't even look forty. What did he know about getting old?

"If I want to treat myself once in a while, then that's what I'll do, Doc. I feel better when I eat my way. A man can't live on salad. Maybe a woman can, but not a man."

"So what are you binging on? Hamburgers and pork chops?"

Walter threw up his hands. "I appreciate your concerns, but I think I have my diet under control."

"Not according to the tests."

"Yes, well, flush the tests. I'm eighty years old! What's the point of staying alive if you can't have a little happiness? I tell you, Doc, death is better than a life without joy."

Dottie fed him another segment.

Walter bit into the sandwich and as she pulled it away they snickered as a long strand of melted cheese hung between his lips and the bread.

"Good?" she asked.

He swallowed. "The best yet. Every time I think your grinders have become the greatest food on earth, it somehow gets better. And I swear it has healing properties. I'm moving around better, no more aches and pains. I can bend over and lift things easier than I have in decades. And my face is clear again—no more red rivers from busted capillaries. I think even some of the hair on my bald spot is coming back."

She ran her non-greasy hand through his hair, just like Agatha once had, just like his mother once had. The nails felt good against his scalp.

"You know I love to feed you," Dottie told him, coming forward with the sandwich again.

Her eyes seemed somehow darker tonight.

He took another bite of heaven.

There was blood in his stool and the stool itself was black. It was as if he'd been consuming nothing but beets and Pepto Bismol. Flushing the toilet, Walter looked in the bathroom mirror. His hair, previously white and thin, was full and had returned to the salt and pepper it had been when he was in his sixties. His chest was high and tight, just like in his army days. He knew Dottie's colorful aura of youth was rubbing off on him somehow, combining with the miracle cure of the grinders to smooth out his wrinkles and put a spring back in his step. These days the neighborhood widows watched him when he went out to the mailbox, waving when he collected his trash bins from the curb. He had delighted at the new attention. He felt better than he had in decades.

But he was bleeding internally.

He would have to move up his appointment with Flanagan if he could.

On his way out, Walter put on his coat but went without his winter cap, wanting to show off his hair to the clerks at the grocery store. He was a regular there and figured they'd notice. He was only going to pick up some over-the-counter stomach medicine. There was no need for groceries anymore, not with Dottie making deliveries for breakfast, lunch and dinner.

"Hello, handsome."

Walter turned to see Mrs. Bloom sitting on her front porch, one of the many widows who'd become friendlier to him lately. It was too cold for her to be outside for the fun of it. She must've been waiting for him again, just as she had been since she'd first invited him over for dinner. It had given him an ego boost, but while he'd always thought Fay was good-looking, she couldn't compete with Dottie. He didn't want to pass up his feedings just to have small talk with Fay Bloom and eat some disgusting home-cooked meal when he could have another grinder.

"Good morning, Fay. How are you?"

"Doing fine. Say, I was planning on baking a pie later. Have I told you about my famous pies?"

"Oh yes, I remember. Three-time ribbon winner at the state fair?"

"Five-time, Walter. The best apple pie you'll ever put in your mouth."

He'd once loved apple pie. Now the thought of it made him want to retch. His stomach pinched even thinking about food that didn't come from Dottie's.

"Maybe you'd like to come by this afternoon?" she asked, giving him a quick glance up and down. "Have some tea and a piece of my pie?"

He had to force himself not to wince.

"Oh, I don't know, Fay. Doctor says I need to stick to my diet, with the diabetes and all."

The old woman laughed and leaned forward in the rocking chair. "Oh, come now. I see you getting takeout delivery all the time. If you can cheat with that delivery girl, you can cheat with me."

Walter tried to smile but his mouth felt full of ash. It was cold outside and his stomach was gurgling audibly. He just wanted to get in his car and go. Why wouldn't this old crone leave him be?

"Maybe some other time, Fay."

He opened the car door.

"All right. That takeout must really be something the way you order it. I'd like to try it sometime."

She was leading him, hoping for an invite. No way she was getting one. He told her the phone number for Dottie's Deli again, though he doubted her geriatric brain would retain the information. Then he got out of there before she could flirt with him any further.

After peeing blood in the urinal of the grocery store's bathroom, Walter bought stomach meds and extra aspirin for the headache that'd been nagging him since Fay Bloom held him up on his way out. He also got some cash from the ATM. When he arrived home he took the medications and sat down to watch a repeat of *Christmas in Connecticut*—one of his favorite films from childhood—but kept having to get up to defecate more blood and blackness. He'd managed to get his doctor's appointment rescheduled for earlier in the week. Now he was considering going to the emergency room. But when he looked at the clock he saw it was twenty past noon. Dottie would be over soon, and he wouldn't miss that even if his intestines were falling out his backside.

Combing his hair in the bathroom, Walter had to stop twice to vomit. It was dark green with black slivers in it. He blinked at what he'd regurgitated. Were the slivers moving?

No, he thought. *They're just moving from the impact.* He'd vomited hard and the pieces were wobbling in the bowl's rippling water. That was all. But when he flushed the bodily waste he could have sworn he saw the black slivers clinging to the sides of the bowl before they fell away.

The doorbell rang just as he finished gargling mouthwash. He practically skipped down the hall.

Dottie smiled, winked. "Hey, Wally."

He loved when she called him that. No one had called him Wally since his days of playing stickball in the streets with the boys—Joe, Mick, Freddy and Georgie—friends who'd been like brothers when Walter was eleven, all of them now long gone.

"You're your usual gorgeous self," he told her. He'd gotten more comfortable with harmless flirting. She seemed to enjoy it just as much as he did. "And those grinders smell better than spring roses."

He'd surprised her with roses multiple times and wished he'd thought to grab some at the store today. He made a mental note for next time. At least he had the thousand dollars cash for her in his pocket he'd taken out of his account at the ATM.

Dottie took the extra-large paper box from the bag. She didn't bring small, personal sandwiches anymore, only party platters of twenty sandwiches each. She titled her head toward the hall.

"Let's go to your room this time."

Walter's smile dropped. His heartbeat was machine gun fire.

"My room?"

She winked again. "Come on."

She took his hand in hers, carrying the platter with the other, and guided him through his own home. He quivered, unable to believe this was happening even though he wasn't really sure what was going on. Surely she didn't mean what he thought she did. Dottie had kissed him before, but only on the cheek in a friendly manner, the way his daughter used to. And he had never made a move on Dottie. She was exceptionally beautiful, but no matter how much younger he'd felt since meeting her he doubted he could handle going to bed with a young woman. He was eighty years old for goodness's sake. But he didn't object as she took him to his room. How on earth could he?

"You just relax," she told him.

He lied down on the bed as Dottie put the platter box on the nightstand and opened it up. The odor hit him immediately, a stench like rotting yams and roadkill cooking under a summer sun. He coughed to get the toxic stench out of his lungs and when he breathed again the foul odor was gone, replaced by the usual smell of warm bread and beef. Dottie sat on the bed, holding a segment over him.

Walter doubted he should eat it when he had this internal bleeding going on, but also felt it could be just the thing to make him feel better. He was like a junkie for her grinders, sick with them and sick without them.

"Open up," Dottie said.

He did. He always would. Chewing the cheesy bread, Walter took the roll of bills from his pocket. Her smile was as warm as the food she served.

"You're so sweet, Wally."

"There's more where that came from," he said with pride. "I've got more to give."

Dottie was stoic. "I know," she said. "Much more. And not just money."

The lights were off, leaving only gray winter daylight to illuminate the room through the thin curtains. In the soft shadows, Dottie's face seemed darker, thinner—almost skeletal. She came in with another sandwich. She was making him eat more of them these days, expecting him to finish several in one sitting. As she inched closer, the smell of death returned to him on the steam coming off the meatballs. Dottie hovered, staring down like a carnivore stares down prey. A glisten of drool shone on her lips.

"I take care of you," she said, "and you take care of me. One hand feeds the other."

He took another bite.

Dottie ran her fingers through his hair and her nails were stronger and sharper than ever before, like knives grazing his scalp.

She breathed deep and something small and black slithered between the gaps in her teeth.

Walter finished the slice and his insides seemed to boil. A horrible gas rose in his throat, his anus and penis leaking in hot stings of pain. He reached up to stroke Dottie's cheeks, his hand now as smooth as a teenager's.

Though he felt like he was dying, he knew it wasn't so. Instead his clock was running backward, his body rewinding with every feeding. He was being unborn, wiped from existence, bite by bite.

The spark in Dottie's eyes was like the glow of a dead moon, their jade green now as murky as a swamp. She grinned with a mouth full of tiny black snakes and fed him yet another grinder.

"Youth is fleeting, but you don't have to worry," she said. "You can just stay in bed as you get sicker. I'll keep making the deliveries, Wally. You have to feed. We both have to feed, now don't we?"

He nodded. That would be just fine. Her darkness was his only light.

"You're an angel, Wally. I really appreciate this."

The coupon was for the deli Walter had told her about before he'd died. Such a sad thing. The poor man's body had simply turned on him in the end. He'd looked so good in the days just before his death, so full of life, so *young*. Fay had felt like a stalker the way she'd always watched his house through her curtains, waiting for any glimpse of him, hoping he'd take her up on an invite even if it meant she had to wear him down and hope for his pity. Walter's youthfulness had made her feel warm in all the places her body had been cold since her husband Jack had passed, and he'd been in the ground for nearly a quarter century. What she wouldn't give just for the company of a man, let alone to feel the gentle touch of one. Maybe some of Walter's youthfulness would have rubbed off on her. She would give anything for a taste of youth.

Fay had never been much for grinders, but Walter had sworn by this Dottie's place. That cute delivery girl had brought him takeout morning, noon, and night. Fay assumed Walter had had a crush on her, but that couldn't be enough to make him order from the restaurant three times a day, could it? The food had to be good if he ate it that often. Now that she'd found a flyer on her door for a free made-to-order sandwich, what did she have to lose? She could always toss the grinder in the trash if it wasn't any good.

The doorbell startled her. It couldn't be the delivery girl this early, could it? Fay had only just called in the order and she hadn't seen headlights or heard a car.

She got out of her chair, using her walker to make her way to the door. Even this small effort strained her breathing, a reminder that she didn't know how much time she had left, and while she knew her sons were busy with families of their own, it hurt that they didn't visit more often now that they all knew just how sick she really was. But that was just part of getting old, Fay supposed. No one in Palm Gardens got regular visitors. Only Walter had had a regular visitor, one he had to pay for.

Fay opened the door.

The handsome young man smiled as he held out her first grinder.

HUNGRY GHOSTS

SYLVIA ANNE TELFER

A S DARK CLOUDS scudded across a full moon, Nigel was dithering outside Marigold Wang's newest Soho restaurant, almost blinded by fancy lanterns blazing around a scarlet door on which a 'Closed for a Private Function' sign clattered.

Foot-dragging to enter was not quite the word. Maybe a sense of wariness was nearer the mark. Accepting the banquet invitation had in itself been a hard decision, but Marigold had been wheedling, and the likelihood of potential sponsors being present was high. After all, a theater owner with current backers baying for profits had to make sacrifices. He shivered in a sudden gust. Oddly icy for early September.

Through the glass, he made out a tiny human shape. Marigold's hand closed on the door handle. *Click-click-click* as her famously long, blood-red nails scratched the surface

"That Wang woman's a veritable click-beetle on her mobile phone," an actor-pal had recently said.

"But she manages. Her deft Scissorhand maneuvers surpass Johnny Depp," he had replied.

The door opened. "Nigel Fox," Marigold said, and bowed him into the lobby.

In a green and red embossed cheongsam, she was a rhubarb stick. Not even a bum curve. Again, a shiver. Was it because the lobby was silent and thick with incense smoke?

"Got fire insurance, Marigold, with all those lanterns outside? And the door's like the entry tunnel of a fairground ghost train."

37

Her face was impassive.

"The Hungry Ghosts must be guided to the table," she said.

"Hungry what?"

"I told you this was a special feast. Zhongyuan. Chinese Halloween."

"You said you were holding a banquet for my potential clients. And wanted to show me you could correct your little catering blunder from last month."

"It is that too. But on this fifteenth night of the seventh lunar month, the gates of hell are opened and ghosts are free to roam the earth where they seek food and entertainment. Who knows, they may join us tonight."

Was she for real?

"Yeah, sure. Say, Marigold, is your heating on? I'm freezing."

She studded her cheongsam collar.

"It is, but when ghosts are near you must accept it will be cold."

This was like something from an Edgar Allan Poe story. Why was he still willing to hire this kook after her catering ruined the private preview of his flopped Chinese production? What a disaster with her duck feet soup. A key potential backer had spewed at the mere sight and fled the theater.

Mental, true . . . but she's still a bottomless pit of wealth, Nigel old boy. And you can get some if you play the cards right.

His footsteps rang out in the marble vault of a lobby reminiscent of the expensive Hong Kong restaurants, in which he had gorged scores of banquets in the days Veronica, his wife, had owned a lucrative chain of fashion shops.

Veronica.

He could not think of her without hatred. Committing suicide after discovering his affair with a Burmese actress had been melodramatic, and later, he had discovered she had cut him out of her will, leaving him penniless. Not one jot did he miss her. But he did miss the lavish lifestyle that had gone hand in hand with being her husband.

As their footsteps echoed down the lobby, he glanced into the many rooms. He was surprised. The restaurant was deceptive from the outside, had appeared small.

"Can you fill all these seats, Marigold? 'Bums on seats' is the catchphrase in our businesses."

38

She smiled, exposing her gold teeth. He hated looking at them. She was like one of those tacky Chinese ornamental figures with painted gold teeth that cluttered Hong Kong night markets. Fucking gold teeth and talons seemed to be indicators of wealth and status in Chinese culture.

'You're a racist, Nigel. You've no understanding of other cultures,' an Indian film director had once said, when he had been sniggering about the Hindu elephant-god, Ganesha.

'When Ganesha goes on holiday, all he has to do is throw his gear in his trunk.'

Marigold's voice returned him to the present.

"All these seats will be filled. My food is very special, and I hired a feng shui master to ensure good luck. Of course, I will have many customers."

"Backers?"

"No need for them. I am rich from my other restaurants."

"Where are the other guests for tonight, Marigold?"

"In here. Now you've arrived, the guest list is complete."

She opened the door to a room.

"No one's here."

"You cannot see them, but they are at the table eager for the banquet. I told you about our custom of setting places for the Hungry Ghosts."

This was getting mental. He longed to be sitting in 'The Jolly Beggar' in Leicester Square with a curvy teenage blonde. He liked them young.

"Singling me out as your sole living guest? You really do want to make up for your catering faux pas."

"You are such a cultured man."

She paused.

"Tonight, you will taste food that will transport you out of this world."

"Marigold, many of my backers were offended by the revolting dishes you served at my play preview."

She arched an eyebrow. He detested people who could move one eyebrow, leaving the other stationary.

"You did ask me to choose the menu. Next time, I will excel. Tonight, I will show you how superb my dishes are."

"You're gonna need to wow me with this feast, Marigold. Not to mention the price better be low, to fix the mistake."

"Come, choose your food," she said.

She led him further down the lobby to an enormous tank jam-packed with marine life.

"You could have suggested this tank for my buffet. It would have added atmosphere to my Chinese theme."

"Not feasible to transport."

"Your duck feet soup was a disaster, Marigold."

She arched the other eyebrow. Giving them turns?

"I am so sorry I shamed you. Duck feet soup is considered a delicacy in China."

"It wasn't to the palate of a sophisticated theater-going London audience."

She slipped her hand into his. It was clammy, fishlike. Amorous intent? Was she delusional? She was nearing sixty, a centimeter from ugly, not to mention she was under five foot tall. He glimpsed his reflection on the tank's glass. Six feet, attractive, a mere forty, and in excellent shape. A score of women were after him.

Then again. She was loaded. Maybe he could screw her for cash for his theatre.

He stared at the marine life.

"Whopper of a lobster crawling by, and just look at that fish by the yellow rock. It's staring at me. It's mouthing 'eat me'," he said, faking joviality.

A flicker of a smile from Marigold.

"That fish is from the Yangtze river. Shall I get my chef to prepare it?"

"Yes, and throw in that lobster. I could eat a horse, if not deer penis."

"I've many delicacies for you, Nigel."

She led him back to the banquet room. The linen tablecloth shone like freshly fallen snow. Solid silver chopsticks, crystal glassware, and porcelain dishes screamed luxury. Paper televisions, cars, and all the paraphernalia that went with offerings to the dead were on a side table.

Each place setting had an embroidered name card. Nigel lifted one written in Chinese. "Who's this?"

"That's Nǚ Guǐ. A special appearance."

"Who's he?"

"She. But I am not allowed to say."

"You're a knotty race."

He walked to the top of the table.

"Who's this presiding?"

"Yan Wang. He is very special."

"Wang? Father?"

Marigold lowered her eyes in filial piety.

"Tonight, you must call me 'Ask Rice Woman'."

"Uh?"

"I am the medium. I relay to the living what the spirits wish to say."

"Can we skip this tripe? I want to talk to you about a theater project."

"First, we eat."

"Any duck feet sticking out from soup?"

"No."

He stared down at her, and sighed.

"Give me an inkling of what dishes I can expect from you for my new stage play venture. I need reassurance you'll be on the ball after the last fiasco, and I also want a heavy discount in compensation."

Her eyes were now downcast. He was making headway with the guilt trip.

"Well, Nigel, perhaps Hangzhou 'Beggar's Chicken' served on lotus leaf. People say that long ago, a beggar roasted a chicken wrapped in yellow mud without plucking. When he peeled off the dry mud, the chicken's feathers were also taken off."

He was elated. He could spin this into another of her faux pas.

"Beggar's Chicken? My rich guests will take umbrage and spew at the sight of feathers."

"Then, I will not ruffle their feathers.

Marigold walked her talons up his jacket.

"My 'Ants Climbing a Tree' is well received."

"Ants? Get real."

"No ants in the dish. It is spicy stir-fried glass noodles with minced pork."

"Then, why the name?"

"Minced pork sticks to noodle strands, and resembles ants crawling through a tree's branches."

"You're a fanciful race. Why don't you just call it 'noodles and mince'?"

"No romance in you, Nigel?"

Another sexual innuendo?

"Has your past faux pas made you a tad boring in your choice of dishes?"

"I have many ideas but your guests might balk at some. Perhaps they might think thousand-year-old eggs are really that age. Some men think I am older than I look."

Bloody non sequitur, or was the bitch being sarcastic? He looked at her scraggy neck. If she came up with a tortoise delicacy, he would find it hard not to laugh.

"Your guests might find these eggs more palatable if I incorporate them in a platter called lahng-poon. It is offered at special dinners. It is sliced barbecued pork, pickled leeks, sliced abalone, pickled julienned carrots, pickled julienned daikon radish, seasoned julienned jellyfish, sliced pork, headcheese and quartered thousand-year-old eggs."

"Headcheese?"

"Not a dairy cheese, but a terrine made with flesh from the head of a calf or pig and set in aspic."

Nigel shook his head.

"Perhaps then 'Liaoning Sea Cucumber'? It ranks as the first of the 'The Eight Treasured Seafood'. Yes?"

Nigel again shook his head.

"So difficult to please you. Do not worry I will not offer you 'Edible Bird's Nest' in case your guests know it is made from the edible-nest built by swiftlets with saliva and feather."

Winding him up?

"Your Chinese cuisine can be cruel, Marigold. I know 'Drunken Shrimps' is made from live shrimps doused in wine and then simmered."

"If you think that cruel, live monkey brain is considered a delicacy. A live monkey is put beneath a table with its head poking up through a hole. Its skull is cracked with a hammer and then a knife is used to prize out its brain. Diners eat while it screams. It is a dish that can cure erectile dysfunction."

"Such suffering so someone can get a boner? Stop! I'm losing my appetite."

She bowed. He hated her humility. He liked brash women. Oh, for a Madonna to sashay in.

"Our guests have huge, empty bellies, Nigel. I can hear the rumbling. We must start the banquet."

"Hope the greedy ones don't scoff all."

"Their mouths are pinholes and their necks so thin they cannot swallow. They were greedy and jealous in life. Those sins led to their rebirth as Hungry Ghosts."

The gibberish was making it hard for him to entertain the thought of screwing her for cash .

"Don't like the sound of them, Marigold."

"Do not fret. At the end of the month, the gates of Hell will close on them for another year."

He sniffed.

"What a stench of alcohol. Not that I'm complaining."

"Warming liquor allows its aromas to escape. But it's not a Jiu Xi."

"Uh?"

"An alcohol banquet. Everyone, from birth to death, should pause for drinking banquets."

"Most of my friends drink like fish, every day. No pauses."

He again sniffed. 'Poison' perfume? That was the scent Veronica always wore. No, his mind was playing him tricks.

She bowed again, a stereotype from an old Charlie Chan television series.

"I can offer you Chinese beer, glutinous rice wine, lychee wine, Mijiu, a type of rice wine similar to Japanese sake, and snake wine, to mention just a few."

She paused.

"Be adventurous, Nigel. Try some snake wine. I can recommend cobra."

"Venomous?"

"Not poisonous after the process. We put the snake in a jar of rice wine. If you do not like the sound of that, snake bile wine is an alternative."

"Marigold, I'm a gourmet, not kamikaze."

"It will increase your sexual performance, Nigel."

How could such a purr come from that dried-up larynx?

"Nigel, Chinese are like the French. We extol cookery and are willing to eat almost anything edible. Allow me to choose the dishes for you?"

"Okay, and 'yes' to the cobra drink. Never let it be said Nigel Fox was lily-livered."

"I'm taking cooking to a high art. We've that in common, The Arts."

He took a sharp intake of air. What did this presumptuous stick insect know about The Arts?

They sat down facing each other. She clapped her hands like an ancient dynastic empress. Four waiters appeared with chrome trolleys.

"Give me an inkling of the menu, Marigold."

"Chinese cuisine is based on opposites; hot with cold, pickled with fresh, and spicy with mild. Color, aroma, taste, and texture are the four criteria."

He suppressed a desire to strangle her. He did not give a damn about the ins and outs of Chinese cooking. He was starving.

"Don't tease, dear. What are the dishes?"

"Not telling you. You might get squeamish and therefore miss delicacies. Many temptations for you; Shanghai hairy crab, salted dried duck, Farewell My Concubine, which is soft-shelled turtle stewed with chicken, mushrooms, and wine."

Could she not stop her verbal cookery diarrhea?

"My mouth's watering. Lay it all on, Marigold."

Dish followed dish. He sampled a pork specialty.

"Unique flavor."

"Dried tangerine peel for zest. My aunt, who is over there, adored that dish."

"I don't believe in ghosts, never mind hungry ones with penchants."

"The living can be Hungry Ghosts, the ones that have all but want more."

She smiled, exposing her horrific gold teeth.

"Talking about wanting more, where's that whopper lobster you promised, not to mention the fish? My belly's a little space left."

"So sorry, Nigel. I will hurry it up."

She whispered to a waiter, who rushed off.

Nigel began cutting noodles.

"Do not cut Shou Mian noodles, Nigel. They are symbolic of long life and good health."

How much more of this tripe did he have to endure?

The waiter glided in and placed two platters on the table. Marigold lifted the lids.

"Lobster with scallions and ginger. Fish cooked chiri style; that is boiled with seaweed, vegetables, and cakes of pulped rice," she said.

"Had lobster this way many times. I'm zooming in on the fish dish."

It was a small dish. Four mouthfuls finished it. He sat back in his chair, patting his belly.

"Dessert, Nigel? Pan-fried water chestnut cake? Red bean paste pancake? Soup? You know our custom of having soup at the end of a meal."

"Not another bite."

She stood up.

"Come, I have laid on entertainment."

She led him to a room with floor space and rows of seating in front of a white cloth screen.

"Sit in the front row. It is for special guests."

"A theater?"

"I plan to have Chinese shadow puppet shows to entertain customers after dinner."

Puppet Shows? Who wanted to watch them, apart from brats into pizza and chips? And fat chance of them coming here.

"I prefer live actors, Marigold."

She cocked her head to one side. She looked like a discarded puppet.

"Why, Nigel? Actors interact with other actors, but their performance is ultimately alone. Thus, the sum total of a personal life enters the equation."

She was talking shit.

"I don't get your drift, Marigold."

"Shadow puppets, having no personal history, are blank canvases. They are much more a joint effort."

45

"Threads pulling the joints? Shadow puppets use exaggeration and heavy dramatization, both hallmarks of a bad performance."

"You have lost the thread, Nigel."

Before he could ask her what the thread was, five Chinese men entered.

"These gentlemen are nicknamed 'the business of the five'. One operates the puppets, three the musical instruments, and one sings."

He was now feeling light-headed. He wished he had not drunk so much of the cobra wine.

"I'm so pissed, I could do the singing. It's all wailing. I know. I once had the ordeal of sitting through a Chinese opera."

"I'm sure you could delight me, Nigel, but later."

This was definitely a sexual innuendo. If he played his cards right, he might be able to get her to part with some cash. He would have to be really tanked though, but he could always plonk the proverbial bag over her head. He would pretend interest in her bloody puppets to please her.

"Can I examine the puppets, Marigold?"

She beckoned the puppet operator. He stared at the lifeless things. Gaudy, transparent, and made of gauze-thin leather, they were absurd.

"I dig this one's face," he lied, holding up a puppet with circles around the eyes.

"The clown. Chinese can tell a puppet's character by the mask. People wear masks. If you analyze the mask, you can get to the soul."

"You're waxing lyrical, Marigold."

She mistook his sarcasm for a compliment and rushed on.

"A red mask indicates morality, a black one loyalty, and a white one deceit. The good puppet has narrow eyes, a tiny mouth, and a nose with a straight bridge. The bad one has tiny eyes, a jutting forehead, and a scowling mouth."

He was almost screaming with boredom. He began throwing caution to the wind.

"Marigold, after some Hong Kong banquets, on came pole dancers. Oh, those spandex girls were felinely lithe. You know, I . . . "

Suddenly, he stopped. He felt dizzy. He was a puppet without an operator.

"That snake brew's powerful, Marigold."

"You have drunk too much. But, come, I have something to show you in the banquet room."

He was barely able to stand. But he prided himself he was a man that could hold his drink. Marigold must not suspect his legs were buckling.

His heart thudded in his ribcage. Veronica's presence was strong. Earlier, he had thought a whiff of her favorite perfume, 'Poison', was in the air. Could Hungry Ghosts exist? Had Veronica come for revenge?

Bizarre thoughts were scorching his brain. Marigold? Marry Gold? He could marry this Wang moron and be again rich. No! He was drunk, not thinking straight.

In the banquet room, Marigold lifted a place name. A scarlet tipped forefinger pointed out a second 'Nigel Fox'. But it was too late. He was now on the floor paralyzed but fully conscious.

"One place for living Nigel and one for ghost Nigel. 'Ask Rice Woman' knows the questions you now cannot ask. But, earlier, you asked about Yan Wang, and got no answer. He is the God of Death. He judges the Underworld. He was presiding at the table."

He could only stare in terror at her.

"Tonight, you ate blowfish liver and ovaries without the safety preparation rules. Your body is swimming in tetrodotoxin. But you are in theatrical company, Nigel. A famed Kabuki actor died after eating sashimi fugu."

She made a pyramid of her fingers.

"Blowfish is the second most poisonous vertebrate after the golden poison frog and far more potent than cyanide. No known antidote."

She paused.

"But I thought, as you are so puffed up about yourself, the blowfish would be more apt than the frog. You did not notice it was the only fish in the tank, and I know how fond you are of fish. Enjoy Mr. Blowfish? Exit Nigel."

She grinned. Her gold teeth seemed now like alligator rows.

"So sorry this is a soliloquy. By the way, the front row of a puppet theater is reserved for ghosts. You caused me to 'lose face', and that is unforgivable to a Chinese person. Also, it has taken me months to regain my reputation as a restaurateur after you gabbled to all London about 'Wang's culinary disasters'."

Her tiny frame now stretched into infinity.

"Revenge is to be savored more than food, Nigel."

He was entering darkness, but he could hear Marigold prattling on.

"A ghost marriage with me? In Chinese tradition, one or both parties are deceased. Possible. But bigamy is out. Your wife is present as a Nǔ Guǐ. They are lady ghosts, who committed suicide after husband abuse. Remember you asked who Nǔ Guǐ was, and again I did not answer?"

Darkness was now almost total.

"Soon your breathing will stop. The lanterns outside were to guide you to the table. You will never re-emerge from your ghost train tunnel."

He dimly saw her holding a wad of banknotes.

"You see Yan Wang on these banknotes? You can use these in Hell."

SEEDS OF FILTH

K. TRAP JONES

"**W**HERE'S THAT FAT bastard at?"
"We're fucking starving over here."
From the back, I heard them complaining. Hell, the whole damn restaurant heard the way they griped and moaned. I despised the three of them. They were here like clockwork every Friday night for all-you-can-eat chicken wings and bottomless curly fries. They could easily sit in another section with a different server, but they never did. I dreaded Friday nights. Nothing gathers all of the local assholes together in one tiny shithole like unlimited wings. Sneaking shots of whiskey between refilling draft beers and cleaning up wet naps was the only way I could remain sane. Stumbling from the back with menus, I rolled my eyes as I approached the booth.

"There's Sir-Turd-A lot, big dumbass motherfucker," Ford said with a smirk. As the leader of the misfit band of asshats, he was brutal and unforgiven in his attempts to berate anyone who he deemed weaker than himself, and that included his friends. He'd gather up his posse and stroll right through the front door every Friday night at 5:00, just as the puke fest of wings was beginning. Same booth, same seats; those fuckers were sticklers for superstition. Unfortunately, I was forced to be a key protagonist in their sadistic, bullying ritual.

Sitting next to Ford was Steven, or who I like to call *Douchebag with a Mullet*. Alone, these three were useless and I could probably squash each one like a blood-filled tick, but together they were inhuman, an unrelenting tornado of insults not letting up until the onslaught devastated their target.

49

"Can you even see your dick?" Steven said, combing his hair. "When you piss, you must have to fumble down there like a blind virgin on prom night."

"Wait, I got a new one," Brian interrupted.

That fucker was dumb as a stack of bricks. Whenever the group would turn on each other, Brian received the ass pummeling. When I was around, it was as if I allowed Brian the night off. I found it ironic how he could easily bully someone else when his friends did the same to him.

"He's so fat, when he puts on a belt, he uses a boomerang," Brian stated, slinging a straw across the booth. Their high pitched, whiny laughter always made my lip curl, but I was in an experimental phase of trying to ignore them.

"You going to order something?"

"Fucking idiot, we get the same thing every week," Steven politely reminded me. "Three pitchers of beer and kick your fat ass into gear by getting us the first round of wings."

I heard what he said, but I was staring through the dust smudged window where my attention was fully on a fine ass woman walking in the parking lot. Her halter top was cut low, revealing the lace trim of her bra and the tan lines of her breasts. Her belly button was pierced with a dangling chain which rattled against her flat stomach. The jean skirt was high and frayed at the bottom; the white strings of denim were highlighted against her tan legs. I lost sight of her for a brief moment until the door chime sounded. Within the grime infested environment of the restaurant, she was a beacon of beauty. Standing in the entrance way, obeying the wait to be seated sign, she had an essence about her; an aura of confidence. Adjusting my stained apron, I made my way over to her.

"Table for one?" I said through a nervous smile.

"Yes, please." Her lips briefly stuck together from the gloss. My senses were heightened; it was peach.

Further thoughts evaded me as the blood flowing south filled my limp dick. Twisting around, I grabbed a menu and swiftly led her to a vacant booth. Her golden hair whipped in slow motion as she swung her ass backward into the seat. When she landed, her tits bounced slightly causing the locket she was wearing to ricochet between her boobs like a tossed poker chip before sinking deep into her cleavage.

"Can I get you something to drink?" I said, trying hard not to stare down her shirt.

"Apple-tini, please." Both her voice and smile were bubbly.

"Um, I . . . um, can I see your ID?" I didn't really need it, but I had to know her name.

"Well, aren't you a saint, you just made my day," she said, unzipping her purse. She fumbled the ID when she pulled it from the wallet causing it fall to the ground. "Oh my, I'm such a klutz."

"Don't worry, I'll get it," I heroically said, dropping to my knees. Underneath the table, she uncrossed her legs, allowing me more room for me to look for the ID. In doing so, the whites of her inner thighs made my mouth water as the smell of her body wash hijacked my nose; it was watermelon.

"How are you doing down there?" she said, at least that's what I think she said.

Her knees opened up more like a hanger door revealing a dark shadow. She had no panties on. I almost lost it when her fingers slid down to scratch the leg. With my hand on the ID card, I needed to head back to the surface, but in reality, I wanted to stay down there until I ran out of air.

"I got it, I got it," I said, hitting my head on the way up. Handing it back to her, I noticed a wide grin on her face. She was holding back laughter. Unfortunately, the others did no such thing. The booth of assholes busted out laughing, slapping the table and pushing each other to catch their breaths. Her eyes looked down as she blushed and snickered. Beyond my belly, I saw it. The sweat pants I was wearing offered no barricade between the erection and the outside world. The cotton material highlighted the tip of my dick like the torch of the Statue of Liberty. I stood their frozen as Ford sidled up to me, putting his arm around my shoulder.

"Someone's pitching a tent," he said. "Mr. Fat Ass, I would like you to meet my girlfriend, Sally."

If it weren't for the amount of grease caked on my face, I probably would've turned red with embarrassment as Sally let loose laughing as she got up. Avoiding my erection, she slid past me, chuckling while looking down. Kissing her, Ford lifted up her skirt to show her bare ass to me.

"You'll never get anything like this, tubby," he said, pulling her to join the others. "Now, go get our wings."

To say I was pissed would be an understatement. I raced to the back-storage room to hide my boner asap. The sound of the door shutting behind me provided comfort, but my erection was not going away. Whenever this happened at home, I usually found relief in my room with internet porn.. I figured that's what I needed now, but how could I run a quick batch before going back out there. Masturbating with my hand never appealed to me, mainly because I couldn't reach low enough with my short dinosaur arms in order to have a steady grip. My method of release usually involved a blow up doll or any type of hole I could fit in.

Looking around the room, there wasn't much to go with, but there was one thing which caught my eye. It was delivery day, so the room was filled with boxes of goods, utensils, cups and what not. Opening up a case of bleu cheese dressing bottles, I thought why the hell not. Popping the top, the hole looked a little big for me and may not have had a diameter to cause enough friction to handle the job. Fuck it, I gave it a shot anyways.

I slowly slid my dick into the bottle. The bleu cheese suctioned around my member, greeting it delightfully well. The chunks of cheese rubbed against the skin as I bent over to gain more leverage. Like milking a cow, I upped the tempo as I was approaching the end game. I unloaded everything I had built up since last night's sock orgy. The aftermath shimmies were in full effect as I pulled the bottle from my welcomed limp dick. Opening a new pack of wet naps, I polished myself off, resealed the lid on the bottle and put it high on the shelf.

"Order up," I heard the cook say as I exited the room. Pulling the tray from the counter, I carried the baskets of wings, curly fries and pitchers of beer through the swinging door.

"Jesus Christ, took you long enough," Steven said.

"We thought you ate the order," Ford added, prompting Sally to laugh. I did my best to ignore them as I put everything on the table and walked away.

"Hey shithead, you forgot the bleu cheese?" Brian shouted across the restaurant.

"And more fucking napkins," Ford added.

"I need barbecue sauce," Steven said.

A migraine crept up my spine and hit my skull with a dirty hoe. Everything blurred until the bell chimed my ass awake with an idea. Heading into the back room again, I pulled down the bleu cheese dressing bottle which I made my love slave earlier. Shaking the bottle to mix everything well, I hesitated. Not because I had a moment of remorse or pity for the assholes, but because the two microwave burritos I had for lunch were starting a civil war in my gut.

The moment my fingers hit the handle of the door, I got another terrible idea. I sliced into the new case of barbecue sauce and retrieved a bottle. Cracking open the lid, I poured some out to make room. Looking at the level, I thought it wise to pore out a little more. The cramps tightened as if I was about to pop out triplets. I quickly removed my apron and dropped the sweatpants.

The first thing that hit my nose was the remnants of bleu cheese on my balls. Clenching my butt cheeks, I placed the bottle on the ground and hovered my ass over the opening like I was a B-42 bomber. It wasn't going to work; at least not that way. I can't even aim a slingshot let alone shoot turds in a straight line. I opted to lean back in a chair and hike my legs out as wide as I could get them. With the bottle in one hand, I created a nice seal around my asshole. When I felt confident, I unclenched ever so slightly to allow a small stream of liquid shit to filter out. I heard the plastic bottle filling up, but underestimated not only the amount of the shit, but the severe power of the extraction. Trying to close my asshole to cut the stream, I inadvertently increased the flow, morphing my ass into a pressure washer. The bottle slipped from my hand and flew across the room as I reached down to plug my ass with my thumb.

Right about then, Beth came in. Beth was another server who I had known for years. I tried to cover myself up, but the aroma of shit-flavored barbecue sauce smacked her across the face. I froze; there was not much I could have done to block the vision, but to my surprise, she simply walked in and closed the door behind her.

"Table 5, huh?" she calmly stated while slicing open a case of ketchup. "Don't worry, I won't say anything. We all have issues to deal with."

I couldn't speak. I was too embarrassed to even form words.

With liquid shit dripping over my fingers, I watched her crack open a new bottle of ketchup and proceeded to pour some out. Reaching under her filthy skirt, she fumbled around until she pulled out a used tampon, saturated with blood. Without much thought, she dangled the dripping red torpedo like a fishing lure above the opening. When it aligned, she lowered the string, submerging it into the bottle. Allowing some slack so that the end of the string hung over the edge, she closed the lid and shook the bottle. When satisfied with her creation, she opened the bottle again and pulled the string. A thick, red blob suctioned from the bottle like a cork as she squeezed the excess, making sure every drip filtered in. After resealing the bottle, she gave it a good shake once again while looking at me.

"It's for table eight," she said, vigorously shaking the bottle while walking toward the door. "You might want to clean yourself up. Those assholes are out there demanding a new round of beers."

Using several wet naps, I was wiping my ass and upper thighs when the door opened again. Sam, the busboy walked in holding a spoon and mustard. He didn't seem to care that I was half-naked, spread eagle with wadded-up brown wet naps tossed about. He sat crossed legged on the floor and started picking the multiple scabs tattooing his forearm. He was very careful to pry each one from the skin in a single piece. Flipping the scab over, he used the spoon to collect the newly formed pus. Opening the mustard, he slid the mucus inside.

"Shitting in barbecue sauce? Nice." He started on another scab. "What table?"

"Four." My voice was shaking, but like Beth, Sam didn't seem to care.

"This is for table six. Those douchebags can eat a bag of dicks." He continued testing the readiness of the other scabs. "Looks like those aren't quite cooked enough. Should be ready for Saturday though."

As quickly as he came in, he left.

With my cramps subsiding, I continued to mix the wonderful concoction of barbecue sauce and liquid diarrhea that Satan himself would be proud of. After collecting the special bottle of bleu cheese, I made my way to the front of the restaurant. A wing to the face greeted me as I approached the booth, but I kept smiling because the owner always reminded us about how great customer service was our number one priority.

"Does this look like anything to you?" Sally held up a small chicken wing bone.

"Sure does! Ain't that right, Slim Jim," Ford said, punching me right in the dick. The impact caught me off guard, but I managed to place both sauces in the middle of the table.

Behind the bar, I pretended to clean glasses, but my eyes were fixated on the booth and the asshats did not disappoint. Ford took a wing and went wrist deep into the bleu cheese dressing. Both Stephen and David double dipped curly fries into the barbecue sauce. As much I enjoyed watching my homemade white sauce dripping down Ford's chin, Sally became the main attraction. Her wing dropped into the bowl and was sinking fast until she submerged all of her fingers to rescue it. She licked the bone, slowly nibbling it to get to remnants of meat. Afterwards, she sucked each of her fingertips; all to my personal delight. As they downed every ounce of my semen and liquefied shit, I was at peace with myself. Beth was leaning on the bar watching her table, and Sam stood near the jukebox observing the mustard being shared amongst his group. Everything seemed right in the world.

"Hey, fuck-nugget," Steven yelled, snapping me out of the dream of content.

As I walked over to the booth, I couldn't help but smile as I observed them wiping their faces with wet naps.

"Waddle your fat ass back there and fetch us some ketchup and mustard," Steven demanded.

Looking over to table eight, I watched a mean looking group of women dipping their grilled chicken wraps in globs of ketchup. Their napkins were stained with smears of the darkened red concoction that Beth created. Glancing back to the bar, Beth winked at me with delight. The women kept going back for more. The way the blobs of ketchup forced their way out of the bottle as they hammered on the bottom was mind numbing to watch.

Table six was squirting mustard on a batch of shared curly fries as Sam cleaned the dirty dishes from the next booth, all while grinning from ear to ear.

For a moment, I imagined myself taking Beth's idea and making my own recipe by going into the ladies' restroom where the owner had installed a separate trash compartment for used tampons in order to avoid clogged toilets. Damn thing was always full and needed to be cleaned every two days; smelled like a murder scene. I could take a bunch of them in a plastic bag, cutting the tip and making one of those cake icing bags like the ones on the cooking shows. Applying pressure and squeezing the bloody mixture from the various tampons, I bet I could filter the stream into another ketchup bottle. I was thinking about reimagining my own barbecue masterpiece by visiting stall three in the men's bathroom. We had given up on trying to plunge that filthy disaster. The variety of shit, cigarette buds and toilet paper were enough to clog Grand Canyon. Even with the murky tide cresting above the rim, people kept taking a shit. With the water level that high, I guarantee their nutsacks acted like teabags. I could use a turkey baster to gather a sample and transform my barbecue sauce to the next level.

It was brilliant; it was foolproof, but it was not right. I needed to stop; enough was enough. I had practically given up on the whole idea until a chicken wing smacked me right in the forehead, snapping me out of my sentimental vision.

"Headshot," Brian announced.

"Did you hear what we said?" Ford said, spilling his beer on my shoes. "Get your Sasquatch looking ass back there and fetch us some mother fucking ketchup and mustard."

A smile crept upon my face.

"Absolutely, I'll be right back."

GRANDMA'S FAVORITE RECIPE

RONALD KELLY

MY GRANDMOTHER WAS a pillar of the community.

Yeah, I know. You hear that about people all the time. But in this case, it was true.

Sarah Plummer was a kind and loving neighbor, a faithful friend to those around her, and a great woman of faith. She cherished the little farming community of Harmony, Tennessee with all her heart and was very active at the local church. Every Sunday morning come rain or shine, you would find her there, teaching Sunday school and playing accompaniment on the organ as the choir sang. She always visited the sick at the hospital and the shut-ins at the nursing home, and she mailed out cards daily, saying "Get well soon!" or "Missed you at church Sunday". She visited every yard sale that was held in Harmony and bought at least one item, however insignificant, just to let them know that she had done her part.

And Grandma baked. She was legendary in town for her confectionary masterpieces and her homemade cakes and pies. Her specialty was cookies. Raisin oatmeal, chocolate chip, and, my personal favorite, snickerdoodles. Whenever she got wind that someone was down and ailing, she would take out her ceramic mixing bowls and flour sifter, her cinnamon, nutmeg, and baker's coca, and set to work. Grandma did everything entirely by scratch. No store-bought cake mix ever tarnished her kitchen counter. Pure ingredients were always used in just the proper amounts; flour, lard, fine cane sugar, and fresh country eggs from Will Turney's farm a mile outside of town. Then came the additions that really gave Grandma's desserts their sparkle. Big Toll House chocolate chips, freshly shred coconut, juicy raisins, pecans, and walnuts. When she was through and the pans of earthly delight were cooking in the oven, Grandma's kitchen smelled like how I imagined the sweet aromas of heaven itself might be.

Then, after the cooling, Grandma Plummer would place an even dozen on a plate and cover it with a tent of aluminum foil. Whenever the townfolk saw her walking through town with a silvery parcel in her hands, they smiled. They knew that she would be ringing someone's doorbell soon and wishing them well, with both kind words and a special treat, the likes of which only she could concoct.

Yes, my dear little grandmother was a saintly woman.

Or so I thought for a very long time.

Sarah Plummer had not had an easy way during the ninety-six years of her life.

She had been born to a hard-pan dirt farmer and his wife, a sickly woman who had been weakened by a bout of typhoid fever when she was a child. Grandma's early years had been difficult, hungry ones and, in the year of 1917, she had lost her four brothers and sisters to an influenza outbreak. She had been the only surviving child.

She had married at the age of eighteen to a man named Harold Plummer, who served as postmaster of the Harmony post office for nearly forty years. He had died of a sudden stroke in 1988. Being a housewife for her entire married life, Grandma lived modestly on Grandpa's postal pension in the little, white-clapboard house they had shared on Mulberry Street.

Like Grandma, I too had been dealt my share of hard blows throughout childhood. When I was four years old, my father was fatally injured at the sawmill he worked at. He fell into a buzzsaw and bled to death before the paramedics arrived. Then a year and a half later, my mother was diagnosed with ovarian cancer. Despite a hysterectomy and numerous chemo treatments, she succumbed to the disease nine months later. I went to live with Grandma Plummer then and thanked the good Lord that she was there to receive me with open arms. She did the best she could to raise me into the man I have now become, and I have nothing but gratitude for both the discipline she provided and the love she gave me during those tender years of childhood.

Despite what people thought, my grandmother did possess something of a temper, however. Whenever someone hurt her feelings or she felt slighted or wronged, she would grow absolutely livid. But that never seemed to last very long. She would always take her Bible in hand and, sitting in her rocking chair on the front porch, pray until those anger lines smoothed from her face and that gentle smile returned once again. Then she would get up, go into her kitchen, and bake a peace offering.

The first time I sensed that something wasn't quite right with Grandma Plummer was shortly after my twelfth birthday. It was a balmy May that year and Grandma's flower garden was brilliant with spring color; marigolds, hyacinth, petunias, and moss roses.

There was a neighborhood dog from down the street, however, that had been trying Grandma's patience lately. Buster was the hound's name and he had dug up about every purple and blue iris that Grandma had planted along the driveway. I had pegged him in the hindquarters with a Little League baseball a couple times, but he kept coming back and wreaking more havoc. I suggested that we buy a BB gun—not necessarily to scare the dog off, but because I really, *really* wanted one at that age. But Grandma would hear none of it.

A while later, she walked out the back door with a leftover piece of my birthday cake on a plate. She sat it down in the grass and soon, Buster was there, chowing it down hungrily.

"Why are you feeding the mangy mutt?" I asked her.

"Because even though Buster vexes us with his bad behavior sometimes, he is still one of God's creatures," she explained. "I'm repaying his transgressions with an act of kindness. Turn the other cheek. That's the way the Good Book says it should be."

I wasn't so sure about that. I stood and watched the dog wolf down my last piece of birthday cake. "If you say so," I mumbled, scratching my head.

The next day, Buster was staggering around in the middle of Mulberry Street, snapping and snarling and foaming at the mouth. The neighborhood kids—me included—watched in horror as Sheriff Tom Stratford shot the dog down with his service revolver. They strung yellow police tape around Buster's stiffening body until a man from the county animal control could come out. He showed up a couple hours later, scooped Buster into a black plastic bag, and hauled him off.

No one in town could figure out how a healthy animal like Buster had contracted rabies so swiftly, with no signs or symptoms to forewarn anyone.

But I had my suspicions.

That night, after Grandma had gone to bed, I got up and took a flashlight from my nightstand drawer. Then I explored the kitchen pantry.

Something had bugged me the previous afternoon, when Grandma had served that piece of birthday cake to old Buster. It hadn't looked right. The sugary white icing with its red-laced baseballs and hickory brown bats had held a nasty grayish tint to it. And, that evening, when I had gone in for supper, I had spotted a bottle sitting on the kitchen counter. A tall, skinny bottle that held a dark liquid. I just assumed it was vanilla extract from Grandma's baking ingredients. Before I could ask, however, she had taken the bottle and spirited it back to one of the shelves in her pantry.

The little closet smelled of cinnamon and garlic as I swung the pale beam of the light around, searching for that bottle. I found it a few minutes later, sitting on the shelf with her spices and baking supplies. Quietly, I reached to the back of the shelf and brought it forward, where I could get a better look.

It was an old bottle . . . extremely old. It was tall and narrow, and sported a single dark cork in the mouth of the stem. A label— yellowed and curled at the edges by age—read: DR. AUGUSTUS LEECH'S PATENTED ELIXIR—CURES A VARIETY OF PHYSICAL

ILLNESSES: GOUT, ARTHRITIS, IRREGULARITY, AND CHILDHOOD ALIMENTS.

A cold feeling washed over me at that moment.

Augustus Leech. I had heard that name before . . . a story whispered over a crackling fire at a local summer camp when I was eight years old. A dark, lanky medicine show man with a top hat full of magic tricks, a song and dance, and a patented elixir that guaranteed to cure all maladies and ailments. He had come to town in the early 1900's and sold his tonic for croup, anemia, and dysentery. And, in the process, poisoned half the children of Harmony.

Legend had it that the menfolk had armed themselves with guns and pitchforks and, like a mob in an old Frankenstein movie, had chased Leech out of town. Deep down into a shadowy place called Hell Hollow . . . never to be seen again.

Some kids in town had dared to explore the hollow, but I never did. I wasn't a child for taking risks. Not with the share of tragedy fate had given me in my younger years.

I picked up the narrow bottle. The glass seemed oily to the touch. I studied it in the pale glow of the flashlight. It was half full of a dark, syrupy liquid. Curious, I wiggled the cork until it pulled free. The contents smelled both sweet and sickening; like cotton candy and jellybeans mixed with dog vomit and the decay of a bloated possum at the side of the road. I didn't breathe it in very deeply. It made me feel sort of lightheaded.

Is this what Grandma had used to poison poor Buster? Or was poison too kind a word for what had been done? And where had she gotten the elixir? The stuff was absolutely ancient.

In the muted glow of the flashlight, the dark liquid seemed to shift and swirl of its own accord. It almost appeared to change colors somehow; from pitch black, to blood red, to pond scum green, then black again.

In the darkness of the pantry, something moved. A mouse savaging for crumbs perhaps. Or perhaps not.

Hurriedly, I corked the bottle and slid it to the back of the shelf where I had found it.

Back in bed, I laid there for a long time before sleep finally claimed me. And, even then, it was not an easy one.

The next time Grandma showed her true nature, I was a sophomore in high school.

Our next-door neighbors, the Masons, had suffered a very bad year. Bob and Betty Mason's daughter, Judy, had endured a long bout with cancer and had passed away the previous week. I was pretty depressed about her death. I'd had a crush on Judy since sixth grade. I had even asked her out to a school dance the previous year, but she had turned me down. Grandma had watched the whole thing from her kitchen window, and I think it made her mad, but she hadn't said anything.

Thinking back, it wasn't long afterward that Judy Mason was diagnosed with leukemia.

I had just stepped off the school bus a few houses down when I saw Grandma standing at the Mason's door, holding a plate wrapped in aluminum foil in her hands. I couldn't help but smile to myself. The Cookie Patrol was on the roll again.

As I made my way down the sidewalk toward our house, I could hear Grandma talking to Betty Mason at the doorway. "Things will be better," Grandma told her in comforting tones. "All we can do is pray to the good Lord for strength through this difficult time."

Mrs. Mason nodded sadly and smiled. "We appreciate your concern, Miss Sarah. And thank you for the dessert. You know how Bob loves your sweets."

"It's not much," Grandma told her. "But perhaps it'll provide a small bit of comfort to you during your time of need."

Betty Mason thanked her again and closed the door. I was nearly to the gate of the Mason's picket fence, when Grandma turned around. That small, gentle smile crossed her lips; the same smile I'd seen a thousand times at hospital visitations and charity bazaars, and at church as she played her favorite hymns on the organ she mastered so well.

It was her eyes that disturbed me. They held none of the benevolence that the rest of her face showed. They were hard, hate-filled eyes, peering from behind her horn-rimmed glasses like tiny black stones. Then, when she saw me approaching, they changed.

They once again became the warm lights of Christian kindness that I was so accustomed to.

"Home a little early, aren't you?" she said. "Well, come on to the kitchen. I've got a fresh apple crumb cake cooling on the counter. I just took it out of the oven."

As I sat in Grandma's kitchen that afternoon, eating my second slice of cake, I couldn't have imagined that Bob and Betty Mason would be dead within a week. The following Thursday, their car had veered unexpectedly across the grass median of the interstate and plowed, head-on, into a tractor-trailer truck. Both had died upon impact.

On the night following the Masons' funeral, I had the strangest dream. One in which I was not a participant, but a spectator.

I was in an old farmhouse. In one room a baby cried. In the other a frail woman wailed mournfully.

I stood in a doorway between kitchen and bedroom. As the woman vented her grief, two neighboring women were silently at work. Lying across the eating table were the bodies of three children: two boys and a girl. All were dead; being prepared for burial.

A man paced around the room like a bobcat on the prowl. His eyes burned with a rage only a father can feel at the loss of his children.

I turned and looked into the bedroom. A baby—perhaps two or three months old—wept loudly from a hand-made cradle. Feeding time had passed, but the infant had been forgotten. And there was another child. A four-year-old girl who sat cross-legged in the center of a big brass bed. The girl didn't seem in the least disturbed by the events that were taking place around her. Her eyes were focused on an object that stood on a cherrywood bureau across the room.

It was a bottle. A tall, skinny bottle with a cork in the top. The label read DR. AUGUSTUS LEECH'S PATENTED ELIXIR.

The bottle was three spoonfuls shy of being full.

The little girl smiled. She was quite fond of Augustus Leech; the medicine show man who had driven his horsedrawn wagon into town and stirred things up a bit. She had watched, enthralled, as he performed incredible feats of magic, picked a few tunes on a five-string banjo, and touted his patented elixir as the "Cure-All of the Ages".

And, when her father wasn't looking, Dr. Leech had slipped her a prize. A playing card with a picture of a fairy princess on the face.

She had placed that card beneath her pillow last night and dreamed that she was in an Enchanted kingdom full of ogres, dragons, and wizards. A place more real to her than the drab town of Harmony had ever been.

Her baby sister continued to cry. Slowly, the girl left the bed and took the skinny bottle from the bureau. She knelt beside the cradle.

"Hungry?" she asked.

The baby continued to wail.

She uncorked the bottle and unleashed a single drop. The infant rolled the dark liquid around on her tiny, pink tongue for a moment. Then grew silent.

No more middle child, the girl thought. *Only me.*

Her lips curled into a smile . . . that girl with my grandmother's eyes.

I woke up in the darkness, my heart pounding. I climbed out of bed and went downstairs . . . to the pantry.

The bottle was still there, even after all these years. But it was only a quarter of the way full now.

A cold feeling threatened to overcome me. I began to recall bits and pieces of conflicts during my childhood. Conflicts that didn't involve me directly, but were always between my parents and my grandmother, my grandmother and friends and neighbors. An accusation of infidelity toward my grandfather. A heated argument over meddling interference with my father. A petty grudge between my mother and Grandma that echoed from years before I was born. Hurt feelings and imagined wrongs done to the matriarch of the Plummer family by townfolk and neighbors. But the dust had always settled and peace was always made.

And, afterwards, there had always been sweets from Grandma's kitchen.

Followed by death.

I began to wonder if she was responsible. That maybe she was poisoning folks with that ancient elixir that sat on the pantry shelf. But my mind couldn't comprehend such a thing. The Masons had died in an unfortunate accident, like my father. A ninety-six-year-old woman can't condemn someone to cancer or a fatal car crash by baking them a lemon meringue pie.

I left the kitchen pantry that night, telling myself that I was being foolish; that my kindly grandmother had nothing to do with the misfortunes of the citizens of Harmony. But I could never erase that dream from my thoughts. And that little girl with the wicked grin on her face.

Several days ago, everything just sort of fell apart for me and Grandma.

It happened on Sunday morning. I was back home from college for the weekend, sitting in a righthand pew of the sanctuary. Church service was proceeding as it normally did at Harmony Holiness. Jill Thompson, the pianist, and Grandma Plummer at her organ, were playing "Leaning on the Everlasting Arms" flawlessly. Then, before they had finished, Pastor Alfred Wilkes rose to his feet prematurely.

The ladies stopped their playing. The entire congregation froze.

Everyone was already on edge, as it was. Bad things had been taking place at the church in the wee hours of the night. Vandalism and desecration.

It had begun two weeks ago. Someone had thrown rocks through three of the stained-glass windows. Then, later, an intruder had stolen the church's 180-year-old King James Bible from a display case in the foyer and set fire to it on the stoop outside.

But the last blasphemous act had been the worst. Someone had defecated on the altar.

Pastor Wilkes's face was long and mournful as his huge hands gripped both sides of the podium. "The devil has been testing us lately, my friends," he said in that deep baritone of his. "At first I just thought it was some disrespectful kids. But after the second incident, I realized that it was something much more serious. It is not an outsider who has committed these sinful acts, but someone in our own midst."

I couldn't believe what I was hearing. A member of the congregation had done those horrible things? A nervous sensation of cold dread began to form in the pit of my stomach, although I wasn't sure why.

"Following the burning of the Bible, the deacons and I discussed the matter and came to a decision," he told us. A grim smile crossed his face. "It's amazing what you can buy at Radio Shack these days."

He then picked up a manila envelope that was lying atop the podium and unfastened the clasp of the flap. "I really hate to show you this," he said, "but God has compelled me to do so."

Pastor Wilkes then pulled an 8x10 photograph from the envelope and held it at armslength for all to see. The congregation gasped as one. The nervous ball of dread deep down in my belly suddenly turned into a cold, hard stone.

Pictured there in the dimly lit sanctuary, with her granny panties and support hose pooled around her ankles was my grandmother . . . smearing her feces across the front of the pulpit.

I groaned involuntarily, as though someone had just sucker punched me in the gut. I heard someone clear their throat haughtily from the pew behind me. It was Naomi Saunders, the church busybody. I could feel her hot, self-righteous eyes burning into the back of my neck.

An uneasy silence hung heavily in the sanctuary for a long moment. Then Pastor Wilkes turned and regarded the elderly woman sitting at the church organ. "It grieves me in my heart to do this, Miss Sarah, but I must ask you to leave us now."

I watched as my grandmother primly turned off her organ and, for the very last time, left the spot she had occupied for countless Sunday mornings. With her head held high, she walked down the center aisle, enduring the stares of shock and disgust that etched the faces of the congregation.

As she reached the rear doorway, I shakily stood to my feet. I couldn't believe the pastor had handled my grandmother's comeuppance in such a callus and tactless manner. Why couldn't he and the deacons have confronted her privately?

Standing there, I stared the preacher square in the face. "This isn't right," I told him in front of everyone.

I looked for some sign of satisfaction in his face, but there was none. "No," he said flatly. "It wasn't."

Outside in the parking lot, we sat in the car. "*Why*, Grandma?" I asked her. "Can you give me a reason?"

She was silent.

"Was it because you wanted the church to buy that new organ last month and the budget committee voted it down?"

She said absolutely nothing in her defense. She simply sat there in the passenger seat, head bowed as if in prayer . . . but eyes wide open.

11

I found Grandma dead the following Monday morning.

She laid there peacefully in her bed, wrinkled hands folded across her chest, a tiny curl of a smile upon her thin lips.

The cause of her death was undeniable. Sitting on her nightstand was a tall, skinny bottle. The stained cork sat neatly next to it.

"Aw, Grandma," I sighed as I picked up the bottle. It was completely empty. "You drank it all." It had only been a quarter full the last time I had seen it, but apparently that had been enough.

The next two days were a blur to me. There was so much to attend to. The proper arrangements were made at the local funeral home; the casket, the vault, the times of visitation and, of course, the funeral itself. After the preparations, I went back to that empty little house on Mulberry Street. The place was a wreck. Along with her will to live, Grandma had apparently lost her will to clean. I made the four-poster bed she had died in, then moved on to the rest of the house. There were dirty dishes in the sink and damp towels strewn across the bathroom floor.

The following day, Grandma was stately and dignified in her burnished, rose-hued casket, wearing a dress she had worn at many a Sunday service. The chapel was Decorated with a forest of flower arrangements, ceramic angel figurines, and matted pictures of Thomas Kinkade churches that played "Amazing Grace" when you wound a music box on the back.

The funeral was almost unbearably long, populated by the folks of Harmony, as well as the congregation that had ousted her from their midst only a couple of days before. As Pastor Wilkes droned on and on about what a faithful, God-fearing woman she had been, I sat there on the front pew and tried to imagine Grandma in heaven. But I couldn't. It simply wouldn't come to me. Trying to picture her in such a celestial setting was like staring at a blank canvas.

After the graveside service, everyone met back at the church fellowship hall for a lunch of covered dishes and desserts. I wasn't very hungry. I just wanted to accept my share of condolences and get out of there. I had much to deal with that afternoon . . . mostly the nagging question of exactly why my last living relative had done the terrible things she had.

I found myself standing next to the dessert table with Namoi Sanders. As the woman stuffed her face, she told me about how wonderful a woman Grandma had been and how they were all going to miss her dearly. I pretty much nodded my head solemnly and thought about how unbelievably delicious the cookie I munched was . . . my second one, in fact.

"These are pretty good," I said. I took another bite and washed it down with sweet tea.

"Snickerdoodles," Naomi said with a smile. "She always said they were your favorite."

I stopped chewing. "Who made these?"

"Your grandmother, apparently," she told me. "We found them on that table when we came to set up this morning."

Dirty dishes in the sink. Coffee cups, supper plates, mixing bowls . . .

"I guess it was one last, loving gesture . . . God bless her." Naomi picked up a greeting card from off the table and handed it to me. "This was with it."

Numbly, I took it. The card face read *"From your Sister in Christ"*. When I opened it, I found there was no printed caption, only Grandma's unmistakably floral penmanship. I barely took two breaths as I read the inscription.

Farewell, my friends . . . May we meet again in the glorious hereafter . . . where the hearthfires shall crackle with warmth and we shall labor together in eternity. I shall see you there. Love, Sarah.

"Sad, but sweet, wasn't it?" said Naomi.

I stared at the handwriting in the card. What had she been talking about? There were no hearthfires in heaven . . . no fire at all. And paradise was a place of rest, not a realm of endless labor . . .

I looked down at the half-eaten cookie in my hand, then at the platter on the table. Only three cookies remained where there had been an even two dozen before.

As I left the church, I wanted to puke . . . but I couldn't. The poison was there to stay.

When I had cleaned the house earlier, I had made the bed . . . but had neglected to look beneath Grandma's pillow. When I did look, I knew exactly what I would find.

A yellowed playing card with a fairy princess on the face.

Now I understood why I couldn't picture Grandma in heaven. She was in a much more sinister place. A fiery realm full of ogres and dragons . . . and wizards named Leech.

MAGICK BREW

NIKKI NOIR

IN TODD'S VISION, his cock was massive as he towered over Mary's kneeling form. From physique to confident stance, Todd's fantasy avatar was dominate in all the ways he lacked in real life.

"*Al-kuhl*. Mary Schmidt cannot resist me. *Avra kehdabra*." He spoke the words in a soft breath and focused on Mary, pleasing him like a sex-starved slave.

In the real world, the flesh of his cock was warm in Todd's hand, but he pretended it was Mary's mouth. Then he added all five senses into the mental visualization. Beyond the warmth, he heard her slurping, smelt the musk of scent and jasmine of her body spray.

"*Al-kuhl*. Mary Schimdt craves my body. *Avra kehdabra*." Todd fell deeper into the vision. The carpet was no longer beneath his knees, nor was the blender resting on the floor just in front of his naked body.

A powerful energy built at the base of his testicles and Todd manipulated his cock faster. Using his mental imagery, Todd directed the surging energy up and down his spine. His breathing increased. He brought his other hand into the action, teasing his balls while the image of Mary greedily sucked his cock.

At the moment of orgasm, Todd's eyes shot open. "*Al-kuhl*. Mary Schmidt swallows me. *Avra kehdabra*." He released pump after pump of hot semen into the blender before him, directing the built-up energy and intentions into the white fluid. After a minute of post-climatic shudders, Todd finally relaxed with a sigh.

Back in the kitchen, Todd put the blender on its mechanical base. He took tequila from the cabinet, then went to the freezer door for ice. As he closed the door, he jumped at the sight of Kevin entering the kitchen.

"Shit, you freaked me out. I thought you had classes all day?" Relief washed over Todd, happy he'd put sweatpants back on when he left his bedroom.

"Hocutt cancelled his lecture." Kevin looked at the blender and ingredients. "Margaritas? Were you planning on getting sloshed and watching rom-coms while I suffered through Punnett squares and mitosis?"

"No. I'm making a special mix for the Halloween party," Todd said, quickly pouring tequila into the blender full of his man-batter. "Mary's favorite. Watermelon." He pointed to the fresh watermelon on the other end of the counter."

"I don't get it. Are you guys even dating. I thought you said she cheated on you?"

"No. Drunken flirting. I just read too much into it."

"Speaking of 'into it', Mary is *not* into you." Kevin opened the fridge and grabbed a beer. "Forget this party, man. You need to stay away from that chick. Much better women out there."

"Mary's not a cheater," Todd said, moving to the watermelon with a spoon. "She was drunk and flirting with some guy. That was it. Everyone has a moment of drunk flirting. She probably never saw him after that. I was just overreacting when I told you the story." Todd scooped large chunks of melon into the alcoholic concoction, smiling. "She and I can work this out. In fact, I think things are gonna turn around for us very soon."

"You guys don't even have that much in common. I mean, sure she's hot, but she ain't the only hot chick at Mesa Community College."

Only hot chick who bothers talking to me, Todd thought. And even then, it had been Frater-Z's magickal guidance that got him that far. Ladies weren't beating down Todd's door. He had a chance with Mary . . . sort of. He wasn't about to let her go without a fight.

"How does my hair look?" Mary stared into the mirror, her friends readying themselves on either side of her.

"It looks fine," Jill said. "Besides, I heard *Todd* was coming, anything would impress him."

Mary shot her a look.

"Wait, wait, wait," Jayda said, adjusting her boobs in the halter top. "I thought that whole mess was over and done with."

"It was . . . it is . . . " Mary looked at the ground. "Listen, Halloween is this guy's favorite holiday. I already invited him before I came to my senses."

"Only took a month," Jayda said.

"I feel like a total bitch about stringing him along. He just like fell in love with me. I thought I'd grow feelings if I stuck with it. I was wrong. I can at least give him a good Halloween send off."

Jayda laughed. "I bet he thinks you're a couple still."

"I told him we were *just dating*, and that it wasn't working," Mary said, going for her eyeliner. "But he could come to the party and we can be friends . . . that's all."

"Yeah, bringing him to a wild costume party when you look this hot and *not* having sex with him is a lot better than just cancelling on him." Jill smiled and looked at the shared bathroom mirror.

"First off, we never had sex. He's . . . Whatever," Mary said. "More importantly, don't act like I'm the only one getting involved in bad rebounds. You forget Jason Armstrong that quickly?"

"Hold up. I think *you're* forgetting about the *assets* Jason had." Jill raised her eyebrows. "If this Todd dweeb ain't packing please do not compare."

"I'm not sure if he's packing. I tried to initiate, but he clenched up. Way nervous whenever things got heavy." Mary shook her head. "I'm assuming he's not. Which is too bad. He talked a big game when I met him. Then it all sort of crumbled."

Jayda laughed. "That's most men. All talk. Tell 'em to whip it out though and suddenly they speechless."

"Not Jason Armstrong." Jill giggled and put away her makeup.

"So he's not hung, or adventurous, or rich? What the hell were you smoking, girl?"

Mary finished her eyeliner and shrugged. "I don't know. Timing was right and there was just something about him. Seemed genuine and down to earth, cute in a . . . sort of way. It hooked me. But it was just a rebound."

"Next time, please do all of our social-statures a favor and rebound with a man, not a boy. This Jair guy you've been messing with, now he's is a step up from your ex. Todd was is a big step down."

"Jeez. Okay. Point made. I should have known the second night out and not dragged it on."

"Oh my god." Jayda's eyes lit up. "Let's screw with him tonight. Guys always talk about threesomes. See if he's down for one. If he says yes, we all call his bluff. Say we'll make it a foursome!"

"Gross!" Jill said.

"He'd die. Todd had no clue what to do with me, let alone three of us."

"Too much porn, no real-world practice." Jill posed in the mirror. "Well, I'm ready."

"Please let's do this," Jayda said taking Mary's arm. "It will be hilarious. Then he won't think you're such a bitch after you never speak with him after tonight. He'll realize it's his fault for being unable to please you in the foursome you so desperately crave."

"That's cruel," Mary said. "And what if he suddenly grows a pair and says yes?"

"Oh, then you on your own, bitch."

They all laughed.

"Are you bitches ready yet?" Jill asked.

They all took a Charlie's Angels pose in the mirror.

"All right, Angel's, let's turn up!"

"You have got to be playing," Jayda said, as they approached the house party.

"Hey guys." Todd waved from the sidewalk in front of the residence. "Figured I'd wait for you outside."

They stopped in front of him.

"What are you wearing?" Jayda asked.

"Mary suggested being Charlie," Todd said. "This is the exact purple. And look at these glasses and hat." He smiled, showing off the large eyewear that looked more like goggles.

"Charlie," Mary said. "As in Charlie's Angels. Not the chocolate factory."

Jill giggled.

"Oh, man." Todd's face grew red. "Sorry . . . "

"It's okay. Don't worry." Mary stepped forward and pulled his arm toward the door. "You look just like him."

"Yeah," Jayda said, suddenly sounding brighter and hustling alongside them toward the door. "Now that I think of it, I wouldn't mind becoming an oompa-loompa later, Mr. *Willy* Wonka."

Mary shot her a look, but Jayda just smiled wider.

"Johnny Depp is always hot," Jill said, joining in the teasing as they headed to the door.

Mary wished they would drop it. She already felt like a bitch and this prank was not helping.

"Oh-kay." Todd wrinkled his brow in confusion.

It had only been ten minutes in the house of EDM, sticky booze, and sweet vape clouds, but it felt like an eternity. Before being able to offer Mary his magickal margarita, a redhead dressed as a bunny handed her a beer. Now, Todd felt like the biggest jackass, hovering by Mary's side as she greeted people he didn't know and barely introduced him. And what was with Mary's friends? It's like they were trying to seduce him before they splintered off from each other to find other acquaintances.

Mary turned from the couple she was talking with and Todd lunged forward. "Hey, look what I brought. Your favorite." He held up the pitcher he'd been carrying.

"What is that?" Mary looked suspiciously at the pitcher.

"Watermelon margarita . . . with real watermelon."

"Oh . . . " she said. "I guess we can have some when I finish this beer."

Something in her face crushed his heart. This was it. She was gonna dump—

"Todd, why don't you—"

"Can we talk real quick?" Todd interrupted, needing to get her alone, otherwise he'd lose her forever to this crowd of beautiful partyers. The chosen ones he'd never been cool enough to compete with. "Please . . . "

"Have you had that pitcher all night?" Jayda appeared next to them.

"Yes," Todd answered, then turned back to Mary. "Please?"

"I don't know, Todd. Can't we just enjoy the party. Have your drink."

"I made it for you. How about a toast?"

Now Jill appeared next to Jayda.

"As long as it ain't roofied, I'm in," Jill said.

"Jill," Mary hissed.

"Yeah," Jayda said. "Let's *all* have that drink."

Jayda's expression made Todd's dick surge. What the hell was she implying? "I . . . " Todd thought he noticed Mary shake her head, but he was too rattled to be sure.

"Yeah," Jill said, mirroring Jayda's sexual hunger. "I'll get the cups."

"Fine," Mary said. "One drink."

Todd allowed Jayda to pull him through to the backyard, Mary trailing behind. As confused and anxious as he was, he felt magnificent; women were dragging him. Maybe he wasn't such a loser.

He looked back at Mary trailing. Pouty lips and pert tits. God, she was perfect. Why couldn't she be as into him as her friends were?

Jill returned with cups. Todd reluctantly took one, realizing he was stuck drinking the semen concoction. Damn, he'd fucked that up. Not that the spell would do anything to him. It was just damn gross! Jayda and Jill looked at him with hungry eyes. Mary looked pained and the squeeze gripped his chest again. Good thing he'd made the magick potion extra strong, since he'd be wasting some on them. Frater-Z had said half a quarter-teaspoon was more than enough. Todd had unloaded a week's worth of cum into that spell. He'd planned on overdosing Mary on his magick brew. Now, hopefully it was enough to even work at all.

Todd poured, saving more for Mary and quite a significant amount less for him. They raised their cups, but Todd froze, unsure what to say. A part of him knew his lust for her was irrational, but he wanted her so badly.

"Uh . . . here's to a good Halloween. Thanks for inviting me."

"Cheers!" Jayda and Jill cried.

He felt nauseous raising the cup to his lips. It smelt like sweet margarita, but he knew what lay just beneath. They waited for him to go first. Well, it wasn't like this would hurt him. It was his own bodily fluid. Girls drank jizz all the time. So, no danger there. And it wasn't like the lust spell was intended for Jayda and Jill. The spell, the intention, was for Mary. And God did she need it if he was gonna have a chance with her.

"Cheers." Todd closed his eyes and swallowed.

He watched them drain the cups.

"Wow, that was great," Jayda said as she walked away.

"Mmm," Jill said.

"Yeah," Mary agreed. "Good job. Thanks." She lingered for a moment, gave a pathetic smile, and went inside to mingle. Todd swore he heard her say 'not funny' to Jayda just before they were out of earshot.

"Damn," he muttered, turning over his cup, spilling the remaining jizz-cohol. He'd blown it. Either the spell worked and Frater-Z was a true magician or Todd was out of luck when it came to women.

The spell could take hours or days to take effect, but he decided to get drunk to help pass some time before heading home. He sulked over to the keg line.

Sex magick is equivalent to blood magick in power. Only seal your spell with semen or blood when you are 100% certain you want this lover bound to you, possibly forever. Todd recalled Frater-Z's word as he stepped one-person closer to the keg. *It's well known that lustful entities can more easily influence a human when intoxicated. That's why the ancients called it Al-kuhl—alcohol— meaning 'body-eating spirit.' When that power is combined with your seed and spell, the individual will crave you. But be careful . . . there is a thin line between pleasure and problems when using love spells.*

Todd stepped forward, pumped the handle, and began filling his cup with the amber liquid. He took a sip of the beer and tried to calm himself. He'd bought the online magician's magick course. Sometimes it felt like the spells worked. Todd had lined up coincidences which led to meeting Mary. Not to mention made some extra cash with money spells and aced all tests last semester. But those could have been coincidences. If this magick love potion worked, it would be actual magick.

Todd checked his cell again. Eleven fifteen. The party was in full swing and he felt more isolated than ever. Perhaps it was time to leave. He'd accomplished his mission. She'd drank his seed. It was time to wait. If it made her as insatiable as Frater-Z claimed, she'd hunt Todd down no matter where he went.

Todd finished the beer, happy he was within walking distance of his apartment. He headed toward the door when Mary sprung out of the crowd.

"You weren't about to leave, were you?" She took his arm.

"I . . . guess I was." Todd straightened up a bit. He conjured false bravado. "Not quite, wild enough for me."

Mary's eyes widened. "Yeah, I hear you. Hey . . . let's do something wild." She pulled him away from the door and toward the staircase.

Todd swallowed hard and let her lead him upstairs. *It fucking worked*! "How about we go back to your place . . . I mean—depending on what you're thinking . . . "

"Don't you dare chicken-out." Mary glared at him on the middle of the staircase. "I don't know what's come over me. But I need you now. You're giving me that dick."

Todd's body shook with excitement.

"Yes, ma'am." Fuck it, he was going for it. A dream come true!

Mary dragged Todd into the first bedroom and pushed him against the wall. She was more dominating than in his fantasy, but that was okay. Mary buried her mouth into his neck. Sucking and licking his flesh, pushing his head against the wall.

The door swung open and Todd jumped, pushing further into

the wall. He almost yelped out a 'sorry', but he saw it was only Jayda and Jill standing in the doorway.

"I told you she brought him up here," Jayda said.

"Better share, bitch." Jill stormed forward followed by Jayda.

Now the three pressed him against the wall. His jacket was pulled apart by a mass of manicured hands. His shirt went next and then the nails were digging into his skin. The sharp clawing hurt, but Todd didn't dare complain. The three mouths sucking on various parts of his torso and neck helped alleviate any pain.

Todd opened his eyes in awe at the three women clamoring over his body. He didn't need to be 6' 1" or have the body of Adonis. They wanted to eat him alive as is and he'd never felt so powerful. A slight struggle ensued as the women fought over his flesh.

Mary pulled away and dropped to her knees. Todd's cock pressed against his pants. As excited as he was, he was also scared as hell. Just relax, he told himself. You gotta keep your nut as long as possible. Leave a good impression, maybe it would help the magick last longer, maybe they could do this every night!

Mary unlatched his belt. The zipper lowered as a sharp pain exploded on his nipples. "Ah." Tod pulled back and saw his nipple pull from Jayda's teeth. "Shit," he said. "Little more gently—Aggh." He pulled the other way and saw Jill gnawing at a lovehandle. "Okay hang on—"

Suddenly his cock was freed, his pants and boxers yanked to the ground. The warm air of the room wrapped around his pulsing member. Todd looked down in time to see Mary sink onto his penis. Fuck, it felt good. It was a searing electric pleasure radiating through his body. She sucked more greedily than he could have ever dreamed. Finally, he had to close his eyes as she popped his cock out and started sucking on his ballsack.

"Aggh!" Excruciating pain flared across his chest. Todd's eyes flew open and he gaped at the bloody hole where his left nipple use to be. "What the fu—"

Jayda lunged up and slammed her forearm into Todd's trachea, pinning him against the wall. "You slab of man-meat," she hissed into his ear. "I just wanna eat you up."

Todd was already drunk and losing the ability to suck in enough oxygen made his knees weak with dizziness. Somehow, he could still feel the warm tickle of Mary's tongue on his balls, but that sensation morphed into a wave of pain as Jayda tore off his earlobe.

Todd stared at her in horror as she slurped down the flesh of his ear. Chunks of blood played on her lips. "And to think, I was only joking earlier. Now I really can't get enough of you, Todd!"

A scream rose out against his crushed windpipe as a new pain tore through his crotch. Above it all, Todd could hear his testicle pop inside his scrotum. He leapt forward, tripped on the pants around his ankles, and fell on top of Mary who was chewing on what he assumed was his nutsack.

The possessed woman rolled out from underneath, then pounced on his chest. "Oh my God, you taste so good. I want more!"

Todd tried to scream for help, but Mary dropped on his throat, and his yell was squashed by a crunching sound. Blood spilled down the inside of his throat. Panic seized Todd and he started to lose consciousness. He could just make out the sensation of the two other mouths, latching on to his quivering body.

Al-kuhl. Body-eating spirit. Fuck you, Frater-Z. You should'a explained how important the dosage was. Fuck you.

Then the world went black.

MERMAID CAVIAR

VICTORYA CHASE

THE PRICE: If you have to ask, you can't afford it. The cost is higher. Never think about the cost if you want to continue.

The place: If you can't find it, you can't pay the price. They don't care about the cost. Not to you or them.

It's an opulent banquet hall. Chandeliers thick with diamond tears that drip but never fall. Chairs of real wood from pristine forests where wolves still hunt young caped girls. Simulated windows splash blue skies blurring into pinks and oranges as cotton ball clouds cascade by, all partially obscured by thick lush drapes pulled back with woven yellow cords braided from the hair of Rapunzels—virgins trapped in towers, their dreams of escape growing into one of the strongest fibers in existence. They glisten gold against the deep black of the curtains made, as the story goes, from the skin of man gone to beast. Man always goes to beast. It's a foregone conclusion.

The dress code is whatever you want. If you can afford to be here it doesn't matter what you wear. There are currently four people here that are not workers. One woman sits alone dressed in what appears to be her wedding dress. Rubies spot blood down her neck and into her décolletage. Another table holds a young couple, man and woman. Both are in suits. He the power dark blue and she in pale gray. They hold hands. Their suits are old or vintage. Threadbare despite the youth of the couple. Perhaps they actually had to work to pay the price.

I'm true rich so don't really care. Or I'm not but pretending today, jeans and a t-shirt that don't promote anything but my toned body.

The menu only contains one item, but it is handed to each person as if we're there for something else. As if we aren't searching for the fertility time or nature has taken from us. They only serve the one thing that can help, if you have the money.

Mermaid caviar.

"The synthetics are lovely this year," I said.

I meant it. You could order classic human, soft skin warm to the touch that glows with life inside. They would even grow with you and have emotions that changed and deepened. If you wanted more intimacy you could program in the flaws of humanity. Perfection is boring in a child.

"Remember Mei? She ordered one with diabetes. It always wants ice cream and she has to talk to him about sugar."

"Diabetes doesn't even exist anymore," Brian said.

"But your child can have it. That's the point," I said. "So you can take care of your kid with diabetes or maybe a heart murmur. Mei was considering a heart murmur. You can lay your head against your child's heart and hear it flutter and you can worry."

"Do you even have a maternal bone in your body?" he asked. "I mean, Jesus, Jess. blood children. That's where it's at. Where it's us."

Blood children were a fad again, and I wanted to yell that at Brian, but he wouldn't see it. He could never see himself for who he was because he had worked so hard to be this idea of himself instead. He was the man who provides. Gender roles were *en vogue* and I hated that. I never really considered myself a woman, with all it's implications, until he told me I was. I let him define me, but to be a woman meant things I didn't understand.

"Don't you want to carry my child?" he said, coming behind me and wrapping his arms around my stomach.

I'm free range human and that was part of what attracted Brian to me. I was self-made from a mom and a dad. So classic. So vintage nostalgia in my creation. So what Brian wasn't—lab designed to be beautiful and perfect. Incubated in a baby farm. Local women in third worlds kept in rooms filled with rows of pregnant women on beds. They are better regulated now than when he was an embryo. Corporations with sleek logos run the farms. With Brian the process was still wild, and so was he. I liked that about him. He was so assured about things even though I could never quite tell what he was thinking. What he was capable of.

"I mean, fuck it all Jess, I'm just asking you to do what your mom did, what women do for their husbands. To love me. To provide me with something so simple. So basic."

He pushed his hands under my shirt and rubbed my stomach, squeezing me tight against him.

"Seriously, what is wrong with you to not want to give birth?" he cooed into my ear. "To not want to be the bringer of life."

His breath went from warm and inviting to hot and damp. He kissed my ear, then my shoulder, and then began to take off my shirt.

"Maybe you just need practice," he said.

Sex was always animalistic and intense. The way he did it was dominance. The way he did it was face away, no contact. Brian was purposeful. He was 'this is a chore' with a happy ending. He was a missionary and I was the land dominated and the native saved.

"We're looking at a baby with some sort of mobility issue," Reese said. She was holding hands with her wife, Janeka.

"It'll be fun," Janeka said. "Like, teaching them how to walk with a missing leg or twisted foot or something. One where we take them to physical therapy three times a week. It'll bring us much closer as a family."

"Brian wants me to carry a child," I said, watching their eyes widen.

"Can people even do that?" Reese asked.

"My mom did, so I guess he thinks I can," I said.

But my mom was a rarity. Raised in the mountains somewhere off the coast of a place that was now completely gone thanks to 'resourcing.' She tried to tell me about her homeland, but I failed to listen. Her country had been fending off corporations for years before her family escaped and went completely off grid. Then suddenly she existed again and became a useful member of society providing me with whatever freedoms I asked for.

Brian loved what he termed my exoticism. It was nice to be loved so specifically.

"Your mom was a throwback," Janeka said, before immediately apologizing. "You know what I mean. She didn't grow up modern like us. She was from a different world. An old one."

"Fairy tales. Like the Rapunzels," I said.

Reese shuddered. She used to be part of the Rapunzel Liberation Front. She rallied against the practice of taking young girls from lands like those my mother walked away from, force fed a diet that led their hair to become the strongest filament out there. No one had actually seen a Rapunzel, although Reese said she came close. A glimpse in a window high in the tower they were picketing. Eyes black with emptiness; hair glistening in the sun.

Had my mother been born a generation earlier she might have been rounded up and used as a heritage human, a being needed for her unaltered DNA. But by the time she was found I was already born and the microbes that kept our air clean were also in her bloodstream, as they were in all of ours. It was too late.

Here's the rub. I am a product of my time. Humans weren't meant to give birth forever. The sex urge may have lasted, but the roles didn't. I didn't need to be a woman growing up. I played with kids at school like everyone else and fashion didn't have a special dictate for me. I went swimming and wanted to be a mermaid because I liked fish and the feel of cutting through the water, not because of some desire inherent in their nature. Not to lure men. I let my hair grow long because of the feel of the ponytail swinging back and forth when I ran.

"It's your duty as the daughter of a natural birth to do the same," Brian said. He rolled over in bed, his blue eyes gleaming. He pulled at the sides of his eyes, a sly mimic of mine.

But I couldn't get pregnant. I had been on medication to suppress my menstrual cycle since five, like most girls, to give them a chance to decide what they wanted to be without the burden and distraction of bleeding. Side effects are never known until they are staring at you. I thought the doctor would be kind to me. Would show compassion. But he looked at my scans and clucked his tongue.

"Brian will be so disappointed," he said.

Brian wasn't friends with my doctor, but he had pull. Privacy doesn't exist when you are married to the son of the Prime Governor of the United Republic. I was lucky to receive his definition of love.

"I've invested so much in you," Brian said when I got home. His anger made him glow. He had a halo of concern, of ire, of incomprehensible emotion around him. He grabbed me and I let him pull me in. "I've invested so very much in you. You will give me my child."

The swirls and whorls of his fingerprints were pressed into my skin and I enjoyed watching them rise.

When I was twenty-one, I decided swimming in pristine pools wasn't enough. I felt a call to the great oceans that my mother spoke of, not the ones we had. I felt the siren's lure. I decided I could swim around the world. I was strong and mermaid was in my blood. After all, wasn't I born a myth? Natural. Pure. A legend among my friends who came from rented wombs. It wasn't natural to be spawned directly from someone you knew. We were all time-sharing.

I thought myself so strong because my arms rippled with muscles. But I was foolish and arrogant in that strength and soon washed up on a beach owned by the Prime Governor to be. It was there her son, Brian, found me, seaweed in my long black hair, clothes torn from being thrashed against the rocks, blood and sand forming scabs across my body. I was there to be saved. I couldn't talk for three days and Brian loved me in my muteness. We married almost immediately and two years later began the quest for progeny.

"It's like the whole tiger testicle or Rhino horn thing that wiped them all out," Janeka said. She hooked her arm around mine. We were out shopping, always a good way to ignore what was going on in our lives.

"But then, half the time they say you're getting tiger balls and it's really like, pig tail or something. The point is that you believe this stuff works."

Brian believed. Mermaid caviar was said in whispers, but then there were the millionaires with children they claimed were truly theirs, homemade, with stretchmarks to prove the struggle was real. Not that such marks couldn't be simulated.

He believed I was a mermaid still and just needed to ingest my brethren so my body could remember. I had washed up on his shores for him alone. I believed in what he told me because it was there. Because his belief was strong enough for the both of us.

He refused to come with me. To the doctors, all of them, or to the restaurant where I could have my dinner.

"Do you think it would be silly if I requested a wine pairing?" I asked Janeka. She was helping us set it all up.

"Yes," she said, hugging me, "which is why I love you for asking."

"How do you even know about this?" I asked.

"Reese doesn't tell the real way we met," Janeka said. "She came to free the Rapunzels, I worked with them. Fed them. She thinks she convinced me my views were wrong, she only convinced me I loved her enough to keep some things hidden."

"So they are real? The Rapunzels?" I asked.

"I made nutrition-dense food to promote hair growth. I'm a food scientist, remember? Nothing more. Anyway, don't tell Reese, it's our little secret. Let me make a few calls."

The Rapunzel liberators and their actions had been growing in intensity. The last attack made the news because the castle collapsed killing all inside. Twelve young girls, hair glinting gold in the sun, were shown lined up next to each other, faces bloodied and covered in soot. The rags they wore burnt showing lithe limbs, also charred from the fires.

"They are probably better off dead, honestly," Reese said. We were sitting at a little Parisian café. The screens around us showed the girls before cutting back to clouds over the Eiffel tower, a fully simulated and immersive experience.

"I mean, the lives they led. Trapped like that. Chained and force-fed Kali knows what to have their hair grow, and for what?"

"For a vital part of our economy," I said, parroting Janeka and Brian's words before I caught myself. He didn't see them as human, just producers of a filament.

"I'm so sorry," I said.

"No, I know it's hard to fight our programming," she said, lightly touching my arm.

"But mermaids, are those real?" I asked. I hadn't told her about the caviar. How I was seriously considering it. How her wife was working with my husband to arrange it for me.

"They're even more of a mystery," Reese said. "There are those in the group who think they are real. But even those people see them as genetic mutations for the idle rich to feast from, not really real. I don't know. But we're talking about them tonight, if you're available."

"Janeka said you had a class tonight? Modern tapestry techniques or something. That you gave up the liberation stuff when you met her."

"Please don't tell Janeka," she said. "Please, I told her I was taking classes but. . . I just can't stop fighting for them. For all of them."

"Because it's hard to fight your programming," I said.

"Rebellion is literally in my genes," she said, a wry smile crossing her lips. "My parents wanted someone ready to take on the world, so here I am."

"And who am I programmed to be?" I asked. Unknown genetics twisted inside me. I thought I was a strong swimmer and ended up stranded. I thought I loved Brian but maybe it was just the idea of being so wanted, of him knowing who I was when I never did.

"A good friend," she said, pulling me closer to her.

"Look, you'll get through this. Maybe Brian will come to his senses and you guys can order a kid like everyone else. Or maybe you'll come to your senses and dump his ass."

"When's this meeting?" I asked.

The meeting was the next day and wasn't so much a meeting as a full-on rescue mission on a reported mermaid holding facility; a basement at a medical school. I learned that mermaids weren't so much a myth as they were a reality. Their scales were pale shimmering blues and greens, each one like the iris of an eye. They were also peeling off, dry and dead. Their eyes, their real eyes in faces so close to human were sunken in, skin pulled taut over high cheekbones and soft jaw lines. Tubes ran in and out of their bodies at various places. They were sideways in the water, hands and faces against the glass looking out, like they were one more breath shy of giving up and floating to the top ready to be flushed.

No one was prepared to face the reality. I think the organizers truly believed they were going to see some PT Barnum trick. Monkey's and fishes spliced together. This was a nightmare of childhood stories. There was tank after tank of floating women, breasts bare and some with milky fluid leaking from their nipples, fingers curling and uncurling as their eyes struggled to focus.

"How do they even harvest the eggs?" I asked.

We fled to the next room, trying to regroup, murmuring about whether mermaids could survive out of water or not. Instead we ran into a horror movie. Flayed bodies hung by their tails like any other trophy fish. Their hair brushing the floor.

I wasn't the only one to fold in two and vomit. It was the way their eyes were still open. Or the way their skin curled at the edges of the cuts, exposing the emptiness inside. Or the frost on their lips. All of this so some could have the vanity of so-called natural children.

I avoided Janeka for a week and lay in bed, pale, sick, mute. At first, Brian took it as a sign that I was already pregnant, his sperm that powerful. He was devastated to hear I was just 'being moody' over something I wouldn't explain.

"You realize you have to eat the caviar," he said. "I've already made the reservations."

"Please don't," I whispered.

"It's okay, sweetie, we'll work through this," he said, stroking my hair.

"Please," I said.

"You can do this for me, can't you?" he said. "You're my little mermaid. You can do this for me and for you. To be who you are supposed to be. A mother."

My mother died in childbirth. My brother was the culprit, not that he lived long enough to know. My family was a fairy tale, too. The way my dad killed himself after my mother died. I was sixteen by then; it was stupid of them to go for another child so late in life anyway. I had told that to Brian shortly after he began insisting I carry our child. But it would be a *coup* for him, he said, to have a natural child. All his friends were getting hybrids. They had kids with the newest genetics and biomodifications. But us, we, him—he could have a heritage baby carried in the real womb of his real wife and wouldn't that be a story. That would be bragging rights.

And he loved me. Why couldn't I realize that? Why couldn't I return those feelings?

I wanted to love Brian, but the images of the mermaids haunted me. In my dreams, my mother's face was superimposed on each and every woman in each and every tank and she was mouthing words in a language I didn't understand. I'd wake up and there'd be Brian holding me and telling me how amazing I was. How beautiful. How I held all the power here and could wield it if only I tried. Telling me it was all taken care of. All I had to do was exactly what he said.

"I love my husband," I told the waiter.

That was the price. Loving Brian. Or maybe it was the cost.

The glass was crystal. The water sacred from a spring somewhere in Russia blessed by Baba Yaga herself. I ran my finger over the rim and heard the siren call of history. Of future. My mother fighting to survive.

The menu was Joshua tree. It was Methuselah. It was a past dying with each fingerprint that told the history of what I was about to eat. The curative powers. The proselytizing in case I suddenly forgot. The fine print that nothing could be guaranteed and nothing refunded. There was nothing about the visions I had of rows of hanging mermaids, empty wombs exposed.

I nodded and the waiter brought over a small bowl filled with sapphire blue eggs. The bowl was ivory or bone or porcelain or something else precious and involved something else suffering. The spoon was matching bone, metal too damaging to the eggs. Maybe the bone and bowl were both mermaid, to keep the eggs fresh. I was to eat all the eggs, wait twenty-four hours, and then reconsummate my marriage.

I placed a spoonful in my mouth and was back on the shore, opening my eyes to the blinding light of the sun, to Brian reaching down for me.

The caviar burst in my mouth, the taste of sea and myth strong, the salt tingling my tongue. There was a brininess of a home forgotten, a tear cascading down my throat.

I swallowed, ready to love my husband. To be the woman he imagined me to be.

CONSUMPTION

S. C. MENDES

"**Y**OU'VE BEEN CORDIALLY invited . . . " Rachel read the cursive script on front, then opened the card. "Oh my God . . . " Her words fell to a whisper as her eyes reread the few lines of text over and over, not daring to believe. Without looking up she shouted, "Babe!"

No answer.

Rachel could hear computer keys clicking under his fingers, and yet she had fallen so deep into the spell of the invitation, the sound seemed far away.

"It's real," she whispered. The need to share pulled her gaze from the card and she walked to Patrick's desk. "Guess what?"

"Just a second." He put up a hand and pecked at the keyboard with the other. "There. Done. What's up?"

Rachel held up the card. "Do you know where I've just been invited?"

"Food Wish Podcast?"

"Pfft, please. This is a hundred times better." She opened the card, grinning. "*Kabzo.*"

"Kabzo?" Patrick's smile dropped. "What the hell is Kabzo?"

"Are you serious? Kabzo—the greatest food event in the world." Still his face was blank.

Part of her was angry. The other part was crushed. "Do you know anything about our industry?"

He's only here for one thing.

"In the past year, I've tried to book you on every food event and channel, and I never heard of no Kabzo."

"It's not like that." Rachel sat down on the couch and looked across the tiny apartment to his computer chair. "You can't ask to attend the Kabzo. Invites are only given to the most esteemed gastronomes. To receive one is like winning the lottery."

"You got my attention. What exactly is this *Kabzo*?"

"No one knows for sure. Except for attendees." Rachel glided her fingertips over the card "Rumors call it the most elusive and exclusive gathering of gourmets. It's held every four years at a secret location. The most exotic and dangerous foods in the world—"

"Dangerous?"

"Pufferfish. *Casu Marzu*. Anything goes from what I've heard." She flushed and her mouth salivated. "They serve dishes most foodies could only dream of consuming."

"So . . . foods that are illegal in America?" Patrick swiveled his chair back to the screen, typed into the search bar, then started reading. "I don't know about this, babe. What's the address?"

"It's here in New Mexico. But I doubt that's where the Kabzo is being held. It's probably just where we meet. Then all guests will be re-routed two or three more times before we get to the actual event."

His laughter stung.

"You really believe this covert bullshit." He scrolled through the search engine. "It's a set-up. You're hot, the star of Food Porn. And this is some fanboy pulling your leg, hoping you'll show up on his doorstep."

"How does some fanboy find our address?"

"They got nothing to do but stalk celebrities and beat off." He pointed at the screen. "Tons of sites saying there's no such thing as the Kabzo."

"You think I don't know that? Think I haven't read about it a million times? But there's just as many websites claiming it *is* real."

"Babe." Patrick swiveled back to look at her. "We need to be focused on building the channel. Creating content and engaging with your fans. Moves that make money. If this is a prank—which it *probably* is—we can't waste time on it."

Rachel looked back at the card. The euphoric wave subsided to a small trickle. Maybe he was right. Was she so blinded by excitement that she didn't see the prank?

"Speaking of time being money," he said. "I cannot get this

website updated with the new forum features. Text Tubby, would you. This is what I'm paying him for."

"You mean Tyler?"

"You know who I mean."

"Would it kill you to be nice? Without him we wouldn't have Food Porn."

"Relax." Patrick stood up and went to the kitchen. "I don't say it to his face." He grabbed a beer from the fridge and popped it open.

"Wonder what you say about me when I'm not around." She folded her legs under her on the couch, crossing her arms, staring off at the wall.

"Fine," he said. "Would you please text *Tyler* and get him to update the forum."

"I told you earlier I'm going to his place tomorrow to discuss new ideas—I'll tell him then."

"We kind of need it updated ASAP."

"Fine." She picked up her phone and messaged.

Patrick took a swig of beer. "You wanna go to O'Kelly's and catch the Laker game?"

"No thanks," she said. "I'm tired."

"Fine. I'm gonna watch it here then."

Patrick sat down on the couch and turned on the TV. They were only one cushion apart and yet she'd never felt further away.

"The Kabzo, Ty. Can you believe it!"

When she gripped his shoulders, Tyler felt the tingles penetrate every layer of his body. "It's a foodie's wet dream . . . " he agreed. "But . . . Are you sure it's real?"

"Don't you start with that too." She sank away from him.

"I'm sorry, girl. I don't mean it like that. It's just so wild to believe it's real. I always figured it was the greatest urban legend in the community—nobody who's been ever talks. Everyone just knows someone who knows someone." Tyler understood her passion for the life, but her face seemed more crushed by his admission than it needed to be. "Okay, what's really wrong?"

She sighed.

"What'd he do?"

"Just being his regular assholey self."

Tyler never liked to discuss Patrick if it could be avoided. It was torture knowing that tool got to enjoy Rachel. But when she vented her frustrations, a small part of Tyler rejoiced in hope they'd break-up. Not that he'd ever have a chance with someone like her, but it was nice to dream.

"He doesn't think it's real?"

"Of course not. But it's more than that. It's his total discounting of my feelings. Wouldn't even discuss. He forgets the whole point of why we started the Food Porn show. It's just a business for him." She mocked Patrick's voice: "I should be filming and engaging with fans and growing the channel."

A slight tremor took hold of her and Tyler reached across the coffee table taking her slender hands in his pudgy paws. Only when she was in distress could Tyler risk a caring touch or pushing his agenda. He ignored the smooth warmth of her skin. "It's okay," he said. "Maybe . . . maybe it's time you think about splitting ways with him. Coming here, upset . . . It's not exactly a rare occurrence."

"I'm sorry to keep doing this to you."

"Don't be. It's him. You even said it. He's more consumed with the money than the lifestyle."

"I shouldn't say that. He's not all bad. He's the reason the show's a success—"

"*You're the reason* it's a success. I don't see him cooking in lingerie or eating in sexy outfits. Anyone can run things behind the scenes. I mean, hey, I'm not too shabby of a webmaster, am I?"

"You're the best." She smiled. "And I couldn't do it without you either. But if Patrick just had that curiosity, that true love of food, he'd see how getting an invitation to the Kabzo could make us the most famous website in the industry."

"If it is real, they're not going to let you report on it—"

"I don't need to report on it. I just . . . I just need to know. To be a part of it. It's a foodie's Mount Everest. My moment of arrival. I've been chosen and I can't believe you're siding with him." The last glow of excitement extinguished from her eyes.

"I'm not siding with him. I'm asking you to look at this logically. Patrick is not passionate like us. He's consumed with the business.

But maybe—just perhaps—you're too consumed by something else to see the truth about the Kabzo."

"You don't think it's real either?"

"I honestly can't say. But the stories . . . The invitation is for you alone. You'd have no one you trust along. There are no cameras allowed. It's more than likely in another country. Rumors have compared it to underground cock fighting rings. Dirty vendors in a wet market, selling—"

"I've also heard it described as the most extravagant of galas."

"That's why it's a legend. No one knows."

"But I *can* . . . " She held up the card.

"Knowing can't possibly be worth the risk, can it?"

She looked away from him and Tyler knew her answer. She pulled her hands from his. "I thought you of all people would understand. Would support me going."

Tyler tried to keep the anguish from his face. He wanted to satisfy her hunger for knowledge. He understood why she never felt satiated for long. Why she thought the Kabzo would end the cravings. He had similar reasons for eating. They were kindred souls. The difference was the weight never showed on her. She was gorgeous on the outside no matter how much she consumed. But on the inside, Rachel wanted to be full no matter what the cost.

"Please. For me, Rachel. Don't go."

Around 4pm the next day, someone pounded on his apartment door. It was so loud, Tyler half-expected to hear the police announce themselves. He inched up to the peep hole and looked out at the face of Patrick.

"I know you're in there," Patrick called. "I need to talk with you."

Tyler checked that the chain lock was secure and opened the door.

"What's up, Patrick?"

Patrick got right up to the small opening. "Is Rachel in there with you?"

"No."

"You lying, Tubby?"

"What's your problem? No, I'm not lying. Last I saw her was yesterday."

"What time did she leave?"

Tyler shrugged. "About this time. Maybe four-fifteen. Did she not come home?"

Patrick pulled back from the crack. "Damn." He turned and paced around the hall. "Where the fuck could she be?" He approached again. "Would you open the door so we can talk?"

"You gonna be pissed and call me names?"

"No."

"Fine." Tyler closed the door and removed the chain. When he opened it back up, Patrick looked calmer. "Come in."

"Did she tell you about this Ka-Kab—ah, that stupid food contest-thingy?"

"She told me about it."

"And . . . " Patrick's voice raised.

"And I told her she shouldn't go. She was annoyed and left shortly after. We didn't even get the next week's episode fleshed out."

"Great." Patrick slumped back on the couch.

"Let's start calling her friends. Maybe we can post something on her platforms as the admin saying she went missing and ask if anyone's—"

"What the fuck are you talking about? We can't do that. We can't say *anything*. We've filmed two shows ahead. Which means we have content for two more weeks. We can find her by then. No one needs to know."

"Aren't you worried—"

"I'm not worried about her. I'm pissed off at her. Big difference." Patrick leaned forward. "Nothing's wrong. She's got her panties in a bunch because we didn't agree with her idea. Probably realized by now how stupid it is and wants to pout on her own. When she's tired, she'll come home."

"What if you're wrong?" Tyler paused and worst-case scenarios pushed into his awareness. "What if she went to the Kabzo?"

Patrick opened his mouth, then paused. He shook his head. "I doubt it."

But Tyler could see he didn't completely doubt it. "Was there a date or time on the invitation she received?"

"No. It was just the invitation with an address."

"Do you remember the address?"

"It doesn't matter." Patrick was up on his feet now. "It was on Monroe street. Somewhere just west of Roosevelt. But it *doesn't* matter. I'm telling you she didn't go." He moved to the window and stared outside.

Tyler knew better than to say anything else.

Patrick turned back to him. "I'm gonna get out of here. If you hear from her, give me a call."

Tyler nodded.

Monroe street, just west of Roosevelt.

After two days without a word from Rachel, Tyler caught an Uber downtown. It was a bustling area with hipster restaurants and breweries, mixed with posh eateries and a park square that often had farmer's markets and small music sets. Any number of addresses could have been on that invitation, but if Tyler could only pick one to help, it would be Madame Hathor's.

It took thirty minutes before Tyler was even admitted to the upstairs loft. He was patted down twice, before he was escorted into her studio apartment above the swanky restaurant.

The room was dim and cool. Madame Hathor was lounging on an oversized chaise, surrounded by trays of varying heights all within reach. She reminded him of a beautiful Jabba the Hut.

"Tyler, Tyler. Oh, it's been so long. Finally, ready for something *exotic* for that little show of yours?" She licked her plump red lips.

"Not exactly . . . "

"Oh . . . " she said, though her face didn't seem surprised at his cover story to see her. "Whatever could you want then?"

"You obviously know Rachel from the show?"

"Quite the dish she is. I bet viewers could just eat her up."

"Has she . . . visited you these last few days?" At that moment, standing between two bodyguards, it would have been less scary talking to a pissed-off Patrick.

"Now why would you think she'd come to visit me?" Hathor smirked and Tyler forgot what a sicko this woman was. She got off on watching him squirm.

"She got an invitation for the Kabzo. It sent her to an address in the square. If anyone is knowledgeable on the event, it would be you."

She laughed and reached for a glass of red wine with her right hand. Her left moved to a cheese, meat, and olive tray. "Pecorino. My favorite pairing with Merlot." She bit, then swallowed, eyes closing, full cheeks flushing with euphoria. "Care for a bite?"

"No thank you." Watching her eat was not appetizing. "I'm worried about her. Is there anything you can tell me?"

"About what?" Hathor licked a finger.

"The Kabzo. Is it real? Is it here in the square. Maybe she's attending or maybe she just went missing. She didn't tell me or—her boyfriend."

The corpulent madame drained more wine, then returned the glass. "I wouldn't worry about Rachel. She's a big girl. She can handle herself. What you need to be focusing on is you." She formed her fingers into a rectangle in front of her eye, framing him within. "You should start your own channel. Or better yet, I could use someone with your talents."

"If you don't want to help me, that's fine. But I already have a job at Food Porn."

"I love that name by the way. It's so poetic." She closed her eyes and inhaled. "Food and sex. The only things that matter in this world." Her eyes snapped open, and Tyler saw wild passion, same as in Rachel. "It's true when you think about it. What else is there? Everything a human does is to improve the quality of their food and sex. People say it's money and power we crave. But it's not. The only reason for money and power is to achieve more appealing food and more exotic sex. To live is to eat and fuck. Wouldn't you agree?"

"Please. Tell me what you told Rachel. I just want to find her."

"Ugh, begging is such a turn-off. Do you ever think that maybe the young lady was testing you and the . . . *boyfriend*. Perhaps you failed. Perhaps she wanted to get away from you."

Tyler couldn't believe that, but the mere mention stole his voice. He replayed her face, her words, was he missing something?

"So there is no Kabzo?"

"I'm fascinated by your obsession with this woman." Hathor took a crystal glass of water and cleansed her palate, then eyed the various trays, settling on a bowl of salted nuts. "If there *was* a Kabzo, you would find it by asking for Ukemoch at Ling Lings market."

Tyler pulled out his phone and began typing in the name. "Where is—"

"It's in LA."

"That's where Rachel went?"

"If she's searching for the Kabzo that's where she went. Forget her though. Tonight's meal is shark fin soup. You should stay . . . ."

"I can't forget her."

Madame Hathor gave a sigh and a pout. "What a pity."

It was an excruciating thirty-six hours waiting for the next flight from New Mexico to LAX. Once he landed, he rented a car and detoured to a hotel only long enough to drop off his single piece of luggage. Then he hopped on the bus to the downtown district and Ling Ling's market.

From there, he was bounced across town from a classy restaurant to outdoor stalls. When he finally got an address in the secluded hills of Napa Valley, Tyler was exhausted and returned to the hotel for a nap.

He woke hours later to a dark room and a ringing phone. He fumbled for the cell in the bedsheets. "Hello?"

"You trying to fuck me?"

"Patrick?"

"You're with her, aren't you?" he screamed. "Played dumb, then ran off and fucked me. Well it doesn't work like that—"

"I don't know what you're talking about—"

"Bullshit! All the passwords are changed. You locked me the fuck out!"

"You can keep yelling at me, but I don't know what the hell you're talking about."

"I've been to your place. I know you ain't there. I know you're with her and if—"

Tyler hung up and pushed off the covers. He switched on the bedroom lamp and grabbed his laptop. He opened a new window and logged on to Food Porn's administer dashboard.

Email or password error. You have three more attempts.

"No, no, no." He tried again, hitting each key with precision.

Email or password error. You have two more attempts.

Tyler ran a clammy hand through his hair. He could see her on the couch, her eyes begging him to be excited about the invitation.

Perhaps it was a test. Maybe she wanted to get away from you . . .

Tyler felt dizzy.

Tyler closed the laptop and lay back on the bed. Scenario after scenario forced its way into his mind. Nothing stuck. Nothing made sense. He pulled out the address in Napa. Every person he'd contacted gave him the same song and dance as Madame Hathor, eventually throwing him a crumb that only led to more questions. No one ever acknowledged that the Kabzo was real but neither did they tell him it wasn't. It was like one big game to fuck with him. And now he was locked out of the website.

Forget her. Forget the Kabzo.

The whole thing was a waste. All his time. All his money. What would be at the address? More questions? Patrick thought Tyler was in on Rachel's disappearance, but he didn't have a clue.

I should be in on it. We're friends. Why wouldn't she tell me—

It was a test. I failed. If I had told her to go to the Kabzo, she would have counted me as an ally and revealed this covert plan to leave.

Tyler looked at the address again.

There was nothing else to lose.

As the rental car pulled up to the gated entrance to the estate, Tyler grappled to concentrate. Chances were he'd have one shot at this. He settled on a cover story, but it hinged on a lot. In his jeans and baggy button-up from Kohl's, he didn't exactly look like an investor, but his options were limited.

He rolled down the window and pressed the intercom button outside the gate. The lines repeated in his head. He swallowed. No answer.

While he was contemplating a second press of the button, the speaker box came to life. "Welcome to Nasso Farms. Do you have an appointment?"

"Hi. No. I . . . I was referred by a business associate. I'd very much like to take a tour. Discuss purchases. I'm on my way out of town, but I couldn't resist. Is a tour available?"

The well-practiced speech sounded foolish now. The speaker box was silent.

"Hello?"

There was a buzz and the iron gate rattled. Splitting down the middle, the bars separated allowing him access.

"Welcome, sir. I am Isiah Hersch. One of the caretakers." The man had grey hair under his square black hat. His body was clothed in a long black coat, buttoned down the front, obscuring all of his body but his hands.

"Tyler Laredo." They shook. "Sorry, for my casual dress. Travel day." Tyler issued a nervous chuckle. "As I said, when my associate knew I was so close to your estate, he told me I had to visit before leaving California."

A soft smiled creased his darkly tanned features. "Of course. A tour and a tasting, yes?"

"Yes, please."

Tyler received a glass of red wine, Isiah informing him there was only one house wine, then they walked the outskirts of the fields. They passed beautiful, expansive gardens. Not just of grapes but various fruits and vegetables. Workers dressed in similar attire to Isiah tilled the fields.

"For a hundred years, Nasso has been here. Crafting artisan food. It is more than a winery. More than a food company. It is a way of life. And everyone who works here is family."

Tyler nodded and took a sip of wine. It reminded him of an Amish community. Everyone working in some capacity for the whole. Only when these workers retired, they did so in the mansion that Isiah was leading them back to. It looked like a castle or British boarding school from a bygone era.

They were only a couple yards from the doors and Tyler knew knew he had to pull the trigger. Forgive me, Isiah," he said, "but . . . I'm afraid there's a bit more to my arrival today."

"Oh?" The man slowed.

"This is gonna sound silly, but . . . I think my friend may have visited here recently." He pulled out his phone. "Here's a picture of her. Did she happen to come by at all?"

Isiah's eyes narrowed a bit, but he didn't seem alarmed by Tyler's farce. He looked at the phone. "Yes."

"She did?" His pulse began to race. "Do you know where she is now?"

"She came to us—much like you have—and was . . . confused about food. Her palate needed reeducation."

"Rachel confused about food?" He chuckled. "Obviously, you haven't seen Food Porn."

"Food porn?" Now the man's face seemed to darken with disappointment.

Tyler choked on his last sip of wine. "Sorry, it's a uh . . . a cooking show. It's not really pornography. Rachel—her name's Rachel Givings—she's very knowledgeable about food."

The man nodded. "Most people think they are knowledgeable on the subject of food. Yet most have lost touch with the reality of the importance of what one ingests." Isiah stopped about fifty yards from the mansion doors. "Eating is a very spiritual and intimate experience. Did you not taste the power in the wine?"

Tyler looked down at the glass. "Oh, yes. It was amazing. About Rachel—"

"Our ancestors put all of their efforts into meal preparation. The entire community, toiling day after day, just for that brief moment when the life-giving force of God would touch their lips." Isiah's eyes saddened. "Mankind has lost that reverence. They eat for pleasure now. A mass-producing business. Consumption without meaning. Nasso Farms will change that."

Isiah continued to the doors.

The confusing conversation, heat, and wine churned in Tyler's mind, tiring him despite his mission.

"It's important that you tell me when she left . . . she's been . . . missing . . . " Tyler felt stupid. The words wouldn't come. How was he so drunk off one glass?

Isiah opened the door, ushering him inside.

"I need . . . I need . . . " Tyler's throat felt dry and his head swayed. "Is this the Kabzo? Is this real? Where's . . . where's Rachel."

He heard the wine glass shatter. His body fell too, but Tyler caught himself on the door handle. He could feel hands around him, lowering him slowly to the floor. The tile felt cool against his warm cheeks. Eyes straining to focus, he saw Isiah bend forward.

"Kabzo is real. But it is not what you think it is."

Then the image faded to black.

Tyler shoveled food into his mouth. Every delicacy he could ever want, all of it, a gorgeous presentation before a mirrored table polished to perfection. Each bite was disgusting though. Tender fruit skin broke, flooding his mouth with rancid juices. Meat was sour and chewy. Maggots writhed in pies.

Voices infiltrated the hellish banquet of his nightmare. Eventually the meal was replaced by a dark room. The only illumination came from candles which lined the walls. In their flickering glow, men chanted. They were the men from the fields. Head to toe in black, they rocked back and forth, their deep voices were all he could hear.

Tyler could not decipher if they were actual words or mere sounds. The chanted tones resonated in his body and it was oddly soothing. Though his body relaxed, the fear in his mind did not subside.

As more of his senses awakened, Tyler could see that he was upright, but not standing. His body was leaning forward at a slight angle, perhaps forty degrees. He was held in place somehow. He tried to move his head but found resistance. He looked down and saw he was naked, a white porcelain basin underneath his body.

"Oh god, what are you doing to me?" His voice was weak against their chanting.

A figure broke from the ranks and placed his hands on the side of Tyler's head. He spoke in a langue Tyler did not understand, then he blew into Tyler's mouth. The sensation repulsed him, and Tyler felt his body convulse. Vomit spewed into the basin and Tyler fell back into unconsciousness.

When Tyler awoke again, Isiah was standing before him. The men and candles were gone. Light entered from a large window.

"Why . . . why are you doing this?" Tyler's voice was weak.

Isiah brought a glass of water before his face. Placed a handkerchief under his chin and tilted the glass. Tyler swallowed until he coughed, and Isaiah withdrew the cup. The liquid soothed his dehydrated throat.

Tyler still felt the straps around his head and arms but could not see what he was bound to, keeping him at a slanted angle, though it felt hard, like a board against his back. "I'm sorry I lied, okay? I'm not a restaurant investor at all. I just wanted to find her . . . " Tyler's body hitched against the straps that held him. "I needed to know if the Kabzo was real or if she'd . . . ditched me. I'm sorry . . . " The tears fell, collecting in the trough below.

"There is no *real* Kabzo. Only our holy order. It is doubtful that whoever gave you this address, knows quite who we are. The legend of Kabzo has taken on a life of its own though, and the mystery serves us well."

"What are you doing to me?"

"Curing you." Isiah walked over to the window. "Civilization has grown sick, mentally and physically, and no one realizes it. People like you and Rachel though, are the most disturbed. Fully consumed. You are the ones who stop at nothing to find Kabzo. When you reach us, our mission is to help you. By doing so, we will heal all of humanity."

Tyler tried to calm his breathing.

Isiah turned back to him. "Do you know why it is unwise to eat pork?"

Tyler remained silent, saving strength, opting to let the man talk.

"Thousands of years ago, rules on what one could and could not eat were always dictated by God to man. Rules that today's men of science scoff at as superstition. And yet those men of science are slowly discovering what our ancestors knew all along. One being the avoidance of swine. Eating pig is like eating man. Pigs are even referred to as 'horizontal men'. Did you know that?"

Tyler could feel hysterics threatening again. "What are you talking about. What do you want from me?"

"To elevate your divine soul." Isiah smiled and returned with the water cup.

Tyler was not too proud to drink again. When he was done, Isiah put the cup down and continued. "Pigs mimic men in many ways. It's why doctors use pig organs in transplants and for growing cells. Eating flesh of a living creature can cause all types of maladies in the body, especially when the DNA is similar to our own. Kuru if it's human flesh, and much worse maladies can besiege one when proper eating is not observed."

Tyler took deep breaths through his nose and out his moth. "Please. I'm trying to understand. I really am. But I don't get it."

"Everything in the universe has a divine essence. The expression of that divine spark depends on the vessel it is encapsulated in. As humans, we are in the unique position to eat in a manner which elevates the divine sparks of our food. Taking less aware organisms and raising them up along with ourselves into high realms of consciousness. The life force travels from soil to plant, searching ever upward for a human to ingest that essence into themselves, then burning the divine calories by doing acts of goodness in the world."

"Doing good? You think this is good? Look at me?"

"We fuel our bodies to carry out service to God. Eating is the most intimate form of union with the universe one can ever have. We are restoring that sacred act. Now do you understand? Do you see what humans have done to the most sacred of acts?"

"You're fucking crazy!" The words shot so violently from him that a bolt of pain seared into his throat.

"The brothers of our order are not crazy. We are not the ones putting our food through slaughterhouses where the fear remains trapped in the blood, the flesh." He approached Tyler and slid two fingers across his tear-soaked face, rubbing them before Tyler's eyes. "No. We do not eat for fun. We do not overeat and lie to ourselves that we need this many calories. We do not value taste over God or price our foods as brands, as symbols of status. Your society has debased food, and as a result your society is mentally imbalanced. Doctors search for medication to cure illnesses, not realizing that the root of all sickness is from what you eat! You are consumed—a Sanskrit word meaning a 'wasting disease'. Nasso will cure humanity though, one person at a time we will raise them up."

"How, huh? You gonna eat me?" Drool sprayed from Tyler's mouth. "Is that how you cured Rachel? Kill us and eat us, then do God's work so we're elevated?"

"Not exactly. As I said, we are to eat organisms of lower consciousness and then raise them to our vibration."

"Then what did you do to her!" Tyler's head throbbed, his vocal cords straining with anger.

"We saved her." Isiah walked away and opened the large double windows, flooding the room with fresh garden breeze. "I cleaned her, prepared her. Bled as much of the infection from her as possible. Then we recycled her. Back to the mother." He was looking out the window at the fields of fruits and vegetables. "Her essence will be brought back up through the roots and then one day, Nasso priests will consume her and unite her with God."

Tyler wretched, but there was nothing for his stomach to void. His throat stretched again with the same result. Isiah came back to Tyler and produced a long steel needle from within his coat. Tyler trembled as the cool needle pressed against the skin of his cheek. Tyler did his best to steady his body as the tip was dragged down his face, fell over his jaw and to his neck.

"Please . . . "

"The Maasai people have drank cow's blood for centuries. They developed a unique method of piercing the jugular yet allowing the animal to live."

"Please . . . Stop."

The man inhaled and pushed. A searing pain bit into Tyler, still unable to move his head. As quick as it happened the needle was gone, yet the searing pain remained. Isiah clamped his hand around

Tyler's throat, massaging, milking the blood into the basin on the floor.

"I will cure you too. And you will be elevated." Isiah looked into his eyes. "I promise."

A WOMAN'S WORK

TONIA BROWN

MARCY WAS WASHING dishes when her husband brought home the dead baby for dinner.

He dropped the child on the table, beside a handful of mail, with a casual indifference he usually reserved for dirty clothes or empty soda cans. A fat, naked baby, with chubby little arms and a full round body. A boy, at least ten pounds, maybe more.

Mark began to unbutton his work shirt and leaned in for a kiss. Just as he always did when he got home. Marcy let him peck her on the cheek while she stared at the dead baby lying face down on her kitchen table.

"What is that?" she managed to say.

"I thought we would try something different tonight," he said.

She furrowed her brow, her stomach twisting in knots. "I don't understand."

"For dinner?"

"I'm . . . I'm supposed to cook that?" she stammered as she pointed at the child.

"Aw, don't be that way. I know it's a little unconventional." Mark patted the naked baby on the rump. "I thought we could look it up on the Internet. Learn how to dress it together." He smiled as he cocked his head to one side. "Dress? Isn't that what they call it?"

"Dress," Marcy echoed softly.

He kicked off his shoes and unbuckled his belt, talking all the while. "Frank gave it to me. After that little romantic trip to the woods, he had more than he and his wife could handle, so he asked if we wanted to try one out. He snuck it into the plant and I hid it in a Foodmart bag in the crisper drawer." He continued to talk as he wandered to the far end of the trailer, to their bedroom. "I thought one of the office snobs found it at lunch, but she was screaming at a mouse that ran under the coffee maker. Thank God. I don't know what they would've done if they found we were using the company fridge for personal food."

Mark kept up his one-sided conversation from the far end of the bedroom, his voice fading to a dull drone, leaving Marcy to stare at the dead baby on her kitchen table. She took a few steps closer to it, eyeing it from head to toe. Its skin had a creamy blueness that was shot through with the crimson lightning strikes of broken blood vessels. Its arms were raised above its head, little fists closed in tight knots at the end of plump arms.

"Frank said if we liked it he could get his hands on another one any time," Mark said. "Wasn't that generous of him?"

Marcy didn't answer. Instead, she reached out and laid a hand on the baby's leg. Cold flesh yielded like putty under her palm. Her stomach lurched, bile burning her throat while she swallowed back a heave.

"Hon?" Mark said. "Marcy? Are you okay? You look like you're about to be sick."

She turned on one heel and thrust an indignant finger at the dead child. "That's a baby!"

Mark started, as if she had struck him instead of spoke. "What?"

"A baby, Mark. That's a baby."

"Really? Do you think so?" Mark went to the table and poked at the dead baby. "It's a little big to be a baby, but what do I know?" He picked the child up under its arms and wiggled it about. Chubby little feet brushed the table while Mark flopped the kid back and forth in a macabre puppet show. His voice rose a few octaves as he said, "I'm a full-grown adult, Marcy. I might be fresh but that's only a bit of extra work for extra deliciousness. Eat me. Yum, yum!"

She stared at him in horror, her arms going limp as her knees felt.

Mark glanced up to her, clearly shocked by her disgust. "Marcy? Are you sure you're okay?" He slowly lowered the baby to the table and furrowed his brow. "If I had known you would get so upset over a fresh turkey, hon, I would've gotten a pack of hamburger."

She looked to the baby, then back to him. "Turkey?"

"Sure." He patted the baby on the butt again. "Frank and his wife hunt on the weekends. They ended up with more than their freezer could hold."

Marcy swallowed hard. A turkey? Of course, it was just a turkey. A turkey that looked like a dead baby. She felt eyes on her and glanced up to find Mark watching her cautiously. No, he was looking at her. It was *the* look. The one he gave her when suspected something was wrong. His judging look.

"Marcy?" he said. "Are you, you know, seeing something different?"

"No," she said without hesitation.

He pressed his lips together and grunted so softly she almost didn't hear it. That damned judgmental grunt to accompany that damned judgmental glare. "Have you been taking your medicine?"

"Yes," she said, much too quickly. Though it wasn't a lie. Not outright. She had been taking her meds. At least, she had until a few weeks ago when she ran out. But she didn't need them anymore. The medicine had worked. It had fixed her. She felt better.

"Marcy?" Mark said. "Have you been—"

"I've been taking my medicine," she said over his question. "Stop treating me like a child." She winced at her own poor choice of words.

He stepped forward and grabbed her by the shoulders, rough at first, then loosening his grip to a gentle squeeze. He breathed a heavy sigh. "You would tell me if something was wrong. Wouldn't you?"

She smiled up at him. "Of course."

Mark locked gazes with her, searching her eyes for the trace of a lie. She continued to smile, keeping her eyes on his, resisting the urge to look at the dead baby again. Mark finally smiled back at her and patted her shoulders.

"If the turkey is upsetting you . . . " he started.

"No." She gently pushed him away and looked to the baby again. Its little fists raised above its head. Its skin that macabre hue of robin egg blue. "It's not upsetting me. I'm okay. Honestly."

"Are you sure?"

"Yes. It was kind of Brian to give it to us."

"Frank," Mark corrected her.

"What?"

"Frank gave it to us. You said Brian. Are you sure you're okay?"

"I'm sure, hon. It was just a slip of the tongue."

He considered this for a moment before he said, "You know, you don't have to help me gut and clean it. I can do it alone."

"Nonsense." She picked up the baby under the arms and moved it toward the kitchen sink. "I can do it. I want to help." It flopped into the sink with a soft slap of flesh on metal. She swallowed another rise of bile and turned to Mark as if nothing was wrong. It was better like this. He didn't need to know what she saw. He didn't need to know how she felt. Not really. He would just get mad about it and that would ruin their evening.

Mark grinned at her. "All right then. Let's figure out how to dress a bird together."

It was surprisingly easy to clean the baby. On Mark's instruction, Marcy split the child from breastbone to groin, spilling its guts into the sink. Red swelled through her hands, running everywhere. No worries there, she had seen blood before. Had it on her hands. In the bed of her fingernails. Running down the length of her thigh. Blood was part of being alive. Part of being a woman. Part of being a mother.

A mother.

That word lingered on the tongue of her mind. A comfortable fit in an otherwise fitful world. Mother. Something she longed for her whole life. A child of her own. She only wished someone had told her how complicated such a thing was.

She found herself comfortably sliding a deboning knife between the thing's ribs. Confidently slicing tissue and scraping fat. Stripping meat from bone. It never stopped looking like a child, and she never stopped smiling. She couldn't let him know what she saw. No matter how much blood there was.

After she cleaned most of the carcass, Mark suggested they should cut off its head.

She rolled it onto its back, raised the cleaver, ready to bring it down between two little rolls of fat that separated its skull from its shoulders, when she caught sight of its blue, swollen lips. Her heart leapt into her throat. The cleaver hit the table with a clatter. Marcy raised her hands to her wet eyes.

"I can't," she said. "I just can't."

"Marcy?" Mark said, enfolding her in his arms. "Don't cry, hon. You don't have to do it. I can do it."

Marcy shook her head into his broad chest.

"You don't want to cut its head off?" he asked. A tinge of amusement rose to his voice.

She couldn't bear the thought of it. Sure, it was just a turkey. Its intestines and fat and bone were stuffed into a plastic bag, and shoved into the garbage can. She didn't see that as part of a child anymore. It could've easily been cast off from a cleaned turkey. But its head. Its little face. Those delicate lashes. That small perfect mouth. She couldn't allow him to do it. She shook her head into his chest again.

"Okay," he said with a chuckle. "We can leave it on. I don't think it matters either way. I think I've seen Chinese restaurants leave duck heads on. Don't they?"

Marcy nodded. She stepped away from his embrace and wiped at her eyes.

"Then that's what we will do," he said. "Get it in the oven. I'm hungry."

"I have to preheat it first," she said, flipping on the oven and setting the temperature. "Find out how long we need to cook it. I've never made one so big before and the store-bought ones usually have instructions on them."

Mark tapped away on his phone while Marcy placed the child in a baking pan. She was worried it wouldn't fit at first, but managed to find the sweet spot by laying the kid on its back. She folded its legs and arms along the length of its body. Just like a turkey. Because that's what it was. Marcy rubbed a generous amount of seasoning on the child's skin, taking care to get it under the folds where they slashed at the baby's flesh.

"Aw crap," Mark said. He glanced up from his phone with a frown. "I have some bad news."

"What?" she asked.

"It takes twenty minutes a pound. That means it take about four hours to cook."

Marcy tutted as she eyed the clock and did the math. "It won't be done until almost ten. That's far too late for your dinner."

113

"Nonsense." Mark waved her words away. "We've eaten late before. I can find a snack until then."

She gave a tired sigh, unsure of what to do about dinner now. Unsure of what to do about the pan filled with a dead baby.

"I love you," he said all of the sudden.

"I love you too."

Mark placed a hand over hers, pressing it into the cold flesh of the dead baby. "You sure you're okay?"

"I'm fine."

"I'm sorry I've been working so much."

"It's okay. You have to work."

"I do. I have to support our family."

She nodded. Family. There was something so strange about that word. Something she felt like she was forgetting.

"You would tell me—" he started.

"I would tell you," she said over him. And she would. Besides, she was going to refill her medicine tomorrow, so none of this mattered anyways. "I'd better put this in or no one is going to eat anything." She opened the now hot oven and reached for the pan.

"Let me get it. It's too heavy for you."

Marcy stepped out of his way, allowing Mark to place the admittedly heavy pan on the rack. He closed the oven and glanced around the kitchen. "Looks like we have some cleaning up to do."

Marcy turned and looked to the kitchen. The child made a glorious mess. Splashes of red painted the counter top and ran rivulets into the sink. A woman's work was never done. "I can clean it up."

"No," he said. "I want to help."

"No I can—"

"Marcy," he said over her. "I want to help you."

"Okay."

And he did. They worked together, like they used to, side by side, cleaning the mess they had both made. Once they were done, and the blood was all wiped away, Mark pulled Marcy into his arms and hugged her tightly.

"I really do love you," he said. "You know that, don't you?"

"I do."

"I . . . " his words trailed off as his attention shifted away from her. "Did you hear that?"

There came a metallic clicking from the front door. The handle wiggled back and forth.

Mark looked down at Marcy. "Are you expecting someone?"

"No," she said and went to see who it could be.

Before she could make it to the door, it swung wide open, pushed inward by a man coming into her home. Not a stranger. No. A man she knew all too well.

Mark closed the door behind him and smiled wide at her. "I am so sorry I'm late. Traffic was a nightmare." He began to unbutton his work shirt and leaned in for a kiss.

Just like he always did when he got home.

Marcy turned to glance at the empty kitchen as Mark pecked her on the cheek. Her vison narrowed on the spot where Mark stood only five seconds before he came in through the front door. It made her head ache to look at the now empty kitchen. Her heart hammered in her chest as her veins ran ice cold. Her breath caught in her throat somewhere between an inhale and a scream.

Mark walked past her and kicked off his shoes. He looked to the darkened back half of the trailer, toward the other bedrooms. Or rather, to one bedroom in particular. "Did I miss Brian?"

The name echoed in her head. Brian, she has said. Not Frank.

She had called the man from work her own son's name.

"Damn," Mark said, mistaking her silence for an answer. "I really tried to make it home before his bedtime."

Marcy continued to stand in silence, staring at the empty kitchen. At the place where the other Mark had spent the last hour helping her skin and debone the dead baby.

"Aww," Mark said. "You're still mad at me. I'm sorry. I know I've been working a lot but like I said this morning, I only do it for our family." Mark unbuckled his belt and inhaled deeply. "What smells so good?"

She finally lost her fascination with the empty kitchen, shooting a glance to the oven instead. The little light on the stove assured her the oven was working just fine. The "turkey" roasted slowly, and would be ready to eat soon enough. She shuddered, her knees buckling under her as she dropped to the floor in a sudden slump.

"Marcy?" Mark said, touching her shoulder. "Are you okay?"

Marcy heard the sound of her own shriek before she realized she was even screaming.

MADE TO ORDER

MARK C. SCIONEAUX

"COME AND GET 'EM! Corn dogs hot out the fryer," Charlie called out as the carnival buzzed and swirled around him. Carnival rides hummed as mechanical levers and arms groaned and twisted. A mixture of gleeful shrieks and shouts filled the air. It was electric. Lights shone, bells rung, and somewhere a man shouted, "You win a prize!" The carnival was alive with people, and Charlie Dogg hoped they were hungry.

He needed this night to be a great night. His business wasn't doing well . . . terrible actually. No one wanted corn dogs anymore. The new trend was pumpkin-spice anything or those frozen space-orb ice creams things that stuck to his teeth and made them hurt. Charlie couldn't see the appeal. It was a chilly October night, and he was *still* being outsold by ice cream. Everyone liked a corn dog. Hell, it was American.

But those times seemed to be gone.

The night ended, and Charlie threw out several dozen corn dogs. He opened the small freezer behind the counter. It was almost empty. Sighing, he sat down and let his face sink into his hands. Tonight was once again a failure, and worse, the witch of a woman he'd married waited for him to return home.

He didn't understand why she took such delight in his failures, but Vickie was a cold-blooded bitch who loved misery. Four hundred pounds of cold-blooded bitch to be more precise, barking out insults from the oversized recliner that she rarely moved from. Charlie couldn't help but wonder what disgusting things were stuck under her fat, sweaty body tonight. The thought made him gag.

He closed down his stand, disconnected the fryer and waited for the oil to cool before disposing of it. Charlie's oil was getting low as well. He'd had to make the tough decision to stop serving fries last week because the cost was eating into the profits. This week, he could barely afford corn dogs, and after tonight's awful sales, he had no idea how much longer Charlie Dogg's Famous Corn Doggs would survive.

Charlie was just about to head out when a small shadow appeared.

"Tough night, huh?"

"Seen better, Rudy," Charlie said as the carnival manager eyed the money box.

"Well, sorry to hear that, but you still owe me my cut for the night."

"Sure thing, boss. Fifteen percent, right?"

"Twenty, Charlie. You know that."

Charlie sighed and rummaged through the box. Grabbing a wadded ten-dollar bill, he handed it over. Rudy snatched it, greedily, his face turning to disgust when he saw the small denomination.

"Jesus, Charlie, that's pretty fucking bad."

"Tell me about it. Try *living* off that."

"I'd imagine it's quite tough."

"It sure is," Charlie said, his voice guarded. He'd never known Rudy to lend a sympathetic ear to anyone.

"Going to be real tough when your shitty little stand gets booted out of here and replaced with someone who can actually make money."

There it was, the true Rudy revealed. Charlie had no words. Nodding his head, he collected his things, walking past Rudy and toward the parking lot.

"Make some sales, Charlie, or peddle your shitty corn dogs somewhere else!"

The words stung like wasps and Charlie made his way to his car as fast as his short legs could carry him. He could hear the laughs coming from the other booth owners. The mocking from his peers hurt.

He knew Vickie would be even more brutal.

"You're such a loser, Charlie," Vickie said, grunting like a hog from her Lay-Z-Boy throne as she watched another episode of *Guess My STD!* Her fat face was slick with popcorn butter and grease. Fried chicken bones littered her lap like an unearthed graveyard. Her breath sucked in with a gasp and exhaled in a raspy wheeze. Charlie sat at the table, munching on a corn dog he had brought home, ignoring her.

He couldn't understand why they hadn't sold. They were perfect. Golden brown but not burnt. The dog inside was flavorful with still a little snap to the casing. The cornbread coating wasn't dry or crumbly. His brain worked in conjunction with his taste buds to identify any seasonings that didn't work, but he couldn't pinpoint a weak link. Out of all the vendors, Charlie was one of the few who chose to make his own food, the rest opting for store bought crap. *Maybe try fresh herbs, toast the spices?* he thought as he chewed and jotted down notes. He felt the small double-wide trailer sway as a large object shifted. Resembling a solar eclipse, a shadow engulfed him, and he stared up at Vickie.

"Where's my corn dog?" Her multiple chins jiggled with anger. "I know you didn't just bring home one!"

"Vickie, dear, I thought you had dinner already. I'd have brought the rest home with me if I'd have known."

"There was more, and you left them?"

"Honey, please, don't yell. I have some left to sell for tomorrow, not many, but a few."

"I don't care. I want my corn dogs!" She stomped her enormous foot down, causing a small painting to fall off the wall.

"I . . . I can go get you some from my booth, I suppose," he said, defeated.

"I'd suggest you do that." She turned and walked back to the small room that held the TV.

Charlie put his jacket back on, sighing as he zipped it up. *Please die of a heart attack*, he thought, shooting daggers at the room emitting the faint glow of the television that never turned off. He slammed the door behind him and walked out into the cold night.

"Get out you bastards!" Charlie said, removing his shoe and throwing it at the fleeing raccoons. The masked bandits had raided his cooler, making off with the last remaining corn dogs he had to sell. Charlie noticed the cooler had been propped open, probably from a competing vendor.

That was the final straw. He was broke, finished, done. With no inventory to sell, he wouldn't be able to turn any profit. Rudy would have him booted, and then what? There weren't many options for a lifetime fry cook.

He opened his wallet and stared into the empty bottom. A crumpled five was stashed behind his license—emergency gas money if he ever were to need it. His car was almost running on fumes. Tonight may be that night. Worse, he couldn't afford to buy corn dog supplies. Even if he was willing to purchase those disgusting, bright-yellow abominations he could find in any freezer section, he didn't have the cash.

Tail firmly tucked between his legs, Charlie made the slow drive back to his home. He tried to close the door as quietly as possible; he could hear the robust snores roaring from the living room.

Abruptly, they stopped.

"Where's my corn dogs?"

"You see, honey, I—"

"Charlie, you sack of rat puke, where's my mother fucking corn dogs?"

"I . . . I'm just getting them heated up for you. It will only be a moment, sweet peach."

"Good, I want three of them. And chips! And a coke! A diet coke!"

Charlie started to pace, his mind racing. What could he do? He needed corn dogs to make a living. He needed corn dogs to shut his boar of a wife up. He needed so much, and yet had nothing. Nothing, but a grinder and a cabinet full of spices—

Well, there was *one* piece of meat in the house. A large, juicy piece of fresh meat sitting in the chair watching mindless filth on TV. Could he really do it? The thought made him nauseous. Yet the thought of him sleeping in the cold made him more nauseous. The handle to the meat clever called to him, beckoned him like a Siren to a sailor. From the living room, Vickie continued to howl.

Voices swirled inside Charlie's head. *Do it. Don't do it. Kill the bitch. Make corn dogs. No, you can't. Do it. Do it. DO IT, YOU PUSSY!!!*

"I'll be right there, honey. Just grabbing your chips." Charlie ruffled the plastic bag in one hand. The other gripped the cleaver tight.

He walked up behind the massive hulk of a wife and dropped the chips in her lap.

"Fuck me sideways, idiot. These are barbeque, I wanted sour cream and oni—" The sentence cut off as the cleaver embedded in her skull.

Her eyes bulged, and a sick moan escaped her lips. Blood trickled down her face, rolling off her neck rolls like tiny waterfalls. Charlie pulled the cleaver from her skull, and brought it down again. And again. Each consecutive whack of the blade echoed the crack of bone and the satisfying plop of metal connecting with brain matter. With each blow, the easier the cuts became until a muddled stump was all that remained.

He fell to the floor, vomiting onto the cheap carpet. The taste of rotten corn dog filled his mouth. He spat, removing the mucous and stomach juices caught in his throat.

He'd done it. Freedom! The gleeful sensation was short lived as Vickie's body relaxed, and her bowels loosened. The urge to vomit surfaced once again.

Charlie broke down her body with relative ease. He was a sensible man and knew that covering his tracks from the very beginning would be a smart move. It had taken all the strength in his small, scrawny body, but he'd pushed the chair to the bathroom and maneuvered it close enough to get Vickie into the tub. He half-expected the porcelain tub to shatter, but it held firm. He stripped her clothes off and deposited them into black trash bags. Using the shower head, he washed her body, making sure any fecal matter was sent down the drain. Selecting a butcher knife, he made surgical cuts to specific locations, and allowed Vickie to bleed out until only a small trickle of blood remained.

He wouldn't need the torso; just the arms and legs would be enough. With mighty hacks, he severed the limbs, trying to minimize the amount of splatter that occurred. Once complete, he placed the four parts in a trash bag, and then into the refrigerator. He bagged the torso and head, or what remained of it, and dragged it to the small back yard. Living remotely had its perks, and this was one of them. A shallow grave became the final resting place of Vickie, the trailer park housewife.

Charlie returned to the kitchen and removed the bag from the fridge. Selecting a plump arm, he separated the skin from the flesh underneath. It was pink, like pork, and speckled with white flakes of fat. It would be one juicy piece of meat. He washed the bicep thoroughly and chopped it into chunks. Mixing the meat with onion, garlic, paprika, and herbs, he ran it through the grinder. The results were perfectly ground meat with the spices incorporated. He removed the grinder attachment and snapped on the sausage maker. Charlie Dogg worked through the late hours of the night, perfecting his newest recipe.

"Why, this is delicious," the man said as he popped a free mini-dog in his mouth. He helped himself to another, and then one more.

"Why not get a big one," Charlie said with a smile.

"Hell, I'll take two!"

Charlie retrieved two corn dogs from the fryer and handed them to the man. He wasted no time shoving the piping hot product into his mouth and biting down. Through painful bites, a smile crept across his face. It didn't come close to the one Charlie had. Record sales followed the entire week.

Saturday night was a slam dunk, and with an hour left before the carnival closed its gates, Charlie sold his last dog. He closed up early and enjoyed the rides for the first time. He was free, but more importantly, he was happy. But something else was different about him now. The rush he'd gotten from killing Vickie was starting to fade, as was the meat he had in his freezer. He couldn't go back to using bland cuts of beef and pork when human flesh provided the flavor that everyone craved, even if they didn't know it. But who would be his next victim? Did he know anyone who truly deserved it? Vickie was a miserable person, and had been easy to kill, but he didn't know many people. Just those who came to the carnival, and those who worked it.

He returned to his booth, and removed the money box from the small safe he kept hidden behind a wooden panel near his feet. As soon as the box made an appearance, it was followed by a small shadow.

"Quite the haul you got there." Rudy stepped into the light. His eyes were fixed on the bulging box.

"Yep, pretty good night. Guess people still like good old American food after all."

"Well, I need my cut."

"Not a problem," Charlie said, handing over a few bills.

Rudy counted the money and chuckled. "Oh Charlie, I'm afraid rent just went up."

"I'm not following." Charlie's eyes were cold.

"I let you slide for so long, barely making any money off you. Looks like those days are over, and I can start recuperating what you owe me."

"And what is it I owe you?"

"Forty percent."

Charlie almost choked. The thought of grabbing the miniature carnival pimp and tossing him into the deep fryer was tempting, overwhelming. At that moment, he wanted it more than anything. Yet something inside him said to stop. He had his next victim. He had what was missing: a reason to kill. *Play nice, Charlie,* he told himself. He counted out the money and handed over another wad of cash.

"Pleasure doing business with you, chump." Rudy turned and disappeared into the night, on his way to steal money from another hard-working vendor. Charlie could almost taste him.
***

Charlie had just opened his car door when the voice barked from behind, making him jump. Turning, he saw Angelo walking toward him. Charlie hadn't said two words to the stout Polish man who ran the hotdog and kettle corn booth and was surprised to see him calling his attention. Angelo walked forward with a purpose. A grimace was plastered on his face.

"Your stand, it is bullshit," Angelo said. "All day, no one wants my hotdogs, but you sell all your corn dogs before carnival even close!"

Charlie tried not to laugh at the thought of no one wanting Angelo's hotdog, but the image was too much. He let out a light giggle, and Angelo looked enraged. The man swung at Charlie, and he ducked it, scampering back to his car, and running behind it.

"Jesus, Angelo. Take it easy, buddy," Charlie said, his hands out in protest.

"You laugh at Angelo! How you like it if Angelo beats you in parking lot? Bet no more corn dogs would get sold." Angelo started to walk around the car to get to Charlie.

"Look, Angelo, this is silly. We're basically coworkers. I made a lot of money tonight, and I'll loan you some. Hell, I'll just give it to you. Consider it a gift from a fellow food vendor."

The fire in the man's eyes went out, and an appreciative look replaced the angry snarl. "That . . . that would be okay, yes."

"Excellent. Just help me move my spare tire out the way. The box of money is in my trunk, and it's a bitch getting that tire out."

Charlie popped the trunk open and gripped the tire. He struggled to pull it out, but it wouldn't budge. Angel stepped forward and the Polish man tugged on the cool piece of rubber. This was the distraction Charlie was waiting for.

Whipping around, he plunged the knife hilt-deep into Angelo's back. The man went to scream, but Charlie clasped a firm hand over his mouth. He could feel the man's teeth start to apply pressure to his hand, but they quickly weakened as air rushed out of the punctured lung. The job complete, Charlie pushed Angelo into the trunk of the car. He looked around, making sure no one had seen him, and was relieved to find the parking lot empty. No cameras were perched on the light poles, and no customers were dawdling around. Just like with Vickie, he'd gotten away with it. Composed, he walked to the driver side door, got in, and pulled off gently into the cold night.

¶¶

"He's gonna need more fennel seed," Vickie said, her fat lips smacking as she plopped a piece of Angelo-sausage into her mouth. "It's good, though. I wish you'd have done this before."

Vickie had returned. Charlie was awoken one night by the sound of something rummaging through the kitchen. His mind raced with terror at the thought of being burglarized, or worse, the cops were on to his murder. It was a silly idea, since he'd never reported Vickie 'missing', and she had no friends or family. But there was definitely someone in the house, and Charlie knew he had to take care of it. He had grabbed the baseball bat he kept under the bed. Gripping it like a major leaguer at a home-run derby, he crept to the kitchen. He dropped the bat immediately when he saw her.

Shoving large amounts of food into her mouth, Vickie stood in the kitchen. Even in death, she was her same obese size. Her skin was gray, and she was vaguely transparent, like a thick smoke screen. Her fat arms jiggled as she held her last reaming body part in her hands, a chunk of thigh meat. She took a big bite of her former body, chewing noisily. Charlie could see the mushy bits hitting the floor below her as they passed through. The sight made him nauseous.

She wasn't mad at what he had done to her; in fact, she never even brought it up. They made small talk, and when the sun rose, she'd disappeared. She returned again the following night, rummaging through the fridge and watching television.

This cycle continued, and sadly, Charlie realized it wasn't much different than when she was alive. But she was pleasant now, less on edge, and Charlie liked that. He even didn't mind scooping out the piles of brown glop she left behind when she went on her binges. She mostly kept to herself, but on the night Charlie dragged Angelo's corpse in, she sprung to attention.

Charlie processed Angelo the same way he had Vickie, and he kept wondering if any of this would jog Vickie's absent memory of the night she was murdered. It didn't. She sat at the table, an ethereal onlooker, watching Charlie transform a hunk of meat into sausage. *Polish sausage corn dogs*, he had thought. *It could be good.*

Vickie appeared to be a fan. After tasting the sample he had given her, he had to concede and whip her up a batch of *Angelo dogs*. He even joined her, having one as well, and admitted that they were pretty damn tasty. Was he developing a taste for human flesh? Was he a cannibal now? All signs pointed to yes, though he didn't really feel like one. A clever murderer would be how he'd define himself if someone were to ask, and he really hoped that day never came. Vickie grabbed the last two *Angelo dogs* and waddled to the living room. Charlie sighed at the strange turn his life had taken, and got back to work, prepping for the carnival tomorrow.

"Polish sausage corn dogs? The fuck is that?" Rudy asked, eyeing the new sign Charlie displayed on his stand.

"Just something different I whipped up. Can't get stale and boring, now can we?"

"I suppose not, but any changes have to be pre-approved by me."

"Tell you what, boss. Have one on me," Charlie said, grabbing a large corn dog and extending it to Rudy.

Rudy snatched it up.

"Charlie, as much as you owe me, you should be giving me free corn dogs until I'm sick of them." He took a big bite, chewed, and smiled. "Damn good, though. Good thing, Angelo didn't show up, probably passed out in an alley somewhere. You should be able to do well tonight."

"Hope so, boss. I have a feeling Angelo may be around here somewhere." Charlie continued prepping his area as Rudy left, pleasantly smacking away at the corn dog.

"We sell hotdogs and kettle corn now, yes?"

Charlie nearly jumped over the stand at the sound of Angelo's voice. He spun around, coming face to face with the ethereal Polish vendor. Angelo looked confused, and Charlie could see the man's eyes darting back and forth, as if trying to figure out where he was. An old woman walked up to the booth, capturing Charlie's attention. He was panicked, thinking the woman would see the ghost and scream. Instead she looked at Charlie, waiting patiently for her order.

Charlie looked at her, then back at Angelo who was transfixed by the splattering and popping grease. The woman gave him a cock-eyed expression, and Charlie thought he probably looked crazy.

"Sorry ma'am, just gets hot back here and I lose my thoughts, what can I get you?"

"Just a corn dog, please."

"We have something new today. Polish sausage dipped in my secret corn batter and fried to a perfect golden brown. Care to try?"

She agreed to that and he handed one over, taking her money and placing it in the small box under the counter. He could see her take a big bite as she walked away, and then stopping to talk to some other people. Charlie's face lit up when he saw her point to his direction while making pleasing gestures. Soon, there was a line at his booth. Angelo remained, standing quietly behind Charlie. He had to make a point of not jumping each time he turned and locked eyes with the somber-looking specter. At least he was the only one who could see Angelo.

The night went on, coming to an uneventful close as people walked away, oblivious to the fact that they were eating and enjoying human flesh. Charlie smiled. It was his first genuine smile in a long time.

Eventually, Angelo made his way over to the hotdog stand that stood dark and abandoned. Charlie watched as he stood there, standing at the counter, expecting people to stop and buy a hotdog that wasn't there. It was a sad sight, and Charlie felt bad for the lost ghost—at least he assumed it was a ghost. He wrestled with the idea that it was all in his head. That this was his guilt manifesting itself into something physical for him to see. He figured he was reading far too much into this. After all, guilt didn't leave piles of mess on his kitchen floor every day. For whatever reason, these ghosts were stuck with him now—at the very least, Vickie was. He wondered if Angelo would stay at his stand all night, and as Charlie packed up, he noticed the ghost never attempted to move.

He was closing shop, cleaning his counters and draining the cooled grease from the fryer, when Rudy made his usual appearance.

"Okay, Charlie, I don't know what you are doing, but those things were fucking delicious. I've been watching you, and even though you've been acting like a tweaked-out druggie all night, jumping at your own shadow and shit, I know you made some good money."

"Yeah, I did all right." Charlie downplayed it.

"I think you did more than all right, and I want my cut. Just went up to sixty percent!"

"Sixty percent? You weaslly little fuck, how am I supposed to pay my bills on that cut? I'm selling corn dogs for a few bucks a piece! It's not some high-priced shit!"

Rudy looked stunned. No one had dared speak to him in such a way, and Charlie could see the little man turning red with anger. "I said sixty percent, you inbred food vendor."

"You can come and get it," Charlie said, counting out the money and slapping twenty percent of his earnings for the night on the wooden countertop. He stared at Rudy, daring him to make a move.

The carnival pimp snatched the money. Stuffing it into his pocket, he extended a one-finger salute to Charlie and stormed off. Charlie shook his head in disgust. He was shaking, visibly angry and upset from the confrontation, but he did it. He told the man off! A feeling of success filled him, and he strutted to his car proudly.

"There's a man poking around outside," Vickie said without looking up from the TV.

Charlie sprinted to the window and looked outside. He could see the top of a hat slowly moving around the large bushes outside his trailer. Grabbing the knife from the butcher block, he quietly walked to the rear of the trailer and let himself out the back door.

The smell of night blooming jasmine hit him, but it was soon replaced by another smell: gasoline. He could see the trail of fluid circling the house reflecting in the moonlight. He picked up his pace as he followed it around the corner. The man was in front the trailer now, the large red can sticking out like a warning sign in the darkness. Like a cat pouncing, Charlie ran, taking caution to not rustle the leaves. He was on the man just as a lighter was produced.

They fell to the ground, with Charlie landing on top. Pinning the stranger down, he brought the knife up, and with a maniacal howl plunged it downward. He repeated this several times until the man stopped squirming. Charlie removed the hat and stared into the face of Rudy.

He had known it all along. The little carnival pimp couldn't get his fat cut, so he came to get his revenge. Charlie looked down at Rudy's corpse. His eyes bulged out in frozen surprise and a trickle of blood flowed from his mouth like a lazy river. *All this over forty percent*, Charlie thought. *What a waste*. He gathered the man up and carried him inside. He would need to be processed like the others.

Charlie threw Rudy into the bathtub, not caring about handling the body with respect. He opened his freezer and saw he was practically out of meat, and not meat from the store, but the good meat people craved. Rudy was a small man, he wouldn't get much out of him, and the thought of selling him for money disagreed with Charlie. The man was scum, and Charlie would rather give him away for free. He looked around the kitchen before spotting the large meat cleaver. He had an idea.

"Vickie, I'm going to need your help for this," he called, and could hear the heavy footsteps approaching the kitchen.

"Wow, these mini-dogs are great! And they're free?" the child said, grabbing another from the platter on the corn dog counter.

"Son, leave some for the other guests," the dad said. "Sorry about that, kid's got an appetite like none other."

Charlie smiled. "He's a growing boy, let him eat."

"Hey mister, what happened to your arm?" the kid asked, pointing to the bandaged stump where Charlie's left arm had been.

"Billy, that's very rude. You apologize this moment," the dad said.

"No, it's all right. I was in a car accident not that long ago. They had to take it. But it's okay, I have a spare one." Charlie laughed, and the boy smiled. The dad appeared pleased. "Now, can I get you folks anything else?"

"Yes, two large corndogs, please."

"Coming right up."

"My friend was raving about them the other day." The dad leaned in "What makes them so good? Secret recipe? C'mon, you can tell me.".

"Well, I'll just say I put as much of me into them as I possibly can." Charlie smiled and handed over the two corn dogs. The dad placed the money on the counter.

They walked away, and Charlie added the money to the box. It couldn't close. His new recipe had been a success. He looked over at Angelo, who gave Charlie a blank stare back. The Polish man continued to pretend to fix hotdogs, though no one stopped at his booth, and no one had reopened it.

Staring down into the cooler, Charlie surveyed his inventory. He figured he had enough to last him for the rest of the week. Then, he'd have to make a tough choice.

Which one of his legs did he like the best?

ROLY-POLY

VIVIAN KASLEY

THE DAY WAS hot and sweat gathered in all her fleshy crevices. Margot trudged into a coffee shop and bought herself two cherry cheese Danishes. A table with three chairs was free, so she sat down and ignored the people who stared at her. She could feel their judgment, *the fat girl who eats two Danishes, and then she needs a table all to herself to do it. The nerve!* She could see the round peeks of her cheeks with each calorie-loaded bite. A tiny burp escaped when she licked her fingers free of icing, relishing the last of her sweet treats.

When she stood up, she could feel her dress stuck in her butt crack, so she pulled it free. She turned around when she heard murmurs and glared at the two college-aged girls gaping at her with smirks on their perfect skinny faces. "Is there a problem?" Margot asked, but the girls just shook their heads. She could hear their bubbling laughter as she threw her trash away. *Fuck 'em.*

Margot wished she had opted to Uber, but the last time she did, the driver kept looking at her thighs in the rearview mirror like they were juicy sugar-cured hams. Her tacky feet slid about her flip flops and sounded like a fart when she walked. *God, I hope no one hears that! Should have worn sneakers, Margot! Only a couple more blocks, you got this!*

The building was an old brownstone, but it looked well kept. She had never been to her friend's new apartment. They hadn't even seen each other in a few years. Even though they lived in the same city, their conflicting schedules never seemed to match up. When Pammy called Margot out of the blue, they talked for over an hour, and by the end of their conversation, Pammy offered to give her something that she said would change her life. When Margot politely declined, Pammy begged her to come see for herself, because seeing is believing. Though she was skeptical, Margot decided to take her up on the offer.

She climbed the steps and pushed a button. "Margot?" Pammy's voice rang out. "Is that you?"

"It is I, the one and only, Roly!" Margot sang out. She wondered why Pammy called her Margot instead of Roly.

Margot's shoulders slumped when she spotted the stairs. Pammy was on the third floor and there was no elevator. *How do they even get fucking furniture up there? I'd probably be a damn bikini model if I lived here for a year!* She sighed, then slowly began to climb them. Her thighs burned and she had to keep wiping away her sunscreen-tinged sweat before it dripped into her eyes. When she finally reached the third floor, she was breathing like an angry bull. She gripped the top of the railing and fist pumped in silent victory. It smelled funny on the third floor, like boiling root vegetables, garlic, and spoiled bologna. *Ugh, gross*, she thought as she made her way down the hall.

The door opened before Margot even knocked.

"Margot! I heard you coming! My smiley friend, how are you?" Pammy beamed. "Come in, come in!"

Margot gasped when she saw her. It didn't even look like her. "Pammy Cakes? You look . . . Phenomenal!" Margot wrapped her arms around her friend.

"I know right? I feel so good, too. I'm a completely new person! Come, sit down, have some herbal tea, and I'll tell you all about my magic pill!"

Margot shook her head and wondered how Pammy did it? She must have lost over a hundred pounds or more. She was acting so weird though, overly happy. *That's not like her? She's usually pessimistic and sarcastic. Well, if the key to being optimistic is being beautiful, I'm screwed. Also, when did she start drinking herbal tea? We always drank fizzy Italian sodas or iced coffees, she hated herbal tea.* Margot sat down and felt a pang of jealousy as she watched her formally obese friend pour hot water into two mugs.

"So, tell me Pammy Cakes, will this magical pill do the same for me? And how much is the damn thing?" Margot snorted.

"What's a Pammy Cake?" Pam tilted her head.

"Seriously? Did the weight loss melt your brain?! You were Pammy Cakes and I was Roly-Poly since elementary school! How could you forget that?"

"Oh—yeah, yeah I recall. Well, I guess I chose to forget that. Shed those painful memories along with my weight, ya know?" She looked at Margot in a way that made her feel uncomfortable.

Margot squirmed in her chair, "Sure, I guess. I get it. So, this pill, is it expensive? I don't have a lot, but I do have some money saved . . . "

"I won't hear of it! I have an extra one, just for you! No charge, I want you to have it." She smiled so wide Margot thought she could see her epiglottis.

"Why?" Margot asked.

"Why?"

"Yeah, why? I mean, I haven't seen you in ages and now you call me outta the blue and offer me this . . . this weird weight loss pill. Why?" Margot searched her friend's gorgeous face.

"Well, you're given two pills in case the first one doesn't take. Obviously, it took for me and I have the extra so I thought of you, because you're my friend." Pammy shrugged. "What're friends for?"

"You mean I'm your only *fat* friend."

"Well, yeah, but you won't be for long!" She grinned.

"Alright, Pammy—sorry, Pam, I'll bite. What is it and what does it do? Where'd you even find out about it?"

Pam brought the steaming mugs to the table and sat across from Margot. She slid a bottle of honey across and then exhaled before she spoke. "Well, I was tired of being fat. I tried it all. Exercise, diet programs, shakes, pills, and you know the whole rigmarole. My insurance wouldn't cover a lap-band surgery, so I felt out of options. I was making my way through a bag of cheddar and sour cream Ruffles when my phone buzzed. You remember Lita?"

Margot nodded, "How could I forget her? She was the other fat girl in school, except she was well liked due to her very popular and attractive older brother."

"Well, anyway, she called me and we chatted about the old days and all that. Then she told me she lost a bunch of weight. I, of course, asked how, and she told me that while on vacation in South America with her friends, she came across a man who was selling these miracle diet pills out of this little bodega. She said there was a long line of people waiting, so she asked them what they were waiting for, and they told her."

"So, you went to South America?" Margot probed.

"No, silly! Let me finish. So, anyhow, I did some extensive research and got my own online. Cost me a thousand bucks! And now, here I am, paying it forward."

"It feels wrong though, like, not legit. Is this one of those freaky pyramid scheme things? I mean, is it even FDA approved? Did you get it from the Dark Web? This shit could hurt people, Pammy!"

"Dark Web—ha! It doesn't hurt people, it makes people better. Do I look hurt?" Pam stood up, twirled, and ran her hands down her perfect body.

Margot shook her head, "No, but . . . "

"Look, you don't have to take it. I just thought I'd offer it to you before anyone else. I have friends at work who could lose a few—"

"No! No, I want it. I just want to know if there're side effects or warnings? Do you know what's in it?"

"There are some side effects, as with anything. Cramping, loose stool, maybe some gas, but nothing too major. No worse than those pills we took in high school that were practically legal speed." She sat down and covered Margot's hand with her own. "As far as what's in it, don't freak out, alright? It's a . . . it's like a . . . tapeworm."

Margot pulled her hand away. "A tapeworm! Are you nuts? Have you lost your damn marbles? You swallowed a tapeworm pill? Those are so bad for you and banned here for a reason! This's fucking crazy, Pam! A worm? A fucking worm? I'm out. No thanks!"

"Calm down! It's like a tapeworm, only it's not. It's a safer alternative. It doesn't hurt you. You lose the weight as it absorbs some of what you eat and when you have reached your goal, all you need to do is eat a bunch of garlic and drink tons of water to flush out your system and voila, it's gone and you're a new person! No pill from the doctor, no anything."

"How do you know that, huh? Lita told you this? For all you know it's a money-making scheme and she roped you in and now you wanna rope me in! How do you know you don't have a giant googly-eyed worm inside of you right now? Have you checked the toilet after you take a dump, see if there's any wiggly worm segments doing water ballet? How about your butt, does it itch, do you drag your ass across the floor?" Margot stood up from the table and crossed her arms. "I'm out, No thanks."

"You're being dramatic!" Pam's face was beet red.

"You just offered me, your friend, a pill with the potential to fill me with fucking worms, Pam!"

"Yes, but they're not bad. Look at me, Margot." Pam stood up. "Just look at me!"

Margot had to admit that her friend looked incredible. It wasn't just that she lost so much weight either. There was no skin baggage, no stretch marks, and she practically glowed. Margot wished to look like that her whole life, to not be the fat girl. She bit her bottom lip and then sat back down. "How do you know this pill will work for me? If it's so damn effective, why aren't more people using them?"

"Well, you know how our government is, they don't want people better. They like people fat and sick. It provides doctors and big pharma with more money and decreases the population. Look, this pill will change the future. I think it'll even be on the market in parts of Europe very soon. And you know how these things go. Once it's approved over there, we'll get on board too. Monkey see, monkey do. We'll just charge an arm and a leg for it and then make people jump through giant hoops to get their hands on it. Capitalism, it could use a lap band, right?" Pam sat back down and sipped her tea, her perfectly French manicured pinky pointed outward.

"Fine, I guess I'll try it."

"Good choice! Because to try and get your hands on it once it does become a thing will be a lot harder, if not impossible. You're going to be so happy you did this." Pam reached over and covered her hand again.

"I guess so. It's just that, well, maybe it won't work for me like it did for you?"

"It will. One pill worked for Lita and I both. She gave the extra to her mother, I believe. Her mother was a real plumper, remember?" Pam chuckled.

"Yeah, I guess. Well, alright. So, can I just swallow it now or should I do anything special before? Like eat a bag of potting soil or something?"

"Very funny! You can take it now if you want, there's no special before stuff or anything. I have it in here." Pam got up and put her mug in the sink and grabbed a small container from the kitchen cabinet. She brought it back to the table and rattled it around, "This's about to change your life, girlfriend. It takes some time, but it will work miracles!" She opened the lid and took out a small cream-colored pill. "Here it is. Your future."

"It looks like a Tic Tac. Well, bottoms up!" Margot swallowed it, then clawed at her throat as she coughed and gagged.

"Margot? Are ok?" Pam came around the table.

"I'm fine, you ninny! I was joking!" Margot snorted.

"Oh, you scared me!"

"So, about how long do you think it will be before I look as fabulous as you?"

"I don't know," Pam said. "I assume everyone is different. For me, it took several months, but you should start to notice a change within a few weeks. Try to eat well and stay away from alcohol. You can call me anytime and we can talk about anything that's going on."

"Well, it's too late now. I took it."

"Yup, you did. It's gonna be great, you'll see!"

Margot wasn't totally sure it would be great, but at this point what did she have to lose other than half of herself. They talked more about possible side effects and what foods to eat to help ease them. They walked around her new apartment and Pam showed her all her new clothes. By the time Pam hugged her goodbye, she was feeling giddy and optimistic.

Walking down the stairs was easier, but it was still muggy in the building. Margot almost slipped out of her sweaty flip flops and tumbled down the steps but caught herself. *Pam seems healthy and looks so fantastic. I feel completely fine right now. Maybe this will work, maybe I will be a new me months from now, too. I can't even imagine being that thin. No more Roly Poly.*

She picked up some fruits and veggies at the farmers market, including multiple bulbs of garlic, just in case. Overhead clouds took some of the afternoon heat away and the walk home felt delightful. Her thighs still burned from her trek up the stairs, but she ignored it. Once home, she made herself a big green salad and chopped up some strawberries for dessert. *A new me, I can already feel it.* Then she let out a gargantuan fart and belch. "Oh my lawd! Jeesh, excuse me! Must be the worm!" She cackled then flopped down on the couch with her salad and turned on the tube.

Weeks passed and though she'd lost a few pounds, it wasn't anything as dramatic as she was expecting. She was constantly tired, bloated, and ravenously hungry. She was mildly disappointed when she didn't notice any wiggling worms in her stool. The frequent gas was embarrassing, at work she blamed it on her squeaky chair or rushed to the restroom before letting it all out. She was grateful for the lack of smell. She called Pammy and told her all about the symptoms, but Pam told her it was all normal and to be patient. *Easy for her to say, miss flawless.*

A few more weeks went by and Margot was irritated. She did everything she was supposed to. She ate fairly healthy, she drank loads of water, and stayed away from alcohol. She had lost 15 pounds, but that was only a dent. When the weekend rolled around, she decided to say fuck it and order a pizza and drink a six pack of beer. *I'm eating for two, aren't I?* She even asked for extra cheese and garlic knots.

Five slices in and three beers later, she sat back on the couch watching a documentary about Inuit people in Alaska. They were eating something they called Muktuk, which was whale blubber and skin. Children giggled with blubber glistening on their faces, eating the stuff like an ice cream cone. Margot's stomach churned. Her hand strayed under her loose shirt and she grabbed a handful of fat. *My Muktuk. I wonder if you could eat human blubber?* She gagged, then farted. *Of course.*

She'd fallen asleep on the couch and woke up to stomach cramps. She wobbled to the bathroom and sat on the toilet. The cramps were ruthless. It felt like she was trying to shit a stalactite. She leaned forward and moaned. Tears sprang to her tightly shut eyes. "Maybe I shouldn't have eaten all that pizza." She grunted. "Or those garlic knots. Ugh." A colossal fart echoed off the bathroom walls and then she was finally able to go.

She couldn't remember a time where taking a shit had caused her to sweat. It worried her. She wiped and gasped when she saw drops of dark blood on the paper. She stood up and examined the toilet, other than the most monstrous turd she ever made, nothing out of the ordinary. *Maybe I should just go to the doctor and tell them what I took?* Exhausted from the strained bowel movement, she decided to call it a night and decide what to do later.

When she woke the next morning, she felt lighter, and when she ran her hands down her belly, it felt flatter. She burped, then rolled on her side and let out a few farts that ruffled the sheets. The smell was foul, like rotting meat and she gagged. A piercing cramp stabbed her abdomen and caused her to jump up and flee to the bathroom, but by the time she got there, it ceased. She looked in the mirror and gasped. Her face was thinner, her hair shinier, and her skin glowed, just like Pammy's. *Maybe I'll give it more time.* She was beyond pleased with the progress, even though she knew in the back of her mind it made little sense. The rest of her weekend was a shit fest, but in the best possible way.

By the time Monday rolled around, the transformation was phenomenal. She knew the amount of weight she lost over one weekend was insane, but the pill must finally be working. She strutted into work wearing heels and a red dress she hadn't worn in ages. It was even a little loose. She beamed as all the compliments rolled in. *So, this's what it's like?*

Guys in the building who never look her way, smiled at her, and female co-workers gathered round like clucking, pecking hens and asked her how she did it. She told them she'd been dieting and working out. They eyed her suspiciously, but she insisted that was all she did. They told her to keep up the good work and give them tips some time over cosmos. Margot basked in the attention. She'd been a ghost at work only last week, now she was front and center, by the end of the day, popular even.

She must've lost over fifty pounds in one weekend. And with the previous fifteen or twenty she'd already lost that was almost eighty pounds total. She still had quite a bit to go, but she felt incredible. It's remarkable how much your face changes when you begin to lose weight. She had cheek bones, *actual cheek bones!* She'd always wanted them. Her double chin was barely there.

At home she gave herself a facial. She plucked her eyebrows for the first time in years and swooned at her own reflection. *Pam was right, this is a miracle, too good to be true!* Something moved inside her eye and made her jump. "What the fuck was that?" She leaned back in. "What the . . . ?"

Margot held her eye open and watched a thin black tendril creep along. There was a slight pressure and it tickled her cornea as it stretched out into several different directions, like a tiny dead tree. *This can't be good. Whelp, it was fun while it lasted, I guess.* The other eye did the same. Tiny black lines crowded the entire whites of her eyes. A cramp shot up from her lower abdomen and raced up into her chest. She clutched her side.

In the kitchen, she held her phone with a shaking hand as she found Pammy Cakes in the contact list. She wanted to punch the screen. It rang twice before she heard her friend's chirpy voice.

"Hello? Is this Margot? Are you there?" Pam asked.

"I'm . . . here. My eyes—they're fucked up! My vision is blurred and the cramps are intensifying. I think I need a doctor!" Margot sobbed into the phone. "Pammy, I . . . is this normal? Please tell me, this's normal?"

"Calm down, it's normal. It all happened to me before the big change. Have you recently lost a lot of weight in a short span of time?"

"Yeah, but—"

"Listen, it'll all be fine soon. Trust me. The new you, it's right around the corner. How exciting! Hooray, you!"

Margot couldn't believe what she was hearing. She gritted her teeth. "Pammy, my eyes look like something out of a fucking horror movie! My cramps are next level, and I'm pretty sure I might be dying! How could you be so happy for me at a time like this?"

"But you're not dying, you're just changing! It'll be over soon enough!"

"You're sure? Like, really sure?" Margot choked.

"Yup, surer than a heart attack!" Pam chuckled.

"Not funny, Pammy. Listen, this's is a lot harder than I– "

"Take it easy, Margot, you'll be fine. Let it take its course. You've come too far." Then she abruptly hung up.

The phone call did nothing to quell her fears, but she was too invested to up and go to the doctor only to be flushed out before she reached her goal. Also, she could only imagine how they would look at her when she told them what she did. She chugged a beer and lay on the couch. "Fucking worm!" she wailed. "You're a damn terror!"

She called into work the next day, unable to hardly move from her bed. Her body felt like it was being tattooed by a thousand needles from the inside out. On the plus side, she felt weightless, having relieved herself of yet another ginormous bowel movement, after another night of painful stomach spasms and obnoxious farts. She'd crawled to the kitchen and grabbed a bottle of vodka. It would've been great at a time like this, but every time she took a glug, something seemed to lurch into her throat and gag her until she spit it back out. She put the bottle back under the cabinet.

"I can't wait anymore! I'll do the rest on my own!" She grabbed the garlic and began to peel clove after clove. The garlic went down easy. She popped several more cloves and downed a couple bottles of water. The burps were putrid, but she continued until she'd eaten almost a whole bulb. There was one tiny clove left. She chewed it and savored the pungent taste. "*Hasta la vista*, bitch!" She drank a third bottle of water.

An extremely sharp pang punched her gut and she hit the floor. Breathing hurt. The worm was clearly displeased with her dining choice. It writhed around maniacally inside of her and she thrashed around the kitchen floor. She pulled down the dish towel, balled it up, and bit down on it to assuage her agony. She kicked her legs in a cycle motion, trying anything to alleviate the severe discomfort. It indignantly rebelled the more she fought. Her skin was cold and clammy as she lay flat on her back.

"Get the fuck outta me you bastard!"

A brutal itching sensation covered her body. Her skin was being stretched tautly in different directions. Her joints crackled and popped. Convulsions racked her body. She vibrated across the floor and tried to call for help, but she could only gurgle. Her tongue felt like a pork rind. It was as if all the moisture in her body had been sucked away. The great waves of pain were relentless. It was too much for her to even try anymore. Her limbs were rigid, like rigor mortis set in.

The body of Margot looked like a mummy that had been unwrapped. It began to separate, slowly at first, like a difficult pistachio nut, but then it swiftly popped open. The shell of Margot lay in thin crisp sheets. As the new Margot emerged, the sheets disintegrated like ash that had been blown by a gust of wind. She stood tall and tilted her head one way, then the other. She pointed her feet like a ballerina, then spun around, kicking the old Margot into to dust.

When she stopped spinning, she coughed several times. She felt something lodged in the back of her throat. It was forced out with several more urgent coughs. She burned with pride as she examined the sticky little cream-colored egg in her hand, it was exquisite. She carefully put it inside of a small container with a lid to harden, then twirled to the bedroom and admired her lithe body in a full-length mirror.

"I'm completely gorgeous!" She smiled. "How splendid!"

Back in the kitchen, she swept up the floor, grabbed the phone, and scrolled until she found a name that looked pleasant. She'd seen how it was done, her finger lingered over the name, then she touched it, and put the phone to her ear.

"Hello?"

"Hi, Kiyah?"

"Roly? Is that you, girl?"

"It's Margot. Listen, I have something that'll change your life!"

PORK ROLL, EGG & CHARNEL

ARMAND ROSAMILIA

MICKEY PULSIPHER SMELLED like death.

He knew everyone in the diner smelled it too, but he was hungry. Always so damn hungry.

"Can I get a cup of coffee? I'm ready to order," Mickey said to no one in particular, since the two waitresses had taken up residence on opposite ends of the counter. Other customers were more important than Mickey.

Not that he wasn't used to it.

He'd been in 'Nam, where it was a different smell of death. Had something to do with the soil and the air. In 'Nam it clung to your uniform and you never got rid of it.

The stench had followed him home. Back to the Pine Barrens. Back to a life he hated, but he had no other life to crawl back to.

His taste buds were shot, too. They'd sprayed him with chemicals. Both sides had done it. Mickey had been given weird white pills by his commanding officers and doused with chemical weapons in the jungles, the yellowed powder seeping through his uniform. Into his water and rations.

"Coffee . . . please," Mickey said, a little too loudly. He hated to draw attention. The smell was doing enough already.

The two waitresses glanced at one another, a silent game of rock-paper-scissor in their look.

"Coming right up," the waitress to the left, the obvious loser of the staring contest, said. "You ready to order?"

"Pork roll, egg and cheese, please and thank you." Mickey always remained courteous. On the surface level he understood the looks. The people covering their noses when he was in town. Children gasped and were dragged away, their stares following Mickey. Even if he waved or smiled they'd screech in horror.

It wasn't his fault he'd ended up this way. It was Uncle Sam. The government was supposed to protect the citizens but had ruined his life.

Even though he'd fought a losing war for them, given it all up.

He knew they'd rush his order. Put it in a to-go box. Give him a big cup of coffee along with the cup on the counter she was filling while covering her mouth as casually as possible.

"I thank you," Mickey said, not only for the coffee but for her discretion and not saying something hurtful.

The general store a block over was going to be another situation he didn't look forward to. The only reason he'd come into town was because his supplies were dwindling. It would be winter soon, and the cold would seep into his bones and hurt.

His cabin had no electricity.

No proper bathroom. He dug pits in the backyard the animals stayed away from.

Even his feces were intolerable.

There was plenty of kindling and wood for the coming months, but he needed more canned goods. Bottled water. Rice and beans.

A five-pounder of pork roll to slice. Three dozen eggs. A block of cheese. A dozen hard rolls. Essentials.

Mickey had his books, too. He'd been dumpster diving behind the stores on Main Street and had come across a box of wet paperbacks. They'd eventually dried in the sun and he put them in order by their title on his tilted bookshelf in the living room.

He'd sit on the porch and read until the sun went down.

His pork roll, egg and cheese arrived in a box on the counter as well as a full to-go coffee.

Mickey didn't bother mentioning he wanted to eat it in the diner. He knew there'd be trouble if he did. Instead he threw a few dollars down, guzzled the last of the coffee in his cup and took the food.

As soon as he stepped onto the sidewalk he heard the diner behind him erupt into normal conversation. Mickey couldn't remember the last time he'd spoken to anyone for more than a few words.

The police cruiser, waiting outside, pulled out, the driver watching Mickey and shaking his head.

He'd never been violent. Never raised his voice except when he was ignored and he wanted to leave as quickly as he could. His money was good, too. The government sent him a small stipend each month as thanks for ruining his life. Enough to buy supplies and ammo for the shotgun.

Mickey would need to spend every last dollar he had in order to make sure he had enough provisions before the snow began.

It was cold today. Not cold enough to get snow, but the gray clouds would open up and throw rain at him, soaking his body before he got halfway home.

Then the real stench would begin.

In the beginning, when he'd returned from 'Nam, he thought a few hot showers would cleanse him. Mickey was wrong. The water, whether hot or cold, increased the smell.

Like rotten eggs stuffed inside a dead carcass, tossed onto the side of the road and doused in excrement. Add in the skunk stench as well as rotten garbage and you got a sense of what Mickey smelled like.

And Mickey wasn't immune to it, even though it stayed with him at all times.

He'd lost count of the times he'd gotten wet and puked.

Mickey had made a list of what to buy so he didn't miss anything. Last winter he ran out of butter and had to trudge the six miles into town in bitter winds and two feet of snow. They wouldn't let him inside the general store because he smelled so bad. He had to shout in his order, put the money under a rock and backup so they could trade the bag for the cash.

He'd need to be in and out.

As he approached the general store, he saw the child in the lone chair to the left of the door.

Mickey didn't know if it was a boy or girl because the features were distorted, like it had been in a fire. Both ears looked like they'd melted and the left eye sagged a couple of inches onto the cheek. The nose was a stump, a bandage across it.

The mouth, though, was smiling, a pink tongue darting in and out.

"Everyone says you smell, mister," the child said as Mickey approached.

Mickey frowned and walked inside.

"Who's the retard on the porch?" Mickey asked.

The old woman behind the counter puckered her lips and shook her head. "You don't say things like that, Mickey Pulsipher. It ain't nice. The boy is slow. He's my grandson and all that's left of my poor Jess." She started crying and turned away.

Mickey had gone to school with Jess about a thousand years ago.

"How old's the retard . . . uh, I mean the boy . . . Jess was as old as me and I'm in no shape to have a damn kid. He adopted from a home?" Mickey needed to get in and out before there was a scene but he couldn't help his curiosity.

The old woman, now shaking she was crying so much, ran toward the back of the store.

Mickey shrugged and went shopping, knowing he'd wasted too much time already.

By the time he'd filled his carry basket with needed items and got to the counter where the meats were sliced, the old woman had been replaced by an old man. Mickey could never remember their names. He wondered if they'd actually ever given them.

"I need a fiver of pork roll and slices of cheddar," Mickey said.

The old man shook his head. "Pork roll ain't come in yet. Hard to get for some reason."

Mickey sighed. "I need it. I really do. When do you expect it? This is important."

"Maybe tomorrow. Ordered four five-pounders, but they said I would only get two" The old man shrugged. "Might not get another for a month or two. Them damn Bennies coming down from the city have a taste for it now, so Trenton only sends the leftovers, I guess."

This wouldn't do. Pork roll was the staple that got Mickey through the winter months. By spring he'd be out and heating up the crumbs of leftover pork roll on his hotplate.

"I'll take both of them. All ten pounds," Mickey said.

The old man held out his hand. "Then I'll need payment for both. Got a few folks that'll be wanting it, too."

Mickey nodded and put the basket on the counter. "All this, too."

The old man grinned. "I reckon I could double the price of the pork roll, too. Start a bidding war for it. Supply and demand."

Mickey wanted to come over the counter and throttle the old man. He hadn't planned on buying an extra five pounds and now he'd need to figure out how to pay for a little gasoline for the generator. "You won't do that."

"Why wouldn't I?"

Mickey didn't like to be ugly, especially with his neighbors, even if they were ugly with him most of the time. "See that retard out front? I'll pull up a chair next to him and chat with every customer in and out . . . if they can get past my stench. I'm guessing folks'll head as far as Philly to get their groceries and not have to deal with me. How's that for selling it to me at normal price?"

The old man relented. "I'll have it delivered to your place of residence tomorrow about this time. Thank you for your business."

Mickey's shack needed repairs so he got to work before the sun was poking over the thick trees. Chopping some wood. Adding some rotten boards to the backside of the shack to keep the wind and coming snow away.

His tools were rusty and cold in his hands, and he only stopped to take a sip of the stream water he'd collected. It was cool, which meant the winter was coming.

By late morning the wind had shifted ugly, and the promise of snow was met. It came down in lazy spirals, a few flakes at a time, just enough to let Mickey know he wasn't imagining it.

"It's here sooner than later, which ain't what I need," Mickey said to the white sky. The faint glimpse he'd gotten of the sun was now a distant memory. He already missed the warmth on his face and chilled fingers. He'd need to dig out his gloves and long-johns.

He never paid attention to the weather. Didn't own a radio and wasn't going to ask when he was in town. Mickey could usually tell when it was going to open up and snow.

This had been unexpected, like a Jersey Nor'easter could sometimes be. They could come out of nowhere, sweep through the Pine Barrens and cover all traces of man. Every road. Every animal trail.

Mickey needed more wood and nails, but he'd lost the chance. Not that he had any more money to buy actual supplies, anyway.

Speaking of supplies . . . where was his damn pork roll? He'd been promised it today. Or was it yesterday? Mickey sometimes had a problem with knowing what day it was. Besides the stench spilling from his pores, he also had short term memory loss. The VA doc said he had a permanent concussion from seeing combat, and his brain got jumbled for longer periods of time now.

Sighing because he knew there was now a shorter amount of time to prepare, Mickey returned to cutting down a few more trees to fashion the makeshift boards. He'd need to collect as much firewood as possible, too.

He heard the clank of the bicycle before he saw it, the loose chain echoing in the silent woods. Mickey looked down the road, or what was left of it, buried under a sheet of white, and stayed in place for long minutes until he saw the bike and its rider.

The retarded boy from the general store.

When it looked like the boy, with a bag slung across his back, wasn't going to make it through the drifts already forming, Mickey sighed and walked down the road to meet him.

The sooner he could get his pork roll the sooner the boy could turn and go back. The snow was starting to come in steadier the last hour, and Mickey feared he'd be trapped inside the shack.

Without pork roll, egg and cheese sandwiches.

The boy got within twenty feet of Mickey, fighting his way through the snow, when he looked up and smiled.

Then his eyes rolled around until only the whites were showing and the boy fell off the bike and slammed his twisted body to the ground.

Mickey was ashamed to admit he'd gone for the pork roll before seeing if the kid was all right.

Turns out the boy wasn't all right. Not by a long shot.

His breathing was labored and he was cold to the touch. Mickey lifted his thin form like he weighed less than the five-pound pork roll.

He brought the deformed kid inside and set him down on the floor, tossing a ragged blanket over his shivering body.

Mickey brought in the supplies and the bike. He tossed some wood into the fire and moved the boy closer to the flames.

"Don't die on me, kid. I ain't got room to store your body until spring," Mickey said.

He put the supplies away, especially the pork roll, which he wrapped in cheesecloth and stored in the old ice box on the small back porch. With no electricity he needed to be careful of spoiling and wasting finite resources.

Mickey kept an eye on the boy for the rest of the day and night. The kid's breathing steadied and he moaned in his sleep. With the fire warming the shack, Mickey fell asleep on the wooden chair in the corner, covered by his favorite blanket.

The boy moaned on and off all night.

Mickey opened his eyes and knew something was wrong. For starters, it was too bright in the shack. Then he noticed the snow covering the wooden floor near the back door, which was unlatched and slightly ajar.

"What the bloody hell?" Mickey stood on rickety legs and shook off the cold. The fire had died sometime during the night and it was so cold his hands shook.

None of that was more than a fleeting thought when he saw the boy, now awake, holding the five-pound pork roll in his hand with Mickey's only steak knife.

"What is it? Spam?" The boy leaned forward like he was going to sniff it, although Mickey didn't think it possible without an actual nose on his face.

"It looks like bologna." The boy smiled, a strange lopsided look. "I'm Alex."

"It's pork roll. That's all you need to know. Some folks'll call it

Taylor ham," Mickey said with disgust. "Them people are wrong. Once had a friend name of Gil. He was a sorry kinda fella. Called it Taylor ham all the time. Stopped talking to Gil. Heard he went north and got a job selling insurance or something."

"You stopped talking to a friend because he didn't call it pork roll?" Alex shook his head. "If I actually had a friend I'd let him call it whatever he wanted to call it." Alex grinned. "Even spam."

"It's not spam, you retard," Mickey said and slammed his fists on the table. "I'll make you some rice if you're hungry."

"I want pork roll." Alex continuing giving his stupid smile. "I won't even call it Taylor ham. Definitely not bologna. Don't want to upset you, Mister Pulsipher."

Mickey groaned.

The snow was so deep outside he didn't think he'd get more than a few feet before he'd be lost, even though he knew the area like the back of his hand.

"Why'd you go outside to get the pork roll?" Mickey asked.

"Can I call you Mickey?"

"No." Mickey stood to get the rice and boil some water on his hotplate. "You want just rice or maybe some kidney beans, too?"

"I want pork roll," Alex said. His one drooping eye stared at Mickey, which made him uneasy. "Want to see what the fuss is all about. Why folks are fighting over it."

Mickey squinted. "Who's fighting over it?"

Alex shrugged. "Marsh family, for one. They asked my uncle for twenty pounds since it's so rare these days. Heard the Whately's down the road paid for thirty pounds. I guess with the factories closing they're trying to get their hands on as much as possible."

Mickey thought he'd faint. "Factories closing?"

Alex nodded. "Before the snowstorm my uncle sent me out to see you. Said you were the smallest order and you smelled. Really bad." The kid touched where his nose should be. "Ain't my problem, Mickey."

"Don't call me Mickey."

Mickey put the pork roll away. No use wasting it. He made rice and kidney beans and shared some with the retard. *Alex*, Mickey thought. *Stop calling him retard. It's offensive.*

He knew first-hand how people could be awful to one another. Denigrating and cruel. The townsfolk had praised Mickey when he'd sacrificed his formidable years and gone off to fight in a war he didn't understand and never would.

When he'd returned, broken, stinking, and a little more off than he'd been, they'd shunned him. The former hero, gone off to fight for their freedom, was now an eyesore.

One who smelled of ungodly stench . . . and reminded them of Vietnam.

Alex ate the rice and beans but complained they didn't taste like anything, how he wanted to try the pork roll, and how he missed home.

"Then go home," Mickey said, taking the two dishes and two forks out the back door and scrubbing them in the snow. He'd barely been able to open the door, and when he had, a blanket of snow had drifted inside and begun to melt.

It had snowed for over a day, and he could barely see across the yard to where the road was. He was trapped until it thawed.

Trapped with Alex.

"Aren't your parents worried about you?" Mickey asked after closing the door and adding more kindle to the fire. "Seems they'll be looking for ya."

Alex shook his head. "They said if the weather got bad to find somewhere warm to stay until it gets better. They said this storm will pile a couple feet of snow on us over the next few days." He grinned, his tongue slithering in and out of his mouth like a lizard. "Isn't this exciting?"

"No. It ain't exciting. It's annoying." Mickey sat on his chair and stared at the melting snow on his floor. He'd need to throw an old towel or two on it so he didn't forget and slip.

"What are we going to do now?" Alex asked.

"Wait until spring," Mickey said with a sigh and closed his eyes. He was trying not to think about the pork roll factory closing and wishing he'd bought the entire pork roll that was left.

It was still night time, although with the snow falling and adding to the sheet, the moonlight made it look like it was first light.

Mickey, bundled up with an extra set of clothes and a second jacket, used his snowshoes to waddle across the landscape.

He'd left as soon as he'd heard Alex snoring on the floor.

It was only a few miles to the Marsh property, but it might as well have been a hundred in the snow.

Mickey knew he was on a fool's errand. By now the bastards had either eaten half of the pork roll, or they were guarding it with their life.

He'd tried to forget what Alex had said. About the families hoarding the precious pork roll. It wasn't fair. Mickey had fought for his country and the right to eat whatever he wanted, which mostly was pork roll, egg and cheese sandwiches.

The Marsh and Whately families had more money than Mickey Pulsipher would ever see, and buying up all the supplies of pork roll was flaunting their wealth.

As Mickey stomped through the snow, sometimes falling through the hard top layer and getting snow in his boots, he became madder than the Jersey Devil.

They didn't respect the savory meat like he did. They'd make it same as pasta or burgers or pizza. It wasn't their staple for a winter diet like it was for Mickey.

He'd slice off just enough each day to make it last. A pound a month would get him just enough pork roll to satisfy his hunger. Of course, he wished he had more money to buy two or three five-pounders for the winter each year. He'd save as much of his government money as he could, but it never went too far.

With the extra pork roll this year he should feel better. He could dip into more of the supply and eat twice as much.

But then, once winter ended . . .

The factory was closing or closed. Mickey couldn't remember how the strange boy had worded it. Not that it mattered.

All good things come to an end.

He'd spent countless days trudging through the jungles of 'Nam, thinking at any moment he'd die, and one thing kept him going. One basic fact: he needed to survive and get back to New Jersey for pork roll.

"I didn't get shot at, have chemicals pumped into my body, and life ruined by that damn smell, only to be denied a pork roll, egg and cheese," Mickey whispered to the snow, which had begun to fall again.

Lights were on at the Marsh residence. Were they still awake, enjoying late night pork roll sandwich? Mickey crept to the nearest window, trying not to make too much noise with his snowshoes.

At first he didn't see anyone. The living room was quiet. The lamp had been left on, next to a chair, in front of the giant television set. Fancy Marsh family probably spent more on the TV than Mickey earned in a year. Maybe two.

These high society ingrates were living in the lap of luxury while Mickey lived in a shack without running water.

Yet, he didn't think anyone in the Marsh household had fought a war for their freedom. They hadn't given it all up like Mickey.

Mister Marsh, wearing nothing but his underwear, came into the living room and sat on a chair next to the lamp. He had a sandwich on a plate, which he set on the table, out of further inspection by Mickey.

"He's already eating it," Mickey whispered, his words steaming from his mouth.

There was no more time to waste.

Mickey trudged to the front door and tried to kick it in, but his awkward snowshoes made it impossible. Instead, it was like knocking at this late hour.

"Just a second," Mister Marsh yelled. "Who is it this time of night?"

"Mickey Pulsipher. You got something that's mine."

There was a pause and Mickey thought Marsh had run off to get some pants and a shirt.

Mickey took off a snowshoe and tried to kick the door open again, but it still held.

"Wait a minute. I'm getting dressed," Marsh yelled. Mickey could hear other voices inside. He'd woken up the family.

The damn pork roll eaters. His pork roll.

Mickey was about to kick the door again when it swung open. Mister Marsh, now wearing a robe and slippers, stared back at Mickey.

"What do you want?" Marsh covered his nose and Mickey could see his wife and two children, a teen boy and small girl, did the same.

"I want my damn pork roll," Mickey said. "I'll pay you for it. But it's mine."

Mister Marsh looked confused. "You're drunk."

Mickey took a step forward. The family recoiled, moving back. Marsh still had his hand on the door. "Leave now, Pulsipher, or I'm calling the authorities. This weather will kill you."

"Is that a threat?" Mickey held up the snowshoe. "Either get me my pork roll or I'll kill you and your family."

Mister Marsh's eyes went wide. "You're threatening me, you smelly old hermit?" He slammed the door before Mickey could make a move to get inside.

Mickey started kicking the door and felt it shake, the sound of wood splintering welcome to his ears.

He'd get inside, knock past the family, and get what was rightfully his.

On the fourth kick the door burst open and Mickey took a step forward.

The shot was jarring in the foyer space, and the .22 round lodged in the meat of Mickey's shoulder.

"You . . . you shot me?" Mickey felt the pain, but it was minimal compared to the biting cold. "It'll take more than that BB gun to stop me."

Mickey rushed forward and swung the snowshoe, connecting with Mister Marsh in the face and dropping him to the floor.

The .22 skittered across the floor, stopping at the feet of the little girl, who was now hiding under the table.

"Get out of my way," Mickey yelled, shaking the snowshoe for emphasis.

The family scattered.

Mickey rushed into the kitchen and opened the refrigerator, a fancy model with handles on it.

No pork roll.

"Did you crazies freeze my precious pork roll?" Mickey was beside himself. He ripped open the freezer portion of the fancy appliance and rummaged through frozen bags of corn and broccoli and meat.

There was no pork roll.

The little girl moaned from under the table.

"Shut up," Mickey said. "Where's the pork roll?"

The little girl shook her head.

Mickey pushed the table out of the way. "Last chance, girl. Where are you hiding it?"

"Get away from her." Mister Marsh, a gash on his head, stood in the doorway of the kitchen. He held the .22 with unsteady fingers.

Mickey grabbed the little girl and used her as a shield, backing out of the kitchen through the back door.

"Give me my daughter!" Mister Marsh shouted.

Mickey didn't want to kidnap her. She was wearing pajamas and would freeze to death. As soon as he cleared the back porch he let her go. "I'll be back for my pork roll."

He ran to the tree line and went to put on his other snowshoe but it was gone. Had he dropped it in the excitement in the house? Mickey didn't remember.

"I'll go to the Whately home and get my pork roll," Mickey said. "Then circle back and force the Marsh family to do the same."

He heard pursuit behind him.

Mickey knew these woods. Every tree. Every ravine. Even in the deep snow and in the dark. He'd easily slip away from them. Maybe he'd head back to the shack first. Get another snowshoe. Some warmer clothes. A proper weapon.

They were coming fast. He could hear them.

Mickey ducked behind a large tree, waiting for them to run past. He could double back and search the house while they got lost in the woods.

"I can smell you, Mickey Pulsipher," Mister Marsh said. "You broke into my house. You threatened my family. You tried to kidnap my daughter, you sick bastard. My wife has called the police. Step out from behind the tree and I won't kill you."

Mickey knew his smell would give him away no matter where he went. He stepped out with hands in the air. "I just want my pork roll. That's all. That's all I ever wanted."

Mister Marsh had a shotgun in his hands, his teen son holding the .22.

Mickey knew the look in their eyes. He'd seen it across enemy lines in Vietnam.

He closed his eyes as they pulled the triggers.

When Mickey didn't return by dinnertime, and well after Alex was sure he'd heard gunshots deep in the woods, he opened the front door. He loved the biting cold of winter and smell of fresh snow. .

He knew he'd need to start home in the morning. His parents would be worried. That part wasn't a lie.

The pork roll factory closing down or the fact the Marsh and Whately families had bought a lot of pork roll *were* lies.

Alex didn't feel bad when he began making pork roll, egg and cheese sandwiches.

"This is for calling me a retard," Alex said to the outside world.

WITH A LITTLE SALT AND VINEGAR

JOHN MCNEE

IVAN WAS A GIANT. A grotesque, hulking monster barely recognizable as a man. At nearly seven feet tall and 22 stone, he towered over every other man at the shipyard. His hard features, indecipherable tattoos, and the scars on his face, arms and back testified to a long life of struggle and hardship, but nobody knew much about him. The only story anyone had to tell was short. He was an immigrant, a refugee from the Eastern Bloc (he never named the nation) and had sought out work the moment he hit port. Carlisle didn't have to do anything but look at the man. He gave him a job loading crates and found him a room to stay above the packing house. Rumor was, Ivan hadn't set foot outside the dockyards since the day he arrived, now some eight years ago. The rest of the men, most of them Glasgow-born, treated him with a rare respect— doubtless owing to his striking build and mean gaze—but they didn't go out of their way to include him in their social gatherings. He was too unnerving a character, this monosyllabic behemoth hewn out of Soviet grit. So he tended to keep to himself.

Only two men on the docks ever came close to knowing Ivan, and they were two of the worst. Paul Cloister and Ewan McLean had both just finished serving custodial sentences (one for manslaughter, the other for theft), when they strolled out of prison and into jobs on the same night shift crew as Ivan. Times were tough, and it was said that when Carlisle was short on men and looking for cheap labor, he'd send someone over to the jail and have them wave a couple of quid under the noses of any fresh ex-cons with nowhere to go.

Cloister and McLean liked Ivan because he didn't talk much, didn't care about women, and didn't understand football, which they presumed meant he was even thicker than they were. They liked him because he was big and scary. He could clear a way through the crowd to the bar at the Coach House and put the fear of Christ into anyone who thought they had a score to settle with either the killer or the thief. They liked him because if they got him drunk enough—which never happened on ale, but sometimes if one of them sprang for vodka—he would sing songs of his homeland, in that crazy language that nobody recognized, but sounded hilarious to them. They liked him because he was simple (or made himself out to be), and would do most anything they asked. And they liked him because he would eat *anything*.

McLean was often asking him things like: "Do they sell Mars Bars where you come fae, Ivan?" or "Wha' boot broon sauce, Ivan? Y'hiv broon sauce?"

Ivan would sigh, shake his head slowly and reply, "Nothing. Nothing we had."

When they managed to get him talking—and Cloister and McLean were the only ones who could—Ivan would tell a little of the life he'd left behind to come to Scotland. The shattering poverty and unending hardship. He spoke briefly of his childhood in a village where the land was spoiled by war, where he and his friends would dig through the soil, seeking earthworms for nourishment. He told of crossing an arid landscape in search of food, and of his joy at discovering the week-old corpse of a mangy dog. He claimed to have drunk the blood from rats and eaten the frozen bark of trees to survive. He talked of living in a city where bullets were infinitely more plentiful than bread, and where the homeless and hungry murdered each other in open warfare, pistols blazing in the streets, all for a piece of cheese or a scrap of meat. He'd spent years of his life eking out a bare existence, forcing into his gullet the most awful things he could find. Anything that gave him a shot of living another day.

Cloister and McLean loved it, even if they weren't sure they believed a word. It was a good story, and at least explained why he seemed to hold Coulter's Fish Bar in such high esteem. Everyone else knew the place was a dump.

Rab Coulter knew a thing or two about running a chip shop. He'd spent decades as an apprentice to his father, learning the ways of the business. When he bought the shed at the end of the shipyard and kitted it out, that was only the start of a grand plan. One day, when he'd saved up enough money from serving all the sailors, dockers and prostitutes, he'd buy a big place at the seaside, sit back and rake it in. That was the plan. But Rab Coulter wasn't just a clever businessman. He was a drunkard, too. And a gambler. And he beat his wife. One night, in the midst of an especially heated argument, he punched her so hard that her neck snapped.

He hadn't meant to kill her, of course. Everyone could tell that. All the local working men could picture themselves in his position. And what with him having a young son left to raise and with Mr. Carlisle pleading for compassion, the police agreed not to take the matter any further.

Over the years, with no wife left to beat and interest in his business waning, Coulter focused his attention on his other passions, leaving the Fish Bar, for the most part, in the hands of his boy, Billy.

Billy didn't know anything about business. He didn't care about hygiene or good service. He barely understood the basics of cooking a fish supper. That didn't mean he didn't still get customers.

Ivan could be found at the corner table of the Bar at the end of every shift. Always the same order—six battered cod and three portions of chips with lots of vinegar. Then he would sit down with a flask of ale and have himself a merry time. Cloister and McLean would join him as often as they could, though they rarely ate. The chips at Coulter's were arguably the very worst in Scotland. Potatoes long past their prime, diced and dropped a few times on the floor, then thrown into lukewarm fat as black as tar, unchanged for a good six months and polluted by all manner of filth, spit, sweat, and dead insects.

Only the unspeakably drunk, the moronic, or the insane would think the food was close to edible. Yet Ivan relished every morsel.

The first night they saw him at the corner table, wolfing down his greasy battered fish with gusto, Cloister and McLean recalled when he'd spoken of the horror of his diet in the old country. And for the first time, they began to wonder if maybe he had really been serious.

"So," Cloister said, "Would you eat a slug?"

"No," Ivan replied. "Not again."

"One little slug," said McLean. "If you used tae do it all the time . . . ?"

"Years of my life," said Ivan. "Never again."

"Fer a fiver?" said Cloister.

"No."

"You said you could eat anyhin'," said McLean.

Ivan nodded. "Yes. Anything. But not for fun."

Cloister and McLean were convinced then that it was all nonsense. They were certain he had been lying, boasting, having them on all this time. Cloister's next comment changed the course of things somewhat.

"I bet if we fried it in batter, you'd eat one," he grumbled. "With a little salt and vinegar."

Ivan looked up from his plate, crumbs of fish clinging to his lips and replied, "Yes. Of course."

"You would?" said McLean.

Ivan nodded. "For five pounds. Yes."

At the end of their conversation, a challenge was set and a new game begun. McLean and Cloister would go in search of something disgusting but objectively edible—not a slug, being too obvious—that they would bring back to the Fish Bar and have fried up. If Ivan could eat it—the *whole* thing, swallowed, not just chewed up a bit and spat—then he'd win five pounds and their unending respect. If he failed, he'd have to admit his whole story was horse shite.

He couldn't *know* what they were serving him until after he'd eaten. That was McLean's stipulation. Ivan had said he could eat anything. They wanted that proven.

Ivan agreed. So too, after he'd been given a quid to keep his mouth shut, did young Billy Coulter.

The week after, Cloister and McLean returned to the Fish Bar with a brown package. They took it behind the counter and showed young Billy, who burst out laughing. Reluctantly, he battered the offending item and dropped it in the fryer just as Ivan entered, stepping sideways through the doorway as his girth demanded. He removed his cap and overcoat and took his throne at the corner table.

McLean carried the plate to Ivan, setting before him what looked like a fairly average sausage supper. Ivan made short work of it, pausing only briefly between forkfuls to take a swig of ale or dish out a little more tomato sauce. Cloister and McLean looked on, fascinated, but managing fairly well to conceal any feelings of revulsion at what they were witnessing. When Ivan was finished, and the plate cleared, he dropped his cutlery, wiped his mouth with the back of his hand and said, "Well? What was it?"

McLean and Cloister exchanged a nervous glance. It was Cloister who ventured the answer. "Horse cock," he said. "You just ate the cock of a horse."

"Ah," Ivan nodded, and shrugged. "Not bad."

The boys lost five pounds that night, and again every week after, as the competition continued. Wee Billy Coulter served up meals of fried mice, beetles, leeches and all the waste parts of sheep, cow and goat, including eyes, guts and genitals. Even, on one occasion, a tumour dug out of the brain of a bull—a curiosity McLean had purchased from a drunken vet in the Lonsdale pub.

Ivan, for his part, never flinched, never faltered. Even when his companions had relaxed enough to brazenly laugh or gasp as he ate, or welcomed in friends to watch, like ogling patrons in a freak tent. Ivan was stoic. Never kicked up a fuss. He ate, took his payment, and left.

Until . . .

"What is it?" Billy was peering into Paul Cloister's kit bag at a glass jar filled with liquid.

"What ye 'hink it is?" Cloister replied, grinning.

Billy shook his head, dumbly. There were things in the jar. Floating around in the liquid, but it was too hard to see.

"Ship came in last night," said McLean. "Carrying 'research specimens' fae the uni. Y'know . . . medical students?"

Billy nodded, though he wasn't sure where this was going.

"We were unloading the crates," said Cloister, "And one o' them broke. Ma pal here—" He indicated McLean. "Rescued these beauties fae a watery grave." He reached into the bag and removed the jar, placing it atop the counter between the salt and vinegar, beneath the glare of the heat lamp.

In the jar floated six pickled human fetuses. They were each no larger than a hard-boiled egg, coiled up balls of white flesh, bulbous heads almost bigger than their bodies. None had any obvious deformities. They all looked completely undamaged. Which made them no less horrific a sight.

"Ah Jesus," Billy moaned, feeling his stomach turn. "I don't know, guys. This is kind of . . . dark. Don't ye think?"

McLean's face was a map of confusion. He looked from Billy to the jar, then back again. "Shut up ya wee poof!"

"Aye," said Cloister, clapping his filthy hands together. "Fry 'em up, ya wee dobber!"

Billy found a pair of thick black rubber gloves in a bucket in the kitchen. He cracked open the jar and emptied the contents into the sink, doing his best not to gag on the smell. When the formaldehyde was all drained away, he salvaged the sick-looking little bodies from around the plug hole and lined them up on the worktop.

He made a fresh batch of lumpy batter, gave all six of the pickled specimens a good coating and dumped them in the fryer, just as Ivan entered through the front door.

"Evening, big yin," McLean called, taking his seat at the table. "Hope you're hungry!"

Ivan grunted a reply, shook off his overcoat and sat down.

Billy wasn't long with the meal. All of ten minutes, which the trio at the table spent in silence, Cloister and McLean both too excited for small talk. It was impossible to tell what the fetuses were once they'd been fried. They'd shrunk a little in the heat and the batter obscured all the detail. Billy piled them on a plate with a side of chips, rounded the counter and took it to the table. He didn't look Ivan in the eye when he set the meal down.

"Go on, son," McLean urged. "Tuck in."

Ivan shrugged, looking tired and disinterested. He picked up one of the curious golden balls in his fat fingers and held it aloft. He turned it over, giving it a brief examination in the lamplight, then opened his mouth and gobbled it down.

Neither McLean nor Cloister made a sound. Normally they were all gasps and cries and howls of laughter, but this time they forced themselves to keep their reactions in check. The event they were witnessing was too important, too bizarre, too downright depraved to be spoiled by their noise.

The first took three chews and was gone. Ivan made no comment on the taste, texture or otherwise. He just speared a second on his fork and continued. The third and fourth followed a few moments later.

Cloister and McLean bit their tongues, gripped their seats, battled to keep themselves from giving anything away.

Halfway through munching on his fifth, it became apparent that his companions' behavior was beginning to get to Ivan. He put his fork down, took a swig of ale, belched and said, "Enough. Tell me."

The silent duo looked to each other, eyes watering, cheeks reddening, shoulders shaking. They started to laugh.

Ivan slammed his hand down on the table. "Tell me!"

The pair were silent again. McLean wiped the tears from his eyes and cleared his throat. "But . . . but, Ivan, pal . . . " He giggled. "Ye've still got all yer chips an' . . . "

"I'm not hungry," Ivan growled. "Now tell me."

Cloister leaned over to his friend and whispered loudly enough for all to hear: "Ye'd better tell 'im, Ewan. Ye wouldnae wanna piss aff a cannibal, would ye?"

McLean completely lost control at that, doubling up and nearly falling to the floor with his guffaws. Cloister joined in, while behind the counter Billy Coulter kept his head down and pretended not to hear a word.

"What means this?" Ivan demanded. "What means . . . ?"

"Sorry, pal, sorry . . . " McLean wheezed, sitting back up in his chair and trying without success to put on a straight face. He went into his pocket. "Look, here's the fiver . . . Ye've done well . . . "

Ivan's expression darkened. "Tell me."

"Alright, alright . . . " McLean sniffed. "You've . . . you've em . . . a-ha . . . ye've been . . . eh . . . "

"Babies," said Cloister, finally. "Wee tiny babies."

Ivan flinched. "What?"

"Aye," said McLean, still grinning. "Fetuses. Y'ken? Aborted or miscarried an' that . . . "

"Babies?" Ivan repeated. He stared down at his plate. "You . . . make me eat . . . babies?"

"I could hardly keep a straight face," Cloister howled.

"Priceless, pal." McLean laughed. "Totally priceless!"

"Babies . . . " Ivan repeated, no more than a whisper. He looked up from his plate, stared across the room to Billy, then turned to look at Cloister, then McLean. The two at his table were still laughing. Looking back at him. Pointing and laughing.

Ivan picked his fork back up, leaned across the table and stuck McLean in the eye. He toppled backward, still laughing, and fell out of his chair. Cloister, closest witness to the attack, stopped laughing, but remained seated. He wasn't entirely sure what had just happened, and was still trying to work it out when Ivan turned on him with his knife—most of the dockers carried one—and slashed his throat open. Cloister stood then, putting one hand to his neck and throwing his other out to Ivan, trying to grab his arm. Ivan knocked the hand away, snatched at the lapels of Cloister's coat, drew him closer and drove the dagger twice into his chest. Cloister's whole body went slack and Ivan dropped him. He lay quivering on the floor as blood soaked through his clothes and spread out in a puddle around him.

"Babies," Ivan said again, panting, his face a map of rage. "*BABIES!!!*" He took two steps toward the door, spun about, and fixed his mad, widening eyes on wee Billy, standing motionless behind the counter. "Babies." Ivan raised up his knife—the blade wet with Cloister's blood—and aimed it at the young chef. He opened his mouth wide and let loose a frenzied roar, then started across the room.

He made it three steps and halted. Looking down, he found a knife in his belly, buried up to the hilt. Ewan McLean's hand was wrapped around the handle. He was still lying on the floor, the fork protruding from his bloodied eye-socket. His one good eye was trained on Ivan as he twisted the blade in his fist and pulled downward, carving through the fat man's guts. Dark blood splashed upon the floor.

Ivan sank to his knees, the knife clattering from his grip. He gazed down at McLean, face full of fury, and turned his hands toward him. McLean squirmed as the giant's hands closed about his neck. He slapped Ivan's face with his free hand, pulled the knife from his gut, stuck it back in, stabbed him time and again, but it made no difference. Ivan would not be distracted from his duty. He clamped his hands around McLean's throat and squeezed, crushing his windpipe between his huge paws.

McLean's mouth opened and closed, pleading without voice. Ivan squeezed harder and McLean's face turned puce, blood vessels bursting in his working eye. His kicking legs relaxed. His right arm went limp. His left hand came uncoiled from the dagger, leaving it protruding from Ivan's belly.

Ivan sank further, falling on top of McLean, crushing his body as he'd crushed his neck. The two of them were face to face, just a few inches apart. The color was gone from Ivan's face. He trembled. His whole body shook. He opened his mouth wide.

A torrent of pale brown vomit erupted out of Ivan's throat. A violent surge of thick steaming liquid that sprayed from his lips and coated McLean's face, obscuring his features beneath a toxic mess. When his stomach had been completely evacuated, down to the very last greasy chunk, Ivan rolled off his deceased, puke-painted friend, and died.

Wee Billy Coulter crossed himself and picked up the telephone.

Fifteen minutes later, Sergeant Mackenzie of the local constabulary was pacing back and forth between the bodies. Mr. Carlisle, wearing tweed and an expression of utter disdain, was standing with his back to the door. "These men," he muttered. "Such animals."

"*You* hired them," Mackenzie replied, grimly.

"A necessity. It can't be helped." Carlisle stepped away from the door, and over to the corner table, to get a better look at Cloister. "But if I'd known . . . "

"What *do* you know?" the Sergeant asked, squatting down over Ivan's body. "About these men?"

Carlisle took a notebook from his pocket and squinted at the pages through his horn-rimmed spectacles. "Well, Mr. Cloister and Mr. McLean were both ex-convicts. Checkered pasts, admittedly. Violent sorts. It's no surprise that they'd end up this way. As for the Soviet . . . " He snapped the book shut. "I can't say. All very sketchy, I'm afraid."

The Sergeant raised himself back up and looked to the counter. Billy Coulter stood there. He hadn't moved since they'd entered. Hadn't moved since he'd picked up the phone and called them. "And what about you?" Mackenzie asked. "You're sure you don't know what their dispute was about?"

Billy shook his head. He'd made up his mind long before they'd arrived that they weren't going to be getting the full story out of him. He could imagine the punishment meted out if he were accused of assisting with the theft of medical specimens. Worse still was the thought of what might become of him if they found out he fried wee babies in batter. The shop would be closed down. He might get jail time. He'd *want* jail time. It would be the only thing that would save him from the wrath of his father.

But he knew what Carlisle and the Sergeant were like. They didn't care about these men or how they died. They'd want to wrap this up quick. Not too many questions. And there was no evidence to tie anything to him. Nothing that would reveal the true reason they'd killed each other. If he just kept his mouth shut . . .

"Well look at this," Carlisle chuckled.

Mackenzie turned to see the other standing by Ivan's vacated seat. "What is it?"

"Fellow never finished his chips," Carlisle replied. He reached down and picked something off the plate.

Billy could recognize it even from across the room. A little golden ball. Ivan had left one—just one—untouched. Billy felt his heart go cold.

A quizzical eyebrow crept up Carlisle's brow as he held the battered fetus up, and he turned to face Billy. "Scampi?" he asked.

The boy had no words but managed one nod of his head.

Carlisle popped the fetus into his mouth, chewed it up and swallowed it down.

"Any good?" the Sergeant asked.

Carlisle cocked his head to one side, made a displeased face and smacked his lips. "Too much vinegar," he said.

THE INSOMNIAC GODS OF BLACKBERRY COURT

CHAD STROUP

HE SHOULD HAVE worn gloves.

His calloused toes shoved in ratty slippers, a frayed robe tightened around his torso, but nothing to protect his hands. Typical.

More garbage bags are piled in front of the curb across the street today. He's certain of it. The heap is growing. But no one's been home at 747 Blackberry Court for days. This, he can only assume. Technically, he's never seen those particular neighbors out and about. Certainly hasn't witnessed them stacking their Great Wall of Refuse. But he's still new to the neighborhood, and he's yet to meet everyone who lives in the curves of the cul-de-sac. Or meet anyone for that matter. He's a man who prefers to keep to himself.

But he can't help but indulge his curiosity.

When he rips open the first garbage bag, he isn't sure what he's looking at. It should be filled with obvious disposables—rotting table scraps, shredded premature offers to join the AARP, empty bags of Fritos. Something similar to what he keeps in his own trash.

It comes to him slowly.

He bites back a shriek, bullies it into a whimper.

The husks of rodents, birds, perhaps a stray domestic animal or two. Each poor creature marked with an imperfect little hole in its head, as if a drill-headed worm had burrowed through its skull and removed a hidden treasure, stolen its most intimate, bestial thoughts. And—mixed among the animals—there's something else. Something his mind cannot comprehend because oh God no nothing like this could ever happen in his neighborhood, no not on his watch.

Upon first moving in, the appearance of the house across the street should have been a red flag. More than just a severe lack of curb appeal, more than owners who have simply gone above and beyond the call of neglect. It's a boarded-up bungalow that's seen better days, its structure's stomach deprived of sustenance. Once-white paint gone grey. The front yard an army of weeds at ease. Cracks on the winding sidewalk so huge that any passersby would, without fail, break their mother's back.

He wishes he'd never crawled out of bed. Never opted to snoop. Not today. This isn't his day. Realistically, it's never been his day. But today, least of all.

The moon is eager, the sun stubborn. As if they'd had difficulty finding this little nook in the neighborhood, the friendly local police have finally arrived at Blackberry Court. To little fanfare. No nosey neighbors. No lookie-loos. No emergency, it seems. It's nothing, really. Only a pile of crudely detached genitalia, left to draw flies in a heat-baked Hefty bag. An everyday occurrence.

He thinks he's going to be sick. But also wants to avoid being sick. If he vomits, his throat will be sore for days. And if he didn't lose his lunch upon the initial sight of the bag's contents—which he's still proud about—surely he's safe now. Except he can't shake the sensation that something might have crawled out of the garbage without him seeing, then found a tiny open wound on his arm to slip into, and was now traveling beneath his skin. Something had to be causing that incessant itching.

The door to the police car slams shut, sounding off like a quick gunshot. It's at this moment that he realizes no familiar sounds penetrate the street. No crickets, no hum of nearby traffic, no anxious buzz of electricity. Were they ever there before? He can't be sure. Again, he's still new, hasn't had time to adjust to the neighborhood's normalcy. And he's not sure he wants to anymore.

The officer—a cornstalk of a woman, her hair pulled back so tight it resembles the top of a rubber mask—questions him, asks if this is his home. The one he is standing in.

He isn't sure how to reply to such a preposterous question. A nervous chuckle spills from his lips.

Damned cop tries to look inside, doesn't believe a word he's saying, asks if this has anything to do with the pharmacies. The ones that were robbed. Without making eye contact with the officer, he points to the curb lined with garbage, where he found what he found, his finger vibrating uncontrollably. Without responding, the officer struts to 747 Blackberry and rifles through the open bag, her only reaction an extended pause. Then she steps a few paces back. The cop doesn't call for backup, only approaches the front door to the old, dead house, her hand at her holster.

From across the street, he watches the officer's every move, his nerves popping and writhing. He doesn't understand why the cop was looking at him the way she was. What did she see? Just a dirty room behind him. Furniture he harbored no pride for. Nothing more, nothing less.

A knock. A call to open up. A moment of waiting that defies the laws of time.

The door flings open, and everything happens so fast that he isn't completely sure it's happening at all. The police officer drops her gun and begins a scream that's never allowed to come to fruition. A fleshy blur pours onto the porch, obscuring his view of the officer. It's like a windshield smeared with bug guts when the wipers aren't working effectively. And then the cop isn't there anymore, the space her body occupied now a swirl of dust.

Then something reaches out for the fallen gun.

A hook. A cane.

A hand.

Maybe none of those things. It isn't something quite that simple, and his mind is far too beyond the melting point to offer any clues or legitimate ideas.

The front door closes. Not a slam. A careful motion, as if anything more aggressive will demolish the house. Attract more unneeded attention.

He bites his lip hard. Draws blood. Despite his best judgment, he approaches the house at the end of the cul-de-sac, keeps a cautious distance. But still closer than he's ever been before.

Every flaw in the structure is visible now. Every speck of dirt more pronounced. Every sign of disrepair digging at his dread.

And the heat of the day grows more oppressive the closer he gets.

Baby steps. No rush. He decides that approaching the front door is out of the fucking question no fucking way, so he steers himself to the west side of the building, once protected by a chain link fence that has succumbed to the elements. No need to hop it. He merely peels the layer of fence away from its posts like a slice of deli meat from wax paper. It falls to the ground with an explosive clang and he grits his teeth.

The sole window on this side of the house is set a little too high to peek into without the help of tippy toes. But even then, he can't see a damned thing. The glass is blacked out from the inside with what looks to be electrical tape, perhaps cheap paint. He considers tossing a rock to break the window, but it's far too early to make a decision so desperate. He eyes the backyard. Maybe he'll have more luck there, the weight of that luck yet to be determined.

A few steps before reaching what may have once been a nice patio suitable for guests but has since become an aboveground cemetery for long-deceased wildlife, he stops. Not of his own volition but because his face smacks into something. Hard. He loses sight of the sun for a few seconds, trades it for stars.

He curses, massages his nose, wipes away a few trickles of blood. After refocusing his vision, he glances around for a pole or a freestanding plate of glass. Nothing. He feels the air in front of him, expecting a shock. He inches slowly forward until his hand connects with something solid. An invisible mass.

Convinced something is there but he simply can't see it yet, he places his hand flat against warm nothingness, reaches up as far as he can and discovers no obvious end to the illusion. He starts to trail his hand horizontally across the invisible partition, then stops when he realizes there's a chance it could go on forever. He can't even begin to deal with that possibility. Too heavy to bear.

He counts his own breaths. It's all he can do to keep the final thread of his sanity from snapping. Decisions must be made. Just bail out now, forget he'd ever left the relative safety and comfort of home. Rewind the darkening day.

Or allow his curiosity to take control, no matter how high the risk.

Options running low. An unseen wall blocking one direction. A dark window preventing a peeping tom's view. The front door, well he's seen the trouble that could lead to.

And the horror of that indescribable hand.

He decides the other side of the property will prove more fruitful. As he passes the front of the house with a wide berth, a low rumble vibrates from a direction he can't immediately discern. The irritated yawn of a giant hibernating bear that has overslept. He stills himself. The sound is coming from underground, a few feet away from where he stands.

A cellar door to his left. This is where the sound is coming from. And the door isn't locked.

He steps past the door to test a theory, this time with his arm fully extended. A few paces in, he jams his finger. The illusion continues on this side as well.

He approaches the cellar door. He kneels and lifts it slowly, peers into the gel-thick murk. An entire hell's worth of heat whooshes out. The vacuum of sound is even more prominent here. His ears plug. He squeezes his nose tight and pops the pressure out. He really should just return home, crawl back in bed, and watch multiple consecutive episodes of *Jeopardy* in an attempt to banish this feverish dream.

Two choices. He can shut the door, scurry away, and do his damnedest to forget any of this ever happened. Or he can feign heroism. Save the cop who should have been saving him. Or arresting him.

Bravery. Stupidity. Twin sides of the same coin.

Only one choice will allow him to continue living with himself. He dips his toes into black soup, and soon he is consumed.

His initial thought: Cellars are known for being decorated with cobwebs. It might even be considered a prerequisite.

Also stains. Dampness. Signs of rodent activity. Something to indicate it's a space a rational person doesn't want to spend more time in than necessary.

Key word: *rational.*

Once he locates a light source—via a string he initially believes *is* a cobweb—he discovers the cellar is immaculate, its floor clean enough to use as a plate and lick up after.

Empty. No shelving, no tools, no storage, no stockpiled canned goods, no forgotten heirlooms. All this space, used for nothing. A total waste.

The rumble subsides, then vanishes. Silence dominates now that he's fully underground. He's swimming on the deep end of the pool, the only sensation of wetness caused by being in a space that could double as a sauna.

Then he sees something he hadn't noticed before. Or maybe he at first believed it to be an illusion. His eyes still adjusting.

A corner.

He moves toward it, hesitating inches away from the turn, unsure he wants to know where the next pathway leads. There's still time to turn back. He should call the police a second time, state what he's seen (and not seen). But they'd never believe him. There would be more questions. And fewer answers.

Holding his breath, he makes the turn. Sweltering wind daggers his face. A long hallway stretches too far to see where it ends. So much space. Far too much to fit directly beneath the house.

He digs a nickel out of his robe's pocket and sets it on the ground, carefully balancing it on its edge. He lets go. The coin rolls forward, continues until he can no longer see it. Then the sound of the nickel wobbling, giving up, and plinking on its side.

Something flickers at the far end of the hallway. Where the heat resides.

Despite his best judgment, he creeps toward it. With each step the ruckus rises again, growing louder and louder into an almost-growl. And someone speaking. A language he doesn't recognize. His heart jackhammers.

Another corner at the end of the hall, which he reaches much more quickly than he assumed he would. The ground is no longer concrete but tightly packed dirt. He allows one half of his face to peek around the corner, his bowels pulling in the opposite direction.

Piles of bodies stacked neatly in rows against the sheetrock. Some animal. Some—despite his best efforts to deny it—human. Some . . . perhaps neither. He can't make sense of the shapes. All he can discern is the one familiar feature they share—an imperfect hole drilled into the skull. A single trickle of blood oozing from each hole, relieving the pressure.

And there are people down here. At the far side of the vast space, their presence lit by a fire pit, its putrid smoke traveling across the room, seeking escape with no success. The people see him but don't acknowledge him.

He squints.

Tweakers.

Of course it's tweakers. He knows their kind well. They've come out of hiding from the valley, set up their squat here in this hellish cellar. They're all pockmarks and soggy hair and gum rot and infected sores. Standard mutants born of meth. Their mouths masticate and their lips slurp on something unseen. They're hardly human anymore.

He chuckles at the thought. A sentiment that feels metaphorical but represents the supposed reality. One of the tweakers in particular has undergone changes far beyond the reaches of methamphetamines, stretched the definition of what could still be considered a man.

And, naturally, this is the one who approaches him.

Warmth and wetness soak his leg. He's frozen in place despite his mind's protests. Before him, an indescribable mass. Long, shivering tentacles, at the end of each of them a begrimed hand. At first, he believes the being before him is a beached octopus struggling to find its way back to water, then he sees a man at the brink of giving up hope but who finally learned his true purpose. A second later, both are as one. Despair and confidence, man and mollusk, in equal halves.

Before he can regain control of his legs in order to run, the tentacle hands surround him, hugging his shape. An act of camaraderie, not of aggression, or so it seems.

He moves to speak, to ask. No sound leaves his mouth.

But vocalized questions aren't necessary. A roar, a voice bringing answers enters his mind. A voice with the cadence of human speech, its timbre ancient, its history unknown.

Let me show you, it says. Let me help you remember.

When they first arrived at 747 Blackberry Court, the tweakers hadn't expected to learn something so deep, so affirming. It wasn't their purpose. But every action, regardless how great or small, creates side effects, ripples in the stillness.

They were unable to sleep no matter how much they craved it. Nothing worked. The methamphetamines had performed their duties far too efficiently. And they couldn't stop cooking fresh batches. Consuming their untainted product.

Despite the poor Wi-Fi so far down below, one in their group dove rabidly into research on her laptop, didn't stop for days until she discovered what they all believed they were truly searching for. All sources, whether reliable or not, claimed melatonin to be the natural key to curing their chronic insomnia. So they came out of their cave and stole as many bottles of the substance from as many different pharmacies in the vicinity as they could manage. Far more milligrams than they ever should have needed. A stockpile. But it still wasn't enough. They guzzled it like water on the driest of days. And it was only a diluted piece of the puzzle. They needed to learn more.

It didn't take long. Determination prevailed. After further digging, they discovered the most natural, raw form of melatonin.

The pineal gland.

The regulator of circadian rhythms.

No need for much discussion. A unanimous decision to move forward.

Their addiction, their ascension, began with rodents, which offered the most structurally complex of pineal glands. They drilled to the spot as best they could, then sucked them dry before the poor creatures had time to perish properly. The last squeals of life kept the bitter pill palatable. Each snack no bigger than a grain of rice, and at first it seemed like it might be sufficient. They dove into deep slumber. And the dreams that came to visit brought clarity. They no longer had to squat in secrecy, worried they'd be discovered and have to relocate. Because their new life was coming directly to them. Collectively they conjured delirium after delirium, each hallucinogenic vision forming something incomprehensible.

Eventually, they settled on the nothingness, the invisible shield that made their new home appear empty, unoccupied from the outside. An illusion that dreamt itself real.

They weren't sure how they'd done it. More agonizing hours of research resulted. Only one answer made even a semblance of sense. Despite dissension among the scientific community, the pineal gland was thought to be ripe with the chemical DMT, causing psychedelic wonder. And the tweakers had managed to tap into the purest supply, so they assumed. But there was a problem that spawned further challenges. The rodent population ran to its limits. The tweakers then moved on to avian subjects, then local pets, of which there were few. But none of these lasted long enough to satisfy.

So they had to assess their options. And do what it took to achieve their ultimate goal.

The postman solved their problem. Even the ghosts who inhabit abandoned homes sometimes still receive credit card offers and grocery store advertisements. But his sacrifice only offered a temporary solution.

The tweakers soon realized the hallucinations were spreading, their unconscious will the cause. The DMT they'd been consuming impacted the closest residents, covered their free will like a thick fog, making them believe all was well on Blackberry Court.

And they would never have the chance to realize just how gravely wrong they were.

The voice continues in his head.

My name was once that of a man's, and I've already lost the letters that formed it. But soon I'll learn my true name. It's calling to me, and I can almost hear it. And it seems yours is calling to you as well. Yes. Can't you hear it? You've been searching for your identity as well, haven't you?

He nods in response. To all of it. The tentacles molest him further. He wants to move to leave to never return. At the same time, he wants to stay. There's a sense of comfort here. Familiarity.

If only we learned sooner, the voice says. What we'd find once we discovered the wonders of the human pineal gland. You see, we've made contact with another world.

Aliens? he thinks.

No. Not quite, the voice replies, now an inhuman gurgle struggling to form English.

He shrugs. What then?

A laugh. A bellow. A pause.

We've found god.

Or—as it may seem—many gods. All of them true, truer than any deity that may have been forced upon you as a child. And they've granted me the honor of merging with one of them. Offering my flesh as a vessel. Soon I will be assimilated into the mass. And I will lead the rest of our group to glory. The gods have removed all carnal desire, much more than even the melatonin had managed. And they asked for a sacrifice to prove my worth, which I offered with no protest. Certain organs no longer serve a purpose. They are merely a distraction. I believe you were the one who found the final remnants of my former self. Out there. My manhood. Soon the others will follow, offering their own respective parts. When they're ready to ascend.

The door to the other side has opened but a crack. And we are working to make room for those who once ruled our world but have rested for far too long. They no longer need to sleep. Not ever again.

But they do need to dream.

And now that you're here, you're fortunate enough to take part in their grand design. Better still, you have a choice. First, you can offer us the sustenance we need, your own delicious pineal gland, and be relegated to a mere footnote in the history yet to be made. Or, you can join us. Let the dreams of the primeval rulers form flesh.

He considers. Decides.

There is one other option, the voice says. Or, more accurately, another possibility.

Is there? And what might that be?

That you've been here all along. With us. A crucial part of our quest for sleep. Except for the moments when you weren't. You were gone for quite a while. We thought we'd lost you, that you'd been caught.

But we're so pleased to see you've returned.

BARREL AGED

SHENOA CARROLL-BRADD

PHILIP BRANDY SPENT the drive to Harriford's distillery alternately giddy and chiding himself to be practical. He'd had to close early in order to make the afternoon appointment—their last available slot until May—but the bar had been a ghost town, anyway. No one would mind, and if this meeting went as well as he hoped, the future looked bright for his little business. Finally, he'd have some good news to bring home to Molly.

As he neared the distillery, Philip passed through a squalid, decaying town that circled his GPS destination like a ring of infection. Everything had to be made somewhere, he supposed.

In his imagination, Phil had pictured Harriford's as small, charming, the way he saw his own whiskey bar. A timely and charismatic savior.

Instead, he arrived at the address to find a boxy, nondescript office building beside a warehouse, bookended on the other side by a narrow brick building whose chimney spewed black, sweet-smelling smoke.

He killed the engine with a sigh and an ever-more familiar sinking feeling. Was he wasting his time in coming here? Should he have gone home instead and told Molly the truth, that they'd poured every cent into an albatross? He'd already taken loans from one bank to pay back two others. Maybe it was time to admit some dreams weren't meant to be realized.

Except . . . yesterday's taste of Harriford's thirty-year whiskey still haunted him.

Before the brand ambassador arrived, no one had ever smuggled booze *into* his bar before.

"Try a taste and you'll understand my loyalty." The man held out a vial the size of a perfume sample between thumb and forefinger, letting the bar lights set it ablaze. With his other hand he sipped the pour of Brandy's best scotch he'd just ordered, grimacing as if it were medicinal. "It takes a whole lotta willpower not to keep the samples all for myself."

To humor his patron, Phil sniffed the vial, finding the aroma at once familiar and strange. The little draught filled his mouth with a pleasant fire and sparked notes of oak, vanilla, and something indefinable. Something that reminded him of how it had felt to marry Molly.

The visitor tossed back his own drink like it was ditchwater. "Remarkable, isn't it? And that's just their thirty-year batch. They have better. They're miracle-workers."

Brandy knew that if he stocked product like that, the bar would soon be in the new-and-exciting realm of black instead of red.

And so here he was, miles from home, about to beg a company without a website or paid advertising, who relied on word of mouth, repeat customers, and brand ambassadors, to help him save his family's fledgling business.

"Right on time, Mr. Brandy. Welcome to Harriford's." The receptionist handed Phil a bottled water. "Normally we'd offer coffee, but it would be a crime to sully your palate on a tasting day."

She conducted him down a short hall and into the office of a man dressed for a funeral.

"Your two o' clock, Mr. Reynolds."

Despite the building's bland exterior, the inside of Reynolds' office was richly appointed with a large desk and wood paneling. Phil nodded appreciatively as he entered.

"Have a seat." Reynolds circled behind the desk and slid forward a single piece of paper.

Philip eased into the opposite chair. "What's this?"

"Our standard non-disclosure agreement. It may seem strange, but we've worked hard to develop our recipes and can't allow any industrial espionage, intentional or not." Reynolds reached across to touch the paper. "This ensures you agree not to divulge anything you see or hear on the premises, on pain of suit." The man smiled. "I'm sorry to begin our business so sternly, but it's best to be clear. We have an exceptional legal team on retainer."

Phil shifted in his seat. "Of course. Perfectly understandable precaution." He skimmed the agreement and signed his name at the bottom.

"Good. Now, our tasting may differ from your previous experiences. Here at Harriford's, we require that you provide a credit card before we pour. Our whiskies are precious. They cannot be wasted. If you complete the tasting, all will be free, no purchase necessary. But, should you wish to leave for any reason or discontinue the sampling, we will regretfully be forced to charge you the full value of the pours, and the bottles they came from." He tilted his head in consolation. "Strict, I know, but this ensures our product goes only to those who are serious about joining the Harriford family. I cannot abide time-wasters, freeloaders, or looky-loos."

"No, of course not." Phil's throat felt tight and dry as he handed over the last card with remaining credit. If he didn't stay 'til the very last drop, his business was doomed. But, how difficult could a tasting be? He'd sampled hundreds of spirits in his life, and today would be no different.

"So glad to find you amenable, Mr. Brandy." Reynolds pressed a button on the side of his desk and leaned over to talk into a speaker. "Swanson, send a tasting flight to my office, please. Eighteen through twenty."

"On the way, Mr. Reynolds."

The intercom clicked off, and Reynolds settled back in his chair. "We're very selective about our customers, you understand, as we have a one hundred percent retention rate."

Philip blinked. "That's an impressive boast."

"Not a boast, Mr. Brandy, a fact. Once a buyer enters the Harriford family, they become customers for life."

If Philip could ensure that even a third of his patrons could be inspired to that level of loyalty, his night sweats and stress dreams could be over. He smiled. "Sounds like you're doing something right."

Reynolds nodded. "We think so. All of our whiskies are made in small batches, using only the freshest ingredients, ethically bought and locally sourced—"

A knock sounded from the wall to the left of the big desk.

Reynolds rose and pressed the paneling with both hands. A door sprang open, and a man in factory whites entered with a polished board holding a flight of stemmed tasting glasses. He set them on the desk in front of Phil, careful not to spill a drop.

"Thank you, Swanson," Reynolds said with a nod.

The man exited again without a word. The wall-door clicked shut behind him.

"You will have already sampled our thirty-year batch, so I excluded it from the tasting. Thirty is the oldest we make, as anything beyond that begins to take on . . . undesirable flavor profiles."

The whiskies before him were deep amber, tingeing almost toward red. He lifted the first taster to the light to better gauge the color.

"That's our twenty-year batch."

Philip turned the glass this way and that before bringing it to his nose. The expected aromas were there, but underlined with something else. A light, energetic note that made him think of clean, excited sweat. He pulled away, breathed deeply, then sniffed again before setting the glass back in its row. "Odd. This is the twenty?"

Reynolds nodded.

"And this . . . ?" He indicated the last glass at the opposite end.

"The eighteen-month batch."

"Ah." Philip gripped the board with both hands to rotate it.

"Stop!" Reynolds stepped forward, fingers splayed. "You must trust that we've presented the samples in the proper order."

Philip paused, shoulders tight. "Oh, okay. Sorry. So, you want me to start with the . . . "

"Twenty. Yes."

"Sure. No problem." Phil lifted the tasting glass, catching the strange scent again, dancing around the more traditional notes. He tilted the rim toward Reynolds in a satirical salute before bringing it to his lips. The spirit warmed his tongue and made his mouth tingle as if he had just broken off a passionate kiss. He sucked in a breath. The alcohol burn seemed stronger than usual for a twenty-year-old whiskey, though there was a secondary smoothness, a satiny mouthfeel that made him think of Molly's birthday-and-anniversary panties. As he swallowed and studied the afternotes, Phil felt a tightening in his groin, as if a lover's breath tickled his ear. He set the empty glass in its holder and stared for a moment, trying to reconcile what he knew of whiskey and what he'd just experienced.

"First impressions?"

Phil blinked at Reynolds, then found himself reaching for the empty glass. He ran a finger along the inside to capture the very last droplet, touched it to his tongue and briefly closed his eyes. Again, he felt a flutter, intoxicating as the beginning stages of infatuation. "I can understand why you'd be proud of it."

Reynolds inclined his head. "I'm glad you approve, and I hope you see now why Harriford's does not stoop to anything so crass as advertising. But twenty is far from our finest year." He waved a hand. "Please, continue."

Phil sipped the bottled water to cleanse his palate.

Next was the fifteen-year whiskey. He sniffed, expecting the same peculiar notes as the first, but this one was noticeably different. It smelled like frustration . . . and potential. He couldn't think of any other term for it. This whiskey was smoother, lacking the pronounced alcohol bite of the first, but leaving a lingering smokiness with a glimmer of skunky tang. Again, he sensed potential in the whiskey, and the intensity of thwarted, repressed desires. His pits felt damp, and when he swallowed, the liquor left a slight scratchiness to his throat, reminding him of the prickle of new stubble. He rubbed a hand over his cheek and waited for the stomach flutter, but it did not come this time. Phil returned the glass with a mild sense of disappointment. "Is the fifteen a good seller?"

Reynolds folded his hands. "Not particularly, no. Doesn't sell as well as the twenty, or the less mature batches, but some prefer it. Stirs up a sort of nostalgia."

Phil wasn't sure he followed, but his gaze and fingers were already on the next taste, the 10-year batch. This one offered notes of lemon and lime, vanilla, and finished with the tiniest hint of rubber, like bike tires, or eraser shavings.

Phil's suspicions didn't fully awaken until he tasted the five-year batch, less seasoned than the average bottle of Jack Daniels. He braced himself for harshness and instead felt heat on his cheeks, warm as sunshine, tasted earthiness and dandelions, with afternotes so reminiscent of sidewalk chalk that he got the sudden urge to go outside and chase something.

The alcohol had clearly reached his head. He felt giddy. He felt . . . young.

Phil's fingers tightened around the glass. His throat and eyes burned, as if near tears. He set his elbows on the desk and folded one hand over his mouth, blinking furiously.

Reynolds leaned in close. "Don't forget your water."

Philip nodded, placing the glass back with its fellows and keeping a hand over his mouth until he could wash the taste of summer from his tongue.

"Did you not care for that one, Mr. Brandy? The five-year batch is one of our top sellers."

Philip shook his head, unable to voice the fear nagging his mind and tightening his stomach. It was preposterous. He was stressed and tired and slightly day-drunk, that was all.

His gaze fell to the last tasting glass, the eighteen-month batch.

His hand stayed put.

He couldn't do it. A good man wouldn't.

A good father wouldn't.

But could he afford not to?

"Do you need a moment, Mr. Brandy? More water, perhaps?"

Phil opened his mouth, stopped, and then wiped a hand over his face. "I don't think I can finish the tasting."

Reynolds cocked his head to the side, brightly alert as a bird of prey. "Feeling ill?"

"Yes." The final glass was a richer amber than the others, so vibrant it could have held the place of honor in a pagan queen's crown.

"There's only one left, and once poured, the liquor cannot be returned to the bottle. It is too precious *not* to be consumed."

Phil stared the taster down, wishing that either it or he would disappear and remove the choice from his plate. "I can't," he pleaded. "Don't make me."

"I understand." Reynolds sat back in his chair and folded his hands. "Our whiskies are richer, more potent than other liquors, and can be overwhelming at first. This is a very common reaction, but I would hate for you to have to pay the punitive fee and waste such a rare chance. The eighteen-month whiskey is the pinnacle of our achievement. Please . . . just smell it, Mr. Brandy. Sample the bouquet."

Philip hoped he was shaking his head. He felt like he was, but his vision held steady as he watched his hand reach for the final glass. He lifted the taster to his nose, intending just to breathe in the aroma and put it down again. He smelled whiskey, and a floral touch, like talcum powder, buoyed by a hint of something else, something . . . impossible.

Fresh skin. Innocence. The indescribable scent of a new baby.

His eyes and mouth watered. His arm ached to fling the glass away, even as his fingers tightened, refusing to cede their hold. He squeezed his eyes shut, trying to will his hand to put the glass down. The scent grew stronger until something hard and delicate touched his bottom lip.

The rim.

Phil's lips parted and he tilted his head back, flooding his tongue with liquor. His breath hitched in his chest. It was a miracle. He opened his eyes, unsurprised to find his vision blurred with tears.

"The eighteen month is our most requested whiskey," Reynolds said softly.

Shuddering and wordless, Phil nodded.

"Our tasting session is now complete. Do you have any questions?"

Again, Mr. Brandy nodded, finding his words at last, though they were feeble and defeated, and their answer would bring no comfort. "How much?"

Reynolds moved aside the empty glasses and brought out a narrow sheet of paper.

Philip cleared his throat and had to wipe his eyes several times before he could focus on the order form. Even then, he was unsure if he read it correctly.

"If you do decide to visit Harriford's," the ambassador had said, *"I'll gladly buy some bottles off you for a quarter over price."*

"*Really?*" *Phil had raised a brow and reluctantly capped the sample. "Why not purchase them yourself?*"

"*They don't sell to individuals, only businesses and wholesalers.*"

A straight, austere list of vintages ran down the center, with their increasingly unspeakable prices ranging along the right side. He scanned the first two lines before dropping his gaze to the final listing.

Philip's heart soared. Even with the ambassador paying extra, there was no way. At last, his failure as a businessman might be his salvation. He laughed. "I can't afford any of this."

Reynolds smiled in a way that made Phillips bones feel cool, and he pressed his fingertips together. "Many new merchandisers find themselves in your position. Our legal department has drawn up an arrangement to ensure both parties benefit mutually. In such cases, the price of the first order is deferred, to be negotiated upon at a later date."

Philip gripped the desk, just as stuck as before. How could he turn away so generous a lifeline?

"Do you wish to call your wife, Mr. Brandy? She's still at work now, but we could get her on the line for you—"

"No!" He sat forward and seized a brushed-steel pen from its holder on Reynolds' desk. Mr. Brandy gripped the cool cylinder as if it were an eject button, hovering over the order form, unable to make a mark. "H-how do you know where Molly works?"

Reynolds leaned in, as if they were buddies sharing a secret. "We carefully vet any potential new sales partners. You understand, don't you? We're both businessmen." He sat back, looking satisfied. "To varying degrees. And once your establishment is selling our product, Molly will have no need to work anymore. I guarantee that. She can stay home with Simon. Won't that be lovely? Isn't that the life you've always wanted to provide her?"

Philip's mouth was too dry to reply, his eyes frozen open, seeing only the totals and wondering at their true cost.

"And besides, isn't sixteen months terribly young to be in daycare all day?"

Phil's hand flew across the paper, made three marks, and wrote down an unforgivable number. He placed the pen atop the paper and pushed both far out of reach, in case he had second thoughts.

Reynolds looked over the order form with a raised brow, murmuring soft sounds of approval. "Excellent choices, Mr. Brandy. You can expect delivery in two to three weeks."

"Fine." Phil shoved out of his chair. His shoulders felt heavier, his stomach ached, and his head tingled, not to the point of true intoxication, but worse than the fuzziness of a mind fresh from waking. He paused for a long breath to stop his voice from shaking. "And send all the documentation to the bar. I don't want any trace of this following me home."

"Of course." Reynolds made another note on the order form before slipping the pen into his inner pocket. "Now that the tasting's concluded and we have your order, would you care to visit the distillery? This is a privilege extended only to our select buyers."

Phil rubbed his eyes with the back of one hand. "No, thank you, I should probably get back to the bar . . . " He glanced up at Reynolds and sighed. They both knew he had no customers waiting. "Yes, actually." He lifted his chin, hoping to project more confidence than he felt. "I *would* like a tour." Seeing how their whiskey was made was the only thing that could dispel his fantastical suspicions. He'd seen the workings of half a dozen distilleries, and nothing would delight him more than the revelation that Harriford's was just like any other.

Reynolds moved to the wall and pressed the catch again to open the door. "Right this way." They stepped into a high-ceilinged grey hall where their footsteps clicked and echoed.

A glass emergency exit flooded sunlight through the end of the hallway. They walked toward it, and Philip felt a sudden sense of relief at this peek of reality. His car was just outside, waiting to take him back to Molly and Simon.

Reynolds halted suddenly and turned to face his right, bringing Philip to a staggering stop.

A huge metal door stood before them, built into the side of the wall. A tiny sign no taller than two inches declared THE DISTILLERY. White letters embossed on black plastic, like the labels Molly stuck on all her craft supplies.

Reynolds pressed what looked like a lit doorbell before stepping back. "Someone will be with you shortly to conduct your tour. Before you enter, I'd like to remind you once more of our non-disclosure agreement."

"Are you not coming in?"

Reynolds shook his head. "Oh, no. I never set foot inside the distillery. My place is in the office, not among the casks. Besides—" he brushed a hand down the front of his suit "—I'm hardly dressed for it."

Before Phil could ask what he meant, the distillery door swung open.

The man who'd delivered his tasting flight emerged, bringing with him a warm, wet, coppery smell.

"Hello again, Swanson. Mr. Brandy here has placed a substantial order with us and wishes to see our workings."

Feeling awkward, Phil stepped forward and offered a small wave.

"I will remain here until you're finished," Reynolds said softly. "In case there are further questions."

Swanson nodded, gesturing for him to follow. "Right this way, Mr. Brandy. Welcome to the Harriford family." He paused for a second, holding up a hand. "Are those shoes waterproof?"

Phil stopped to consider his footwear. "I-I don't know. Is that a problem?"

"Nah, that's all right." Swanson slapped his shoulder, drawing Phil's attention to a rusty stain on the man's white sleeve. "We can bag 'em." He smiled and stepped backwards through the huge distillery door.

With increasing tension growing in his neck and shoulders, Phil followed.

Philip Brandy emerged from the distillery not long afterwards, pale and sweating, with a hand clapped over his mouth.

Reynolds stood in the hallway, just where he said he'd be, wearing an expression of kind condescension. "How far did you get?"

The big door slammed closed again.

Philip staggered over to sag against the wall.

"I am going . . . to call . . . the police," Phil panted between heavy swallows.

Reynolds's voice remained even. "You are free to do so, Mr.

Brandy, but the Harriford family is large and wears many names. Our distilleries reach across the country and overseas. We have remained in business for over a century, even during Prohibition." He leaned forward to catch Philip's eye. "Especially during Prohibition. We have never feared the police."

Phil swallowed hard, trying to fight the images seared into his mind, the slickness of the floor, the terrible smell . . .

"I must also remind you all sales are final. Your order cannot be canceled, refunded, or returned."

"Fine!" Philip bared his teeth. "I'll pour it out. I'll smash every bottle!"

Reynolds gave him a humoring smile. "They're yours to do with as you wish, Mr. Brandy, though destroying them will not negate the deferred cost. Another water before you go?"

"No." Philip backed away, pointing over his shoulder with a thumb. "No more drinks. I want to get in my car and go home. I don't want to think about this anymore. I don't want to be here anymore . . . " His other hand, outstretched behind him, closed around the emergency exit's push bar. "I just want to go."

Reynolds raised a hand in a solemn wave. "Drive carefully then, Mr. Brandy. We'll be in touch."

Philip burst out into the afternoon sunshine. The warmth on his skin reminded him of the five-year whiskey. He hurried to his car and ducked behind the wheel, fingers curling and releasing as he stared through the windshield. His throat and stomach clenched, his head felt light and unsteady, and his vision blurred. Phil leaned out the window and threw up a car payment's worth of whiskey. His nose burned and tears coursed down his cheeks as he lost the most expensive lunch of his life.

Phil cleaned himself off with fast food napkins from the glove box until at last, empty and numb, he started the car and headed home.

He'd barely paid attention to the desolate town on his first pass, but more citizens were out and about now. He passed a young man hobbling along with a crutch and an empty pant leg.

Philip shuddered. There were plenty of reasons why someone might lose a leg, he reminded himself.

Most of the storefronts were dark and boarded up, all except the pawn shops, convenience stores, and fast food drive-thrus. The sign outside Empire Pawn boasted a blowout sale, seventy percent off all wedding rings.

What wouldn't people sell to keep their families fed?

What wouldn't *he* sell?

Phil pulled to a stop at a red light, lost in thought until movement caught his eye.

A stringy-haired woman entered the crosswalk in front of him, clutching a swaddled infant to her hollow chest. She didn't look his way but the child did, and the face staring back was much older than the body size first indicated. Closer to five, he realized, and the swaddling clothes were layers of dingy bandage encircling the child's truncated body.

Phil's stomach seized. He needed to puke again. He rolled the window down and stuck his head out, but no matter how he heaved, nothing splashed onto the cracked asphalt below. He had read once about a town in Florida where the locals were so poor they began amputating limbs for the insurance money. How long had this arm of the distillery existed, feeding off the desperate? And how long had the town been withering in its shadow, offering itself up for harvest?

The car behind him honked.

Phil jumped and hauled his head back inside. He carefully avoided eye contact with any more pedestrians until he'd escaped the city limits and put miles of highway between himself and Harriford's.

All Phil wanted was a shower and the comfort of home, but the family couldn't afford to keep Brandy's closed all day, even if only one patron came in.

Phil poured a finger of his standard, a peaty twelve-year scotch. It was his comfort drink, his go-to, but the whiskey smelled slightly off when he raised the glass to his lips. It smelled . . . flat. Watered down. Phil held it up to the light and checked the bottle, but the color seemed right. He took a sip.

Mr. Brandy lurched forward, nearly spitting his scotch across the bar.

He'd been robbed. Someone had broken in and replaced all his liquor with tinted rubbing alcohol. He scraped at his tongue, trying to purge the chemical aftertaste.

Philip pushed the glass away, grabbing a bottle of twenty-year-old bourbon. He sniffed it, and again, something seemed wrong. Phil poured a shot with mounting panic, lifting the glass to his lips. It wasn't as bad as the first, but still revolting. He couldn't stomach a second sip.

"My God." Phil leaned his elbows on the counter, cradling his head in his hands. "Holy shit, we're ruined."

Desperate, he reached up and pulled down the bottle of fifty-year-old scotch he had served to the man who'd introduced him to Harriford's. He'd never allowed himself the indulgence before, but he had to know. His hands shook as he lifted the bottle directly to his lips.

Finally, something drinkable. His most expensive whiskey now tasted like the stuff in plastic bottles, ten bucks for 1.75 liters.

He shook with silent tears, his hand tight over his mouth. Philip Brandy loved whiskey only slightly less than his wife and son, and now it offered him no pleasure. He thought again of the stranger, and of the face he'd made upon tasting this scotch. *Is that who I am now?*

That night, he barely spoke and sat on the couch with Simon squirming on his knees, watching TV without seeing anything. Every now and then, he leaned forward and touched his nose to his son's scalp, inhaling his special scent. When it was time for bed, he brushed his teeth hard enough to make himself gag, and curled up facing the wall.

After putting Simon down, Molly came in and tried to cuddle against his back.

The press of her flesh and the thrum of her blood sent him straight back to the distillery, covering him in a sick sweat. He might have saved the family today, and he couldn't even bear to tell her.

The shipment from Harriford's arrived fifteen days later.

Philip called the ambassador, not trusting himself to open the case alone. "I want *half* over price," he demanded, once the man arrived.

"Done." The man rubbed his hands together with a sound that made Brandy's skin crawl. "Which years did you buy?"

Phil cut open the box and shoved it forward.

The ambassador folded back the flaps, carefully lifting out a couple bottles. He whistled low, under his breath. "I'll take these two."

Phil glanced up quickly, checking the labels. "Fine." His voice cracked, and he brought a hand up to massage his forehead. "Take them."

The man pulled out his wallet and laid a thick stack of bills on the counter. "Can I get a glass?"

Philip shoved the nearest tumbler at him. "Quick. Taste it and go." He raised a tight smile to a young couple who entered and settled in a booth by the door.

The ambassador opened one of his bottles and inhaled sharply.

Phil caught a whiff of that indefinable infant smell and turned away. He squeezed his eyes shut, listening to the other man pour and drink a reverent swallow.

"With Harriford's on the menu, you'll never know another quiet night."

Brandy looked back to see the man staring deep into his glass.

"Nor a peaceful one." He closed his bottle with visible regret. "Keep my number. For when you order more."

"I won't." Phil's hands clenched into fists on the bar, hard as bourbon barrels. "Damn you for bringing this into my life."

The man gathered up his bottles, clutching them to his chest as tight as that woman had held her ruined child. "I'm sorry. Really, I am." His voice dropped to a hiss. "But I *had* to bring you in. They won't sell to me! And you've tasted it. You know."

He had. And he did. And, thanks to this man, he would never be able to forget.

Philip narrowed his eyes as they shared a silent moment of understanding. "Get out."

The ambassador nodded and sidled away, eyes down. "Keep my number," he repeated.

After serving the couple who whispered to each other, sweet as the splash of twenty-year batch he'd snuck into their cheap drinks, Philip Brandy took stock. He surveyed his rows of beautiful, fine, undrinkable whiskies, and felt a tightness growing in his throat, a dryness that could only be quenched by one thing.

Against every moral fiber in his body, Phil grabbed the ambassador's empty glass and poured himself another splash of damnation.

ABOUT THE CONTRIBUTORS

Chew on This! is **Robert Essig**'s third time in the editor's seat. He has also edited the anthologies *Through the Eyes of the Undead* and *Malicious Deviance*. He is the author of over a dozen books including *Shallow Graves* co-authored with Jack Bantry (Death's Head Press), *Mojave Mud Caves* (Thunderstorm Books), and *Stronger Than Hate* (Death's Head Press). He has published well over 100 short stories. Robert lives with his family in East Tennessee. He can be found on major social media platforms and occasionally at robertessig.blogspot.com.

Robert Bose has a fondness for tentacles, picnics, church parking lots, and expensive Bourbon—in any or all combinations. He's the publisher and editor of many books and anthologies for Coffin Hop Press and The Seventh Terrace, and the author of various twisted short stories including the fiendish collection, *Fishing with the Devil* and *Terrace VII: Wall of Fire*. When not writing, editing, publishing and running unfathomable distances, he spends his time annoying his wife, pestering his troublesome children, and working as a software architect for an economic forecasting software company.

Tonia Brown is a southern author with a penchant for Victorian dead things. She lives in the backwoods of North Carolina with her genius husband and an ever fluctuating number of cats. She likes fudgesicles and coffee, though not always together. When not writing she raises unicorns and fights crime with her husband under the code names Dr. Weird and his sexy sidekick Butternut. You can learn more about her at: www.toniabrownauthor.com

Shenoa Carroll-Bradd lives in southern California with her brother and dancing dog. She makes some killer vegan bacon and has been learning German in order to sing along with her favorite bands. Her short fiction has appeared in nearly three dozen anthologies and been produced for audio on several fiction podcasts. Keep in touch at facebook.com/sbcbfiction or, for free fiction and links to live readings, visit sbcbfiction.net.

Victorya Chase is a writer and educator currently living mostly online. They are still proud of having their novella, *Marta Martinez Saves the World*, published by Apokrupha press and available on Amazon and other online stores. Their short stories have been seen in journals and anthologies such as *Lamplight Magazine, Cemetery Dance*, and the *Journal of Unlikely Entomology*. Parts of their memoir have been featured in *Ninth Letter, WaterStone Review*, and other magazines.

Sarah L. Johnson is a curly hair gladiator, bookseller, editor, publisher, teacher, and all around side-hustler. Her short fiction has appeared in *Vastarien, On Spec*, NoSleep podcast, *Shock Totem*, and the Shirley Jackson Award winning *Twisted Book of Shadows* (Haverhill Press). She's the author of *Suicide Stitch: Eleven Tales, Infractus* (Coffin Hop Press), and *Terrace VII: Wall of Fire* (The Seventh Terrace). She is rumoured to have a family, and a number of cats.

K. Trap Jones is an author of horror novels and over a decade's worth of short stories appearing in numerous anthologies. Specializing in splatterpunk/extreme horror, he draws inspiration from Dante Alighieri and Edgar Allan Poe along with his appreciation towards narrative folklore, classic literary works and obscure segments within society. His novel, *The Big Bad* was nominated for the 2018 Splatterpunk Award. His novel, *The Sinner* won the 2010 Royal Palm Literary Award. As a product of the '80s, he likes his movies bloody and his music heavy. He is the owner of The Evil Cookie Publishing and is also the Co-Founder of The Splatter Club. He can be found lurking around Tampa, FL."There's a new generation of horror writers bursting onto the scene, and Jones is one of the leaders of the pack."—EDWARD LEE, author of *City Infernal, Header*, and *The Big Head*

Vivian Kasley hails from the land of the strange and unusual, Florida! She's an educator and a foodie, who also loves to write and travel. At a young age, the horror genre opened its arms to her to which she ran headfirst and stayed to cuddle. Her stories have appeared in Blood Bound Books, *Dark Moon Digest*, Gypsum Sound Tales, Grinning Skull Press, HellBound Books, Castrum Press, and Sirens Call Publications with more on the way, including her first novella. When not writing, she's enjoying time with her other half, snuggling her fur babies, eating something weird, or reading in a bubble bath. You can learn more about her here: https://www.facebook.com/bizarrebabewhowrites/ or amazon.com/author/viviankasley

Ronald Kelly has been writing horror tales set in the American South since the small-press days of the 1980s. A former author for Zebra Books, his published works include *Fear, Undertaker's Moon, Blood Kin, Hell Hollow, The Buzzard Zone, The Essential Sick Stuff*, and *The Halloween Store*. He lives in a backwoods hollow in Brush Creek, Tennessee with his family and a psychotic Jack Russell terrier named Toby.

Chad Lutzke has written for *Famous Monsters of Filmland, Rue Morgue, Cemetery Dance*, and *Scream magazine*. He's had dozens of short stories published, and some of his books include: *Of Foster Homes & Flies, Stirring the Sheets, Skullface Boy, The Pale White, The Neon Owl* and *Out Behind the Barn* co-written with John Boden. Lutzke's work has been praised by authors Jack Ketchum, Richard Chizmar, Joe Lansdale, Stephen Graham Jones, Elizabeth Massie and his own mother. He can be found lurking the internet at www.chadlutzke.com

John McNee is a Scottish horror author known for the books *Prince of Nightmares, Grudge Punk* and *Petroleum Precinct*. His short story collection, *John McNee's Doom Cabaret*, was published in spring 2020. He can easily be found on Facebook, Twitter and YouTube, where he hosts the horror-themed cooking show *A Recipe for Nightmares*.

S.C. Mendes is a teacher, real-estate investor, and author with a penchant for the occult. He's published many short stories and articles under various names. *The City* is his debut novel and the beginning of the Max Elliot saga.

Nikki Noir writes erotic thrillers, extreme horror, and bizarre plotlines. Her *Black Planet* series is available now from Blood Bound Books. You can find her short stories, reviews, and more on her website www.RedRumReviews.com.

Armand Rosamilia is a New Jersey boy currently living in sunny Florida, where he writes when he's not sleeping. He's happily married to a woman who helps his career and is supportive, which is all he ever wanted in life . . . He's written over 150 stories that are currently available, including horror, zombies, contemporary fiction, thrillers and more. His goal is to write a good story and not worry about genre labels. He not only runs two successful podcasts, Arm Cast Podcast—interviewing fellow authors as well as filmmakers, musicians, etc. and The Mando Method Podcast with co-host Chuck Buda—talking about writing and publishing, but he owns the network they're on, too! Project Entertainment Network. He also loves to talk in third person . . . because he's really that cool. You can find him at https://armandrosamilia.com for not only his latest releases but interviews and guest posts with other authors he likes!

Mark C. Scioneaux is a Bram Stoker Award® nominated editor and author.He is the author of numerous short stories appearing in various anthologies; most recently "A Very Trying Time" in *Distorted Mirrors*, published by Gyldendal of Denmark. He is the author of *Family Dinner, Slipway Grey, The Director's Cut*, and *Dead on the Bayou*. He is also author of the "Splattire Series" with books that include *Cannibal Fat Camp, Die, You Zombie Crackers!*, and *America's Next Dead Model. Horror for Good: A Charitable Anthology* is an award-nominated anthology for charity he edited. He is a graduate of Louisiana State University and currently resides in Baton Rouge, Louisiana with his wife, Kristin

Chad Stroup is the author of the novels *Secrets of the Weird* (Grey Matter Press) and *Sexy Leper* (Bizarro Pulp Press) and the comic series *Hag* (American Gothic Press). He has published several short stories in magazines and anthologies such as *Shock Totem, Worst Laid Plans, Forbidden Futures, Chiral Mad 4, Lost Films,* and *Splatterlands,* and his dark poetry has appeared in all volumes of the HWA Poetry Showcase. Stroup received his MFA in Fiction from San Diego State University. Follow him on Instagram or Twitter @chadxstroup.

Sylvia Anne Telfer is an international award-winning Scottish poet/author frequently published in magazines and anthologies. From a focus on writing poetry, in particular in her Scots language and with emphasis on portraying society's marginalized, she is relishing the thrill of writing horror and sci-fi—delving into the murkier side of herself, and is attempting new media art (a horror story in itself) to illustrate her poems/stories. She is a campaigner to halt climate change, a feminist, pro-Scottish Independence and an equal rights activist, who after years of living in Africa, Far East and Middle East, now lives alone in an 'old Scottish miners' row' but minus the obligatory cat.

Kristopher Triana is the Splatterpunk Award-winning author of *Full Brutal, Gone to See the River Man, Blood Relations, Shepherd of the Black Sheep*, and other scary books. His short stories have appeared in various anthologies and magazines, including Cemetery Dance and Flame Tree Press's *Chilling Horror Short Stories,* and his books have been published in multiple languages. His latest novel is *They All Died Screaming,* available now from Blood Bound Books. Triana lives somewhere in New England. kristophertriana.com, Twitter: @koyotekris, Podcast: *Vital Social Issues 'N Stuff with Kris and John Wayne*

www.ingramcontent.com/pod-product-compliance
Lightning Source LLC
Chambersburg PA
CBHW032000170626
46807CB00006B/2582

* 9 781940 250465 *